SO-ABA-744

VIENNA NOCTURNE

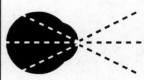
This Large Print Book carries the
Seal of Approval of N.A.V.H.

VIENNA NOCTURNE

VIVIEN SHOTWELL

THORNDIKE PRESS

A part of Gale, Cengage Learning

GALE
CENGAGE Learning·

Farmington Hills, Mich • San Francisco • New York • Waterville, Maine
Meriden, Conn • Mason, Ohio • Chicago

GALE
CENGAGE Learning®

Copyright © 2014 by Vivien Shotwell.
Thorndike Press, a part of Gale, Cengage Learning.

Thorndike Press® Large Print Peer Picks
The text of this Large Print edition is unabridged.
Other aspects of the book may vary from the original edition.
Set in 16 pt. Plantin.

LIBRARY OF CONGRESS CATALOGING-IN-PUBLICATION DATA

Shotwell, Vivien.
  Vienna nocturne / by Vivien Shotwell. — Large print edition.
    pages ; cm. — (Thorndike Press large print peer picks)
  ISBN-13: 978-1-4104-6495-8 (hardcover)
  ISBN-10: 1-4104-6495-4 (hardcover)
  1. Storace, Anna Selina, 1765-1817—Fiction. 2. Mozart, Wolfgang Amadeus, 1756-1791—Fiction. 3. Sopranos (Singers)—England—Fiction. 4. English—Austria—Vienna—Fiction. 5. Large type books. 6. Vienna (Austria)—Fiction. I. Title.
  PS3619.H682V54 2014b
                                    813'.6—dc23   2014000143

Published in 2014 by arrangement with The Ballantine Publishing Group, a division of Random House, LLC

Printed in Mexico
1 2 3 4 5 6 7 18 17 16 15 14

*For my parents,
Hudson and Janet*

A PARTIAL GUIDE TO PRONUNCIATION

While not meant to be exhaustive, this guide might help readers from hesitating over some of the foreign names in the novel.

The first "A" in "Anna" may be pronounced either like the "a" in "father," or like the "a" in "fan," as the reader prefers.

"Benucci" may be pronounced "Ben-OO-tchee."

"Lange" may be pronounced "LANG-eh."

"Marchesi" may be pronounced "Mar-KAY-zee."

"Rauzzini" may be pronounced "Rowd-ZEE-nee."

"Storace" may be pronounced in either the

English way, "STORE-us," or the Italian way, "Store-AH-tchey."

THE CASTRATO

He spoke first of her breathing, then of her bearing and strength. He showed her, with lightness and ease, with playful, wry animation, how *he* breathed, as he had been trained. Such training as he had undergone could not be replicated. But he would do his best, if Anna would try. She said she would.

He exhaled in a hiss from full, strong lungs while she counted out the seconds. Her own exhale she could not sustain long, but it was wonderful failure, failure that might someday be overcome. He demonstrated for her, too, the *messa di voce,* the placement of the voice, in which he sang a single note from softest to loudest and back again, and touched, along the way, all the gradations of loudness and softness between. She failed here, too, but still he made her feel already taken, already touched, with the fever of aspiration — to

9

learn and master everything. It would be like becoming an acrobat, Rauzzini said. Soon enough one might fly. Already he was pleased with her, already praising her quickness and skill. He said that in time they would begin two-note scales, then three notes, then as many notes as could be contained in the measure of a single breath. She had never in her life felt as dancing and vivid as now. She forgot herself. He did not sing much, but when he did, the sound went all around her and through her body. It was as though her soul became huge with life and joy, and she could not believe that she had been so nervous, nor that she had not been more.

The year was 1776. Her name was Anna Selina Storace. She was eleven years old. She could play harp and guitar and sing anything by sight. Her elder brother, Stephen, was a prodigy on the violin, and had been sent to Naples to study at a conservatory. Her father was Italian, a double-bass player who had lived in London for twenty years and who arranged and translated Italian burlettas for Marylebone Gardens. He was a hopeful man who was always losing money. His unhappy wife, born Elizabeth Trusler, was the daughter of the proprietor at Marylebone, a pleasure resort just outside of London, not as plush or posh as Vauxhall or Ranelagh but characterized by the Truslers' simple, rustic food: fruit tarts from their own gardens, and cheesecakes, cream, and butter from the sleek dairy cows that lowed and grazed in the lawns behind the theater. There were breakfasts, balls, and fireworks. The patrons were not wealthy but neither were they poor.

Anna had sung and danced in her father's burlettas at Marylebone for as long as she could remember. She was a lively, clever child who wanted only to be pleasing to everybody. Her eyes were large and dark and mutable and seemed to express more depth of feeling and quickness of mind than were found in many an adult. Her thick, black-brown curls made Mrs. Storace despair that she would be taken for a Gypsy. Her stature was small and neat, and she carried herself gracefully, after her mother, who in times of greater prosperity had had a French dancing master.

The night before her first lesson with Venanzio Rauzzini, Anna had hardly slept. Every quarter of an hour she'd woken to see if it was time to get up, but it was always the depths of night, everyone asleep but herself, her heart fluttering with excitement and her feet too hot. At last the sky had

11

lightened and she'd heard Bridget beginning the morning chores.

"Up already?" Bridget had said.

Anna had looked at the good woman with solemn eyes. "It's the most important day of my life."

"Then you'd best get more sleep, my love," said Bridget, but she gave Anna her bread and butter and let her stay.

The morning had lagged on as the night had done and then suddenly it was time to dress and go with her father to Rauzzini's house in Covent Garden. When they entered the castrato's apartment, three small dogs trotted down the hall to greet them. "I never thought he'd have *dogs,*" she whispered.

"He doesn't have children," said her father. He licked his lips and tugged his wig, which was too small. There were mirrors on the walls. Anna was afraid she looked shabby. The servant opened the tall inner doors and the dogs rushed before them into the drawing room, which was decorated richly in red. "Salutations," said Venanzio Rauzzini, turning with an easy grace to meet them.

He spoke in Italian — a high, sweet, full voice. There were rings on all his fingers, and at his breast, a pin in the shape of a phoenix. He wore a fine blue coat and jew-

12

eled buckles on his shoes. His large, heavily lidded eyes had an expression of dreaminess and calm, and his face was as round and as smooth as a boy's. He possessed an unusually tall frame, with wide, plump shoulders, gangling arms, and ample legs, and yet he carried himself so proudly, and moved with such elegance, that according to his reputation he could not enter a room without drawing every eye upon him to admire.

"You're very young," he remarked.

"I'm just small," Anna exclaimed. "I'm already eleven."

"Already?" he said. He gave her a warm look. "I'd have taken you for ten at most. Well, then, come with me. We'll leave your father with my pups. You can play with them later, if you like. They've come all the way from Munich."

She followed him to his music room, which smelled of books and cinnamon, and felt instantly relieved. Here she belonged, here she was home, with this purpose and this teacher. He held in his mind the knowledge she required. She need only convey to him now that she was better and brighter than any little girl on earth.

"She's a pearl," said his servant when the

13

Storaces had departed.

Rauzzini looked at the other man and smiled. "Yes."

He felt unexpectedly lively in the wake of the little girl's visit, could not suppress his smile. One wanted a purpose, after all. One wanted a project, a pet. He had everything material but no children and no family. To be a castrato singer was to be a man from an alien land — not even a man. And yet even such a man might long to have a child. One could have wealth and favor, one could populate one's house with trinkets and dogs, yet in the dinginess of London, and the remorseless, accelerating march of time, there was aimless, itching spleen. Each day his own singing — what he lived for, for which his young body had been violated — relieved him of that spleen. But he could not sing forever.

He glanced along the row of mirrors. He had been an orphan in Rome, and until he had been given to the conservatory — gelded and sold, like a piece of cattle — he had never looked closely at his own face. But after that great change, the singing masters had made him stand before a mirror every day so he would not grimace, nor make any sign of strain, while cycling through the musical scales. When he had

14

first looked into the mirror he had been struck at once by the thought that in this unfamiliar face lay the melded images of his unknown parents, their lips and cheeks and eyes. He had thought that if he studied this face long enough, this face that contained theirs, he might someday meet them again, on the streets of Rome, and say, "I am your son. I have become a great singer." For he believed that he had been born to a poor girl who had given him away.

He had liked to imagine her, his mother, while lying on his cot at night. That was the only time in the conservatory when he was alone and quiet. All the rest of the day and night the young castrati spent singing. They sang psalms as they dressed in the morning, as they washed and walked. They sang in nightly vigils. *Figlioli angiolini,* they were called — little angel boys. They stood watch over the corpses of dead children. For this service the conservatories were paid high fees. It was on such a vigil that Rauzzini, as a boy little older than Anna, had fallen in love with singing; as he stood in his white cassock, motherless, and comforted the poor dead children, who were far worse off than he, and their veiled, grieving relations. He had loved the ceremonial ritual, the candles, the lateness of the hour; loved the importance of his task, which could be done by no other, and the sweet sounds that released like butterflies from his finely coordinated throat. He had understood then how powerful he could be, and how admired.

His voice could fill the largest hall, be heard from mountaintop to mountaintop, yet it was so beautiful — he was not arrogant, it was simply a fact — that it would not have waked an infant at arm's length. Not one in a hundred of those *figlioli angiolini* had grown to have a voice and technique like his. He had been blessed by God, and by his own determination.

He'd had a storied career in Rome, and later in Milan, where the young Wolfgang Mozart had written him an exquisite motet. After Milan he'd gone to Munich, but his mistress there — the exquisite Elizabeth Bauer, just seventeen, with skin like silk and constellations of freckles and moles — had made a mistake with their rendezvous. The old duke had burst in upon them. The duke was a jealous man at best, but there was particular shame in being cuckolded by a castrato. Most people did not know the extent to which a man like Rauzzini might still serve a lady, but Elizabeth knew, the sweet girl. She had a mole on her left but-

16

tock that he would carry in his heart forever.

She had sent him a rose the next morning and told him her husband intended to kill him. So to London he had come. He liked the fog. His humors were thick and hot, and made his joints ache, as if the heat of the man he would never be had backed up and poisoned his blood. He liked what cooled and quieted.

He had read a review of the Storace girl in the paper, but had not believed there would be anything interesting about her. He had been happily mistaken. She was a treasure. She would be his student and sing in his own operas, for he wished to compose.

He had been about her age when his life had turned from one thing to another. At the conservatory, the regular boys had mocked the young castrati, who were fed on broth and eggs and meat while they, the instrumentalists, were half starved. They had divided themselves into *integri* and *non integri,* whole and not whole. Remembering this, Rauzzini tossed his head in the mirror. None of us were whole, he thought. The fellow who'd done his surgery had been usually employed in extracting teeth. Most castrated boys died from infections. But Rauzzini had lived, had grown brilliant and handsome, and the voice had been good,

17

the voice of a boy in the body of an almost-man, only fuller and more masterful than any boy could muster. But Anna required no injury. She had everything she needed.

One look and he had cherished her. The absurdity did not diminish the feeling. Intelligence, openness, heart — these qualities attracted him, these rang upon his life's purpose. There was no higher art than music and no purer musical form than song. The voice of such a child must brim the soul. For the preservation of his own childhood voice he had been castrated. Yet now it need not be so. This girl, this pearl, this new daughter, would grow into a fine young woman. She would lose nothing. Neither her heart, nor her joy, nor her confidence. She would be celebrated. She would have everything he had, and everything he had not.

Cupid All Armed

The Royal Opera House glowed with hazy light, its air filled with heat and smoke and rumbling noise. On the ground, there was not room to move and yet movement was constant. Now and then someone lost his supper, and the mess was absorbed with sawdust, and the stink dissolved into the rest of the stink. There were pickpockets and food vendors and three men for every woman, and when these women were groped and squeezed, they whacked the men with whatever implements they had at hand. The crowd on the grounds pressed against a row of spikes set there to keep them from overflowing onto the stage in occasional riots. They threw orange peels upon the stage boards. The set burned above them, a hot apparition. The singers and dancers sweated and strained upon it, in costumes decorated with feathers, baubles, and anything that might catch the light. For ten minutes, twenty, the audience's attention held, for favorite singers, arias, or intervals of ballet, and the applause then was raucous and long. But soon enough there would be a lull of confusion, and food was thrown, and men stood on benches shouting at one another, and lords in the boxes dallied behind curtains with their mistresses. Anna's mother said the opera house was full of harlots. Had it not been for the debts, she said, she would not have allowed Anna to sing there, not so young. And because of this, for the first time in her life, Anna was grateful to the debts, and bowed before them, and wanted to kiss their hands, because there was nowhere on earth she would rather be than inside an opera theater.

She was thirteen. The Cupid costume showed her legs from just above the knee. She had not shown her legs since she was a small child. The stockings were white and the breeches gold. Her white legs would catch the light and everyone would look at them. Her mother was not happy about the costume, but Cupid was a boy; he could not have had his legs covered.

Anna had never done anything like this. The audiences at Marylebone had been perhaps one hundred people, the stage small, the music simple and easy. Standing in the wings before her entrance, she breathed deliberately, as Rauzzini had taught her, and straightened her shoulders. "Trust your heart," he had said. "Wrap your heart in the strongest silk, and don't let anything tear it, nor burn it away." From the stage came the sounds she yearned for — the orchestra, the cheers. Upon her cue she stepped onto the boards, noticing in passing a stray orange peel that had not been swept up. She wanted to knock it away with her foot, but that would have been out of her part. So she pretended that it did not exist. There, before her, were the heads of the players in the orchestra, there her hopeful father smiling at his double bass. Everything was as they had rehearsed, but now it was night, and the air was hot and smoky, and in the broad, vaulted space before her, pushed against the spikes, standing on benches, leaning out of balconies, eating, drinking, talking, and embracing, two thousand faces turned to Anna with her bow and arrow, her golden pantaloons, her silver wings, her blazing stockings. Two thousand hearts lived with hers, and she did not know where was the silken armor Rauzzini had meant for her to wrap around her heart. She felt her limbs grow weak and uncertain, felt the two thousand faces begin to turn away.

But then she saw Rauzzini in the wings, dressed all in red with his face brightly painted. He played the hero. He met her eyes and his face told her that he trusted her, and that because he trusted her she had no choice but to see it through. She looked at the bow and arrow in her hands, and lifted them in the air. Though she could not hear, she watched the concert master and found her entrance. Into the wall of faces she launched her unwilling voice, launched it with the imaginary arrows, while Rauzzini watched from the wings, while the silk singed and peeled but did not dissolve. She did not know why he had trusted her. For a moment her mind was a blank and she could not remember anything. Then the music and the stage drew her back. The opera house became a circle of dim light in which she sang and danced as if she were alone. At a certain point she knew it must be good, because she was aware that the murmur of the hall had quieted, but she did not allow herself to dwell on it. The aria finished, the applause was ready and re-sounding, and she stood for a moment feel-ing the confused and muddy-minded release of a condemned thief who has been spared

22

at the foot of the gallows. "Bow!" Rauzzini shouted from the wings. "Bow!" He was laughing. The applause went on. Anna gave a start, flourished her arm, called up a radiant smile, and bowed like a boy, one leg extended before her. Then she ran off the stage and into her teacher's arms.

NAPLES

Rauzzini said there was no steadiness in music. One could not hold music in one's hands. One could not taste it, nor see it in the air. It vanished almost as soon as it was made. Music for them was an offering. That was what it meant to sing. It meant being in love with the audience, having that ardent munificence, withholding nothing. Only then would the voice truly be beautiful.

Anna did not quite understand. She was only fifteen. But she said she did.

He had taught her to sing a line, to sing as though she were speaking, to sing softly and loudly. He had taught her how to move, how to gesture, how to pronounce the language, and how to have appropriate musical style and inflection. Everything that was necessary. Now it was time, he said, for her to sing in Italy. Italian opera was all, and Anna could not sing as she wished — as a prima donna — without first establishing herself there.

So she was leaving. Anna's mother and father would go with her and in Naples they would be reunited with her brother, Stephen, who was studying at the conservatory.

"You must promise to care for yourself," Rauzzini said to Anna a few days before her departure. She had come to his studio, as familiar to her now as her own home, for a last lesson. He kept blowing into a handkerchief. "You must promise to stay safe and well and never cross through danger, nor associate with bad people."

"I won't," she said. There had come over her face a kind of ashen sobriety unsuited to a girl of fifteen. She had not taken off her hat. It was askew. Her face was blotched and distressed with tears. "I hate saying good-bye. I can't bear it. We have to go on a ship, and nothing is packed and everyone is in fits and it's all because of me." She smiled weakly. "Make me sing, maestro. I'm afraid I'll forget on the voyage how to sing."

Without difficulty they slipped into their usual routine, and one would not have known it was the last lesson except that he did not correct her as assiduously as usual. He was helplessly sad. She sang beautifully, with dear honesty and true instinct. Her

25

cheeks brightened and her loveliness was restored. She had grown up. Her figure was womanly, her waist neat. Her darkly lashed eyes could entrance every soul, her brows articulate any subtlety of comedy and wit. Her lips were clever and full, and her smile — her father's smile — almost devilish in its charm. But it was her voice, now, that Rauzzini cared for; the voice he had helped shape, the voice that had become as dear to him as his own child's. He lapsed in correcting her because he was trying to burn the sound of it into his brain. It was impossible, and yet he must try.

The voyage to Naples brought out the worst in everyone. The air was bad, the sailors unsavory, and the quarters more like a sick house than a ship. They were trapped. Nothing happened. A nothing to end all nothings. Theirs was the weariness of bodies not allowed to move as they should and unable, after enough time, to recall how such movement felt. Everything was monotony, stomach cramps, bad breath. They dreamed of vegetables.

But Anna had her guitar, and where there was a guitar, there could be music and good cheer. Even Mrs. Storace remarked how soothing it was to have Anna's guitar on the

26

ship. An hour spent listening to Anna idling upon the instrument was an hour free from pain. That was a blessing, Mrs. Storace said. She was very glad Anna had brought the guitar.

Mrs. Storace was a woman whose position in life did not reflect her sense of her own refinement. She was always reading books and poetry, and the more moral they were, laughed her husband, and the more tedious, the better. Though her husband was some twenty-five years older, all the youthfulness and playfulness were his, which she took for folly. He had no head on his shoulders, she said. He was a great grinning salesman, a seducer, a philanderer. He had left three mistresses in London, she was sure. Had it not been for her daughter, Mrs. Storace said, and her absent son, she would have committed herself to a convent.

She was always wincing at some thing or other. When readying to volley a criticism she would first sniff through her nose and stare into the middle distance. Her husband was all vagueness. He threw himself into the air and expected to be caught. When Mrs. Storace was angry with Anna she would say that she was just like her father. But her mother loved music and was softened by it. She could never know how pleasant she looked when she listened to her daughter, how her forehead relaxed and her breathing slowed. But Anna could see it, and it made her play more sweetly. She did not mind the conditions on the ship. She wouldn't have minded if the journey had been twice as long, or if there had been no food at all. The tedium, the discomfort, the sailors who stank of rum — the rats and fleas, the dirtiness of her clothes and of her own person — could not overcome the bigness of the sky at sea at night. If ever she felt sick or upset she need only remind herself, "I am going to Italy. I am going to see Stephen," and that would cure her. She would have been ashamed to feel ungrateful. She missed Rauzzini's advice, his wit and his laughter, but it was for this he had trained her. She must sing in Italy. It had been fine to sing in London as a child, when her youth had made her something of a wonder, but all anyone wanted now were Italian divas; they would not pay good money to hear one of their own, not unless she had sung abroad, in all the great houses. Anna should stay away just long enough, Rauzzini had said, for her countrymen to forget she was English.

She hoped Stephen would love her as much as she intended to love him. He had left when she was ten. She remembered playing games with him, and how patient and jolly he had been, and she remembered how he had practiced his violin and harpsichord all day behind a closed door, but when she tried to recall his face she could not. All they had was a small portrait of him that Mrs. Storace had drawn before he departed. She said it was not a bad likeness, but neither was it a good one.

They arrived in the Naples harbor. The long illness of the journey lifted. Anna's father could not stop smiling — he remembered, he said, everything, even after twenty years. Mrs. Storace stretched and felt the life returning to her limbs. And Anna could not believe it. They were there. They were nowhere else. It was another world from England and they were in it.

They stayed with Mr. Storace's elder brother, a merchant. Stephen lived at the conservatory. After they'd washed and eaten they sent for him. Everyone was nervous. At the least sound from outside, Mr. Storace would jump up and go to the window. Mrs. Storace's face was pale and her eyes bright. "I'm afraid I won't recognize my own son," she said to her brother-in-law, through her husband. Mrs. Storace had some Italian but refused to use it, because she was embarrassed by her errors. "I'm afraid he shall not know me." Her brother-in-law murmured his sympathy. Mr. Storace jumped again to the window.

Anna could not sit at all. She had barely eaten. She wanted to run to the conservatory. And suddenly he was there, Stephen, her brother.

There was a moment of hesitation. He stood in the doorway, in the uniform of the Conservatory of Sant'Onofrio, the white tunic and the black sash, his hair curling to his shoulders and his eyes shining with suspense, this boy of seventeen whom they had not seen for five years. Then they were falling upon him, laughing and crying, squeezing him to death and saying they would never have known him and would have known him anywhere, for he had the same dear look, inflection, and manner, a light-boned, thoughtful young man with pleasant features, his sister's eyes, and his father's middling height.

They said his name a hundred times, "Stephen, Stephen," smiling and looking into his face, touching him to make sure he was there. He seemed like a dream to them, and they to him; it was as if there had been some sorcery.

"Anna," he said. "Do you remember me?"

She could not let go of him. She was weeping loudly and laughing. She had given herself hiccups. "Stephen!" she said. "Stephen!" and he kissed her cheeks and said he would have known her in any country.

Later they had a concert for each other. First Stephen played on his violin, with the easy pride of mastery, that they all might admire him. Such tones and notes! The instrument became in his hands like a human voice. They watched him greedily, his serious brow, his slender, steady limbs. There was no flaunting about Stephen. He had always been quiet. It was astonishing that he had ever been sent away, and that he had managed. But he had mastery and grace. Anna's intentions were fulfilled. She loved her brother completely.

"Now you must sing," he said to her, and she readily complied. Her uncle had tuned his harpsichord, though he said it was little better than kindling, and she sang to her own accompaniment. Stephen, delighted, said there was not a better soprano in Naples. Everything refreshed. Mr. and Mrs. Storace smiled and did not hate each other. Mr. Storace's brother felt he now knew what it might have been like to have had children. Stephen seemed to grow taller. And Anna, with everyone she loved all around her, tried to make her gaze wider, her ears more true, to fix in her memory this moment of her family together and happy. She loved her father with his pattering speech and his bad puns and clumsy feet. She loved her unfamiliar uncle. She loved her mother in all her nerves and severity. She loved her brother, who shared her face but not her affect, who lived in certain of her memories and was absent from others. He had never met Rauzzini. All that part of her life, and so much more, he could not know, just as she could not know of his. But he was her own brother and no one else's.

The next day, they visited Stephen's conservatory. He had already completed his studies, and now he taught some of the smallest boys and played concerts here and there. He took Anna to see Giovanni Paisiello, a famous opera composer who taught singing and counterpoint at the conservatory. Anna sang for him and he was pleasantly surprised. He said he would recommend her to his friends, and would offer small parts to her in his operas. But as the months went on, nothing to speak of came of Paisiello. She sang a few solo cantatas for him at the cathedral, but they paid very little. Finally he said he could not gamble on a little English girl. "She must sing more in Italy," he told Mr. Storace. "She must spend some years here."

"How is she to sing in Italy if no one in Italy will hear her?" asked Mr. Storace.

Paisiello shrugged. "How does one do anything?"

Her father wanted her to sing for Jommelli, who had taught Farinelli, but he would not hear her. He said he was too old to give time to the English.

Cimarosa was in France, and would not return until the new year. Mr. Storace had translated several of Cimarosa's operas and corresponded with him. He'd set his hopes on Cimarosa. Cimarosa had promised on his honor to help Anna. He had said nothing about France.

All of the family but Stephen got sick with feverish indigestion. For two weeks Anna did not leave her bed. And they had to eat, and be kept in good clothes, if they were to mingle as they must with the aristocracy. Yet the aristocracy did not invite Anna to their concerts and salons because they did not know who she was. And even if they had known, they would have assumed that she could not sing, because she was English.

In the spring her father determined to go

back to England and raise capital. He would be gone most of the summer. While he was there he wished his family to leave Naples and try their fortunes elsewhere. Naples had no use for them. There were too many singers in Naples. He was not a superstitious man but he believed they would have better luck elsewhere; that this whole year, nearly, had been cursed by some fog of confusion or disorder. But while he was in London he died of an infection. Mrs. Storace and her children were left alone with very little money, and debts now in Naples and London both.

L'INGLESINA

For months they did nothing. As the weather cooled, Stephen, who had been giving music lessons for too little pay, began to talk of pawning his violin, while Mrs. Storace volunteered her modest jewels. Then a letter arrived from Paisiello. He had found a position for Anna at the Pergola theater in Florence. The miracle was arranged: she would sing *seconda donna* to the *primo musico* of the famous castrato Ludovico Marchesi. Stephen would play second harpsichord in the orchestra there, and that would provide enough funds to send him back to England, where he would settle whatever affairs Mr. Storace had left unfinished.

"This is a great honor," Mrs. Storace admonished her daughter. She had been shocked by the death of her husband. She took hardly any food and seemed to shrink into the earth. "You must do everything to

35

perfection, and offend no one."

Anna was too pert, said her mother, and lacked deference.

"Don't worry, Mama," said Anna with a smile. "I'll be an angel."

"You're not the prima donna yet," said Mrs. Storace. "And you'll never be if you carry on as you do. They think of you as an English child with bad Italian."

"My Italian is perfect."

"Then something else is wrong. How you move. You must take smaller steps and be careful not to knit your brow."

"Yes, Mama."

Anna thought of her father every day, of his hopefulness and his daring. He had wished for his children to have the sort of musical career that had been denied him, and somehow it seemed her fault that he had died, because he had gone back to England for her sake. But she could not allow herself to think like that for long, because then she would not have been able to sing.

They arrived in Florence and began to rehearse, and almost immediately she knew that she could not keep her promise to her mother to be an angel. She did try.

Had it been anyone else she would not have

objected to kneeling. Ludovico Marchesi had done it simply to abase her. She knew he had. In the few days she'd been in Florence he had done everything to cross her. He had stepped on her toes, deliberately stepped on them, when he passed her in the wings. He had given her wrong directions and wrong cues and doubted her abilities openly and at every turn. Anna had done him no wrong. But Stephen said she was a threat. Although Marchesi was one of the most famous singers in the world, and all of Tuscany was coming to hear him, the castrati were dying out. The profit was going to be in comic opera now, in opera buffa. Castrati were rubbish for buffa, Stephen said. They sang only serious opera. They played gods and heroes, not ordinary people. Ordinary people did not sound like castrati. Besides, the French found the castration of boys abhorrent, and the sentiment was spreading.

"You must be lower down when I'm singing this," Marchesi said to Anna. "You must kneel."

"Signor," she said with a soft smile. "I do not see how you could appear any taller."

A ripple of laughter went through the orchestra. The stage manager looked uneasy. Marchesi narrowed his eyes. "I am supposed to be standing on a mountain," he said, as though with infinite patience. "You must appear lower."

Anna regarded him demurely. She thought of her father. She was now sixteen. They lived on bread and water. At last, with a graceful inclination of her head and a supple billowing around her of skirts and ribbons, she knelt.

"Ah," Marchesi exclaimed. He spread his arm to the orchestra. "Now we may begin."

Anna, swallowing bitterly, kept her eyes down. His voice was not as beautiful as Rauzzini's, nor as elegant — not nearly — but the sound was loud and brilliant. Still, he had no taste. He was all embellishment and show. There was no naturalness, no honesty, no simplicity. His diction was lazy and incomprehensible. He was all vowels — vague, lazy vowels — with no consonants to mark the sense. One could hardly make out the line of melody for the frills and leaps and runs of adornment he heaped upon it. It was ornamentation in the old style. To Anna it sounded pompous and ridiculous.

She lifted her eyes to watch him sing the end, the part for which he was most acclaimed, a cadenza so dramatic and daring it had been named for him, *La bomba di Marchesi,* the bomb of Marchesi, a dazzling *voletta* of octaves ascending by semitones all the way to a high C. A miracle of a cadenza, a feat of humanity, which none on earth could match or mimic. And in that moment she got her idea.

"But you can't," whispered Stephen. "You haven't practiced. We'll be run out of town."

It was the first interlude. A ballet was playing on stage, and after the ballet would come a short comic intermezzo. The whole evening's entertainment would go on for some five hours. All of Tuscany was in the audience, and perhaps beyond Tuscany, including, Anna had heard, an impresario from La Scala theater in Milan.

Marchesi had sung his *bomba* in the first act, and had received a twenty-minute ovation. The rest of the act he'd strolled around the stage with as much boredom and nonchalance as if he'd been in his own home. He'd taken pinches of snuff and talked to his friends in the audience. He had talked, on stage, through the entirety of Anna's first aria, as though she were not singing — as though she were not there. The whole audience, in fact, had talked through her aria. She could hardly blame them. Her character did nothing, said nothing, knew nothing, and the aria was repetitive and simpering

39

and thus sounded like nothing. Her only purpose was to let Marchesi rest his throat. Nor could she do anything to redeem her part — not with a text like that, music like that, and everyone talking.

Marchesi was supposed to be a prisoner in chains but he wore a plumed golden helmet and was impeccably powdered and pomaded. He was supposed to have an injured arm, but he gestured with both arms vigorously. He had talked through her aria. He had trod on her foot. And the whole of Tuscany was there.

"All you have to do is hold the cadenza and make sure the cellist waits for me," she told Stephen. "He never pays attention."

"Ludovico Marchesi is the most famous castrato in the world," said her brother, as if fending off the devil.

"Just make sure you hold that cellist."

The Pergola theater in Florence was smaller and more refined than the Royal Opera House in London. In the boxes the aristocrats lit their own candles and feasted on their own food trolleys. Ladies beat the air with lacy fans. Nowhere was superb singing more prized than in Italy. The Italian audiences spoke of certain singers as though they were gods.

In all her years of trying, Anna had never

40

been able to contrive a convincing imper-
sonation of Rauzzini. She was a fine mimic,
but his voice was too different in color from
her own, and his manners too elusive. But
Marchesi's every word and action were
steeped in contrivance, and made him as
easy a target as any.

She was standing alone on stage toward
the end of the final act. As if from a great
distance, the orchestra began the introduction to her aria. *I am Ludovico Marchesi,* she
thought, hearing in her mind his honeyed
voice. She had had no time to practice.
Someone would have suspected. But she
had imagined what it would sound like, and
how it would feel.

Even before she began to sing she felt the
change in the hall like a great warm wave.
She pretended to take some snuff. Some-
body laughed. Then they were all laughing.
She had them. She was Marchesi and yet
she was not Marchesi, she was something
charming and light, and she *had* them. She
could keep them as long as she wished. She
strolled about the stage like a languid cat.
She sang without consonants. She remarked, aloud, during the orchestra's ritor-
nello, in her perfect, ringing Italian, that she
was not in good voice tonight — that she
had eaten too much rum and pudding. She

41

sang a few extravagant and unnecessary ornamental roulades, and though they were ridiculous, they were also impeccable, the technique flawless and clean. Then it was time for the cadenza. Composing herself, and dropping, at last, the appearance of nonchalance, she took to the front of the stage. Stephen, at the second harpsichord, sweat beading down his face, put up one hand to hold the cellist. Anna took a breath and stretched out her arms. This was her triumph. For she sang a *voletta* of her own, having never practiced one in her life, a *bomba di Storace,* just as quickly and accurately as Ludovico Marchesi himself, up and up by semitones in leaping octaves, all the way to the high C, a great victorious scream, as if the top of her head had popped open and light was shooting from the middle of her forehead, and it was the feeling that counted, of being a hollow body full of rushing air, empty and full all at the same time, and it was the surprise, the unfettered joy, in her brother's face, that counted, and the knowledge that Marchesi was listening to her match and ridicule and best him, and that everything would be all right at last because they were on their feet, the Florentines, stamping and hollering her name, until she heard nothing else — *"Brava*

La Storace! Brava L'inglesina! Brava, brava!"

Of course they fired her immediately. The manager apologized, for in spite of her temerity she had been a thrilling success. But Marchesi was *primo musico* and had powerful friends and backers. Anna requested her fee for the evening's performance and was granted it — more money than she had ever made for a single night. Marchesi would have made ten times more. Her mother was in tears and would not speak to her. Stephen thought it was all his fault. But the next day Anna's name was in all the papers, and on everyone's lips, and there was a letter of invitation from La Scala to sing *prima buffa* — leading lady — in the spring.

Several months later, from the port city of Livorno, Stephen departed for London. He would address their debts there, organize the family's possessions, and sell the house, as Mr. Storace had intended. Anna and her mother went on to Milan, stopping along the way to concertize.

LA SCALA

They had two clean rooms in Milan, with a sitting room between them, up three flights of stairs. Another singer lodged next to them, an Irish comic tenor named Michael Kelly, whom Anna had met in Florence. He was a slight young man of about twenty, with long, flaxen hair and a round, birdlike face, and specialized, he said, in "Lechers, windbags, and doctors." He had taken a room next to theirs on purpose and promised Anna's mother that he would protect them from thieves and scoundrels. Mrs. Storace said privately to Anna that she was not convinced he could protect *himself.* Michael spoke with great rapidity and his dress was extravagant and costly, often at the expense of his food. His voice was penetrating and reliable, not particularly winsome, and he was fond of cards.

"Isn't it grand?" he asked Anna downstairs at the inn over a chicken. Her mother was upstairs with indigestion, having had a disagreeable reaction to her first Milanese water. "Here we are kings and queens. I don't think many young fellows from my town would've imagined themselves singing at La Scala." He stretched his arms behind his head and grinned.

"Have you met the other singers in the company?" Anna asked. "Are they nice? Are they very old?"

"Oh, yes, jolly fellows all. Trust them with my life. There's Mandini and Benucci who are much alike. Mandini's not as good as Benucci but he's an upright fellow, elegant, lean. Benucci's tremendous. He's a cannon. Great fun. What, how old? Middling of age. Younger side of middling. Then there's the basso, Bussani, great booming fellow, and his pretty little wife, Dorotea. She's the only other lady, almost as young as you, I should think, but not nearly as good. She's a good old ham but the voice isn't much. She goes with Bussani, you see. Then there's you and me."

"I hope they like me," she said.

"They won't be able to help it, my dear!"

"Is Benucci the *primo buffo*?"

"Him or Mandini. You'll look well with either of them. Mandini you don't have to worry about, he's got a wife. Oh, she sings,

45

too; I forgot about Mrs. Mandini. And Benucci — well, he's a good chap, sings like a cannon."

The following morning Anna and Michael went to La Scala to sing through the first act with the rest of the cast. Michael had been there a month already, and the others longer, but the former *prima buffa* had departed for another engagement. The opera was by Antonio Salieri, visiting from Vienna. He did not know Anna's voice but she had told him its compass in letters. She had received one aria by post in Livorno, but otherwise today would be her first encounter with the opera. The first performances would be in four and a half weeks and the other two acts were still being written.

Opera buffa was the new, modern comic Italian opera, born from commedia dell'arte. The music was natural and the language conversational. Serious opera, opera seria, was in the old, grand style, the plots complex and often mythological, vocal prowess the most important element. The singers in opera seria sang their long, demanding arias in turn, one after another, without much interplay between them. The plots were so complicated, and at the same time so similar, that it was not worth the effort of the audience to follow them, and the words were often distorted almost beyond comprehension by the feats of vocalism — *fioratura* and roulades, ornaments and cadenzas — which were among the greatest arts of the castrati.

But artifice now was out of fashion. These days, one could go to the opera to laugh. One could see ordinary, lower-class people on the stage, in natural, comical situations, such as were encountered every day. The ordinary man could be as entertaining as Zeus — and everyone knew an ordinary man. The music was simple, transparent, and tuneful; everything that music should be. One could understand the words.

Anna — a clever girl with a witty stage presence, a fetching figure, and a talent for comedy — had arrived at the perfect time. She would play cunning maids and dexterous shepherdesses, girls of the peasant classes who fell in love with noble gentlemen, outwitted all those who plotted against them, and finished their lives in happiness.

Mrs. Storace went with them to the theater, though Anna wished she would not. Still they were almost late, having gotten held up by a fish cart, and arrived out of breath at the small rehearsal hall where the other singers, the stage manager, and Salieri were waiting for them.

"Are we late?" shouted Michael, in his quick, Irish-inflected Italian, pulling Anna by the hand. "Fish cart, fish cart! But I've brought her, here she is, our new girl, and her excellent mother."

The singers had been loosely arranged at the harpsichord, and now as Anna and Michael went to meet them — her mother took a seat to the side — they rose to greet her. Anna, flustered and nervous, received these impressions of them: that they were friendly and kind, loud and informal; that Mandini was refined; that Bussani's young wife had a lack of grace that only increased her charm. Salieri had a tight face and a drawn-down mouth. But he, too, seemed kind, or kind enough. Indeed they were all happy to see her there, and she was immediately re-assured. But when Francesco Benucci took her hand she felt a shock to her heart — so firm was the touch and so warm — and she flushed red and hot.

"You must be my Dorina," he said.

"Am I?" she asked, and everyone laughed.

They began the rehearsal. Anna could read almost anything by sight, and Salieri was experienced enough that he had written nothing that would show her ill. She was aware of them all listening to her — the opera would largely fall on her shoulders — but the feeling invigorated her and only made her want to sing her best. As soon as she began, she saw the other singers smile and whisper to one another, and she knew then that they liked her.

After that it became simply a matter of play between them, a game of words and music and physical exertion that they embarked upon together. They were strong singers, with swift minds and open good humor — arrogant enough to think they could stand on a stage and dogged enough to have done the work to get there. They earned their way with their voices and bodies. It was changeable work and fickle, which time and fashion would remove, but which they loved so much that none of them would have changed it.

At first Anna could hardly look at Benucci. Everything Michael Kelly had said about him was true. He had thick, dark brows and dark hair, and alert, warm eyes spaced slightly far apart. His expression was energetic and intelligent. He had a firm jaw, a wide, infectious, dimpled smile, and a reverberant and unself-conscious laugh. His voice was as beautiful as it was powerful, his neck and torso broad and strong, ideal

49

for singing. He was taller than Mandini but shorter than the giant of Bussani. And Anna saw that Benucci was loved by everyone, and that he made them laugh and lighten. She saw that they all looked to him, that even Salieri looked to him.

She had never had to play a lover before, not as she would have to now. She had never kissed a boy or gentleman as a lover would. She had hardly even been to a ball. And now Francesco Benucci was beside her, with his laugh and his smile, with his voice that was one of the strongest and most beautiful natural male voices she had ever heard, and she would have to pretend to be in love with him, to be his match and his ideal.

By the end of the rehearsal she had become more comfortable, as though they all were friends already. But every time Benucci looked at her, she felt as though she might fall over.

"Who was your teacher?" he asked quietly.

"Venanzio Rauzzini."

He gave an approving nod and leaned back on his heels, his hands loosely at his waist. "I knew him in Rome. Fine singer. Fine lineage. Porpora taught Rauzzini. He did well by you."

"You knew him?" she exclaimed. "What was he like?"

He smiled thoughtfully but did not have a chance to answer, because Dorotea Bussani was coming over in her carefree way to say how well Anna had sung and how much fun they would have. "You aren't stupid," she declared, clapping Anna over the shoulders. She was a striking girl with a long face and reddish hair; everything about her seemed lanky and open. "We always get stupid girls who stand like poles, it's *agony,* can't do anything except prop them up and wait for it to be over. But *you're* smart and we'll have such fun. You know how to *entertain*! You know what it's all about!"

Dorotea had grown up in a family of traveling performers, which was where her husband had discovered her when she was only fifteen. There were almost thirty years between her and Bussani. He was a comic bass of the first class, with a rumbling voice and a sardonic manner.

"Marvelous," said Stefano Mandini in velvet tones, taking Anna's hand to kiss it. He had an aquiline nose and a broad, steeply sloping forehead. Everything about him was precise and well contained. Anna had liked his singing very much. His voice was not as beautiful as Benucci's, nor as loud, and his manner was less passionate, but the technique was without flaw. Man-

51

dini could probably sing anything he liked, and he gave one the impression that he did so not to entertain, as Dorotea did, but because it was a physical challenge that happened to provide him with an income. "I think we'll find ourselves lucky to have you," he said. "I think you're the piece we were missing."

"Brava," said Salieri with a wry smile. "When I heard how young you were, I was afraid you'd embarrass me. Now I'm afraid I might embarrass you."

"Oh, never!" said Anna.

"Look it over, tell me tomorrow if there's anything you want changed. There's not much time, but time enough."

"You sang prettily," her mother conceded on their way home. "And you looked well."

"She was an angel, madam," cried Michael Kelly. "Those are the best buffa singers in the world and your daughter holds her own among them."

"You are too kind, sir," said Mrs. Storace. "I enjoyed your aria, as well. Very nice Irish tenor."

"I thank you, madam," Michael declared fervently. "I am neither a large man, nor a great one, but with my voice I hope to seem so."

"That is all one can ever do," said Mrs.

Storace, and she talked with Michael all the rest of the way home and through dinner. She liked having a gentleman to speak English with. Anna, lost in daydreams and fatigued by the rehearsal, was glad to stay quiet.

A few days later they began staging the opera. They memorized their parts as they went along. They were well trained in memory and the music fell into familiar tropes and patterns. Sometimes Salieri would alter something or other. He was a dry, thin gentleman, with a square head and a habitual, wincing frown; a man at once smooth and sharp, who held the rigor of an ascetic while yet, at least according to Michael Kelly, enjoying his women and his drink.

The men all knew one another from previous engagements and acted like brothers. They were scrupulously courteous with Anna and Dorotea. Only Michael treated Anna as a friend, with frankness and unreserve. She supposed this was because he was not handsome, although he had a pleasant expression, boyish and birdlike. At any rate, she could be easy with him.

Benucci said very little to her. He let the others talk. He seemed, on purpose, after that first day, to situate himself far from her when they weren't rehearsing, and whenever she caught his eye he would find a reason to turn away and say something to Mandini or Bussani.

Nevertheless Anna felt his presence keenly. He would tap her shoulder and say, "Well done," or, "Very fine," and when she found in their staging some interesting motion or turn of phrase, his approval was open and genuine. When they sang together there could be no appearance of reserve. They must look into each other's eyes, argue and exclaim, laugh, dance, despair, declare their love and their hatred, and then again their love renewed. On stage they had a rapport, a secret, silent dialogue that could be indulged in nowhere else. They spoke in glances, in movements of head and hands, in inflection, in touch — all there, on the open stage. Dorotea remarked to Anna that she had never seen a leading couple so well matched. They acted as if they already knew each other, she said. She had never seen Francesco Benucci better than he was now. All the other sopranos had been too dumb — they hadn't known what to do with him.

Anna shook her head and demurred, but in her heart she felt it was true. Francesco Benucci had found his match. That was why he wouldn't talk to her, and why, on stage, his hand seemed to linger in hers a moment longer than was necessary. It was wonderful and strange. She thought only of him. Her only project was to make herself better, for him. Her Dorina would be sparkling, vibrant, bright — everything he deserved. She slept with the windows wide open and in the morning the air was filled with honey. It seemed impossible that this should be her life, that she had made it this far, and no one had told her, not even her mother, that she must go back to London. Young ladies of sixteen were not supposed to live like this, in the honeyed air, singing on the stage with men. Yet it was so.

Love's Confinement

In the bowels of the theater were all the magnificent ropes and gears and pulleys of the stage machinery, as complex and fine-tuned as any clock or warship. These great works of wood and rope were pulled and pushed and held down by stage workers, moving the flats of painted scenery to create spectacular effects. It was a dark, churning space, crowded with men who must work in silence at the limits of their physical strength, and whose any mistake might kill someone.

Anna and Benucci retired to this space below every night, near the end of the last act. Once there, they would fold themselves into a small wooden closet that the workers would gingerly raise through a trapdoor in the middle of the stage — so that the two lovers might emerge at last in a state of final marital bliss.

They had to practice it many times for

safety and timing.

Benucci went in first, with his wide, fox-like grin. A lattice above the door let the light in. He held out his hand to Anna and she stepped up to join him, turning so her back rested snugly against his front.

He settled his arms around her. "Comfortable?" he asked, his voice sounding at once above her head and through her heart.

"Oh, yes," she said.

The men slid the door shut.

"Just rest against me," he said in a low, easy tone. "We'll be out soon."

She realized that she had been holding herself rather stiffly, and she sighed a little and let her head lean back against his shoulder. He had large, nice hands, and they held her easily. His face inclined in such a way that his calm breath touched her ear in soft and stroking intervals.

The men outside were talking. It was so dark and quiet where Anna and Benucci were that it seemed the outside must be far away. Anna could not help herself. She lifted Benucci's hand and put it to her left breast. Her heart beat so fast that she thought she would faint.

His hand held at her breast and his breath caught. Still they did not move. Then he sighed through his nose and circled his hand

and pressed there so that she was pressed totally against him. And then she took his hand and put it under her bodice and he pressed and squeezed there, while his other hand stroked her hip. She had never been held so raptly, so completely, with such open ardor.

There was a rattling at the door. Benucci quickly took his hands away. Anna giggled. She thought her eyes must be as big as an owl's. The man outside explained what they were working on. He said that everything was very safe.

"Are you all right in there, or should we let you out?" he said.

"Perfectly all right," said Anna.

"Not causing a stink, is he?" asked the man jauntily. "Not getting too ripe for the young lady?"

She smiled and said, "Signor Benucci perfumes himself in roses."

The door closed again and the box lurched and seemed to hesitate. Benucci twisted down to kiss her and she turned up to meet him. They made no noise but rustling and sighs, the soft wet *tsks* of lips meeting and drinking and parting. There was a holler from without and the machinery cranked into motion, lifting their conveyance into the air. The sensation of weightlessness, of

58

unhinging, brought a moment of fear, and with it, of greater exhilaration. Benucci pressed himself against Anna and flicked his tongue along the side of her neck, just near her shoulder, and she did not know or care where she was in the world or what she did, as long as there was this, forever. She was made of fluff and nothing, was wholly released, though she had never been so confined.

Up and down they went, more times than they could ever have hoped. If the compartment was constrained, if she could not turn totally to face him, at least they were alone. When they stepped outside it seemed at first they could hardly look each other in the eye, but then everyone remarked how well, how naturally, they moved and sang, as if they'd been working closely all their lives. And almost every other night, for more than a month, they could step into that lifted space and for five or ten minutes be alone together again, alone in their secret, before the door would slide open and they would come forward, flushed and laughing, to general applause, to sing their last number and be married for the hundredth, the five hundredth, time, just as all lovers dreamed.

LETTERS

Dearest Stephen,

I have not forgotten you. We have been so busy. There is no time to eat or think. If only you were here.

We are sorry that things are in such a dreadful state. When Mama read you were ill she went quite pale. We are enclosing some banknotes. Please do all that is necessary and for God's sake take care. If you die there I shall never forgive you nor speak to you ever again.

I am so happy, except for missing you. It is all a dream. Send me a drawing and an English song. Do send them.

Have you met Maestro Rauzzini? Once you have met him you shall understand me better.

There is a buffo singer here who is quite drôle. His name is Francesco Benucci and we sing together like a charm. Someday you will meet him. He's got the blackest eyebrows you ever saw — they are almost blue. But we laugh and laugh. I have never met such a fine buffo. After you meet him you can write him an aria.

Your silly sister,
Anna

Dear Anna,

Glad you've not forgotten me! I have written about the business matters in my letter to our mother. There is much to be done.

I love it here and never want to leave. I'm English and that is all. And you are becoming more Italian by the moment, aren't you? I met your Rauzzini and heard him sing. The voice, my God! He sang something Mozart wrote him. Extraordinary, humbling. He liked my Italian and said I resembled you, and told me I should stand taller and not apologize for myself.

Be careful of that buffo. If his voice is as good as you say and his eyebrows as black, I don't trust him. Remember your virtue and your worth. You are too young for buffos. I fear you are too soft. Why didn't Rauzzini give you some of his steel?

I sold a watercolor to the father of one of my pupils and walked around as if I'd been knighted. I enclose a sketch and a song.

Ever your,
Stephen

Dearest Stephen,

I'm dismayed you are so happy and so English. You'll never come back to us! Don't worry about the buffo, he's the best gentleman I know. Rauzzini gave me his phoenix pin and that is my steel. Next month I'll be seventeen. Tom Linley was friends with Mozart, don't you remember? In Italy when they were boys.

Benucci is really very grand. He makes me laugh till my sides hurt, and he sounds like a lion. Now I must go. I have already learned your song by heart and am singing it to you now. Can you hear?

With greatest affection,
Anna

P.S. Rauzzini is right, you mustn't apologize, at least not for yourself. It's good to apologize for some things, for instance if you tread on a lady's foot or behave badly, but you should not apologize for your nature — after all, didn't you sell a watercolor? But I'm sad you sold it, for it means I shan't see it.

A New Maid

Benucci had a three-month engagement in Rome, and would be gone some four or five months in consequence. Mandini would take his place in the interim, as primo buffo at La Scala. Anna had known of Benucci's impending departure for some time, but still it was horrible and she did not know what to do. For all their secret affections, and for all that she felt they were linked in their souls, still they barely spoke. There was never a chance — someone was always with them. She thought they had an understanding, and that he must love her, but he had never said he did, nor admitted that he wished to marry her. There could be no harm in marrying — there was nothing to prevent them — and yet somehow she was afraid to make it come to that. Her mother would say she was too young. Dorotea Bussani had married at fifteen and she was happy enough, but Dorotea had been poor.

Benucci was not like Bussani. Anna was afraid he might not love her. When they were with others he pretended as if she were nothing to him, and at times it did not seem like pretending. So she stayed quiet. She was confused and uncertain. Her doubts sometimes were as strong as her longing, and she had nobody to talk to, no confidante. She would not see him for four or five months, and after that perhaps never again. Perhaps he would not wish to return.

But then came a sudden security. The whole opera buffa company from La Scala was engaged to sing their Salieri opera in Venice, for Carnival. They would go there after Benucci had returned from Rome. He would sing it with them. Everything would fit perfectly. Though the thought of being apart from him for almost half a year was unbearable, Anna would be reunited with him in Venice, in the richest and most decadent city that had ever been born, and when he saw her again she would be worldly herself, and beautiful and proud, and he would be amazed and enchanted.

"May I write you?" she asked him. It was their last performance before he departed. They were standing backstage during the duet between Mandini and Dorotea.

"Write me?" He smiled. "What would you say?"

She bit her lip. "Why, what people usually say in letters."

He sighed and touched her waist. "I don't like letters."

"Oh," she said, and moved away. Then Dorotea came crashing off the stage wanting to be complimented.

Anna wished to cry, but there was nowhere to do so safely. But when she went into the compartment with Benucci at the end of the last act, for the last time, he held and kissed her as usual, and whispered into her ear that he would see her in Venice, and she could not help herself, she abandoned her heart. He contained all her life. They would see each other in Venice, and in Venice she would be changed, changed almost beyond recognition. She would persuade her mother to give her more freedom.

After Benucci left, Stefano Mandini was her primo buffo. He was expert and precise on stage, sang clearly, acted well, never had to be told anything twice. They were doing a new opera by Sarti, and there was no closet, no reason to be alone together. Mandini was true to his wife. Anna could relax with him. Her thoughts were no longer frenetic and confused. She did not have to be always censuring her feelings. She slept more soundly and spoke more easily with the other singers. The five months passed almost without her noticing. They left Milan and arrived in Venice a few weeks before Benucci was due there, and she thought, as she gazed upon that beautiful city, a city like a painting, that perhaps she did not need to live for him after all. She was almost eighteen, and had made more money in the past year than she'd ever dreamed.

One night, soon after their arrival in Venice, Anna was out with Michael Kelly and her new chaperone when she noticed a girl playing guitar and singing popular songs in a corner of one of the casinos. The girl was tall, with a long face, a pointed chin, and a dark complexion. The Carnival mask she wore was unadorned, and her dress plain. Anna could not tell if she was pretty. But the voice was lovely.

"How do you do?" Anna asked warmly, approaching and introducing herself. The girl offered a shy smile and said she knew who Anna was.

Anna laughed. "Do you?"

"Everyone knows you."

"They think they do. But what's your

name? You've such a pretty voice."

The girl's eyes were shadowed by the mask. Of course that was the appeal of the masks; they gave everyone so much mystery. "Lidia Martellati."

"Not your real name, surely?" *Martellati* meant "little hammers" — a technique for singing fast scales. And Lidia was not a common name.

"The nuns wanted to call me Mariateresa."

"Nuns?"

Lidia glanced around the room and shrugged. "I came from a music conservatory. I escaped."

"All by yourself? But who is there to protect you?"

"Why, no one."

Anna bit her lip. "Are you — then I suppose you must be someone's mistress." She could not think *whore;* this girl looked nothing like one.

Lidia smiled graciously. "No, I'm chaste. I play and sing, and work for a seamstress. I have a cousin who helped me."

"Look here," Anna said. She blushed suddenly and felt shy. "Would you ever consider — I don't suppose you should — might you like to be my lady's maid? I already have one but I can't stand her. She's over there.

She's my chaperone. She watches me at parties and sleeps in my bed. But she snores. Do you snore? I like you. I know we don't know each other, but I think — I daresay we could be friends. I don't see how I could do anything but like you when your voice is so pretty. We could try it out for a few weeks. You'd stay with me, and talk with me, and unpin my dress and hair at night. I've others to do the rest."

In the face of this outburst Lidia seemed at a loss. She pressed her hands together and looked very thin indeed. Then she smiled and touched her heart and said, "I'd like that very much."

Anna clapped her hands. "Splendid! Come see us tomorrow afternoon. Here's my card. But you must act sober and dour. That's what my mother likes and it won't come off if my mother doesn't approve."

Lidia was from the Infanta orphanage in Naples. While in service there she had been trained in singing, guitar, cello, and violin. She had played in the girls' orchestra and sung in duets and trios. Her voice was a sweet alto. It might have been a voice for the stage, had she learned to breathe properly, but she did not like to sing loudly and she did not like everyone staring at her. But music was all she knew, and since she did not care to become a nun, and no one wished to marry an orphan who was so tall and boney, she had at some peril come to Venice alone, from Naples, to make her way as best she could. The night Anna met her she had not had a good meal in three days.

Mrs. Storace looked Lidia over and pronounced her underfed and swarthy. However, she said, she liked the sternness of her bone structure and the modesty of her garments. Anna explained about the chaperone's snoring and said that Lidia could read in Italian, Latin, and French, and was eager to learn English.

Mrs. Storace said, "She appears all right and proper. She is not loud but neither is she *mousy*. She is not afraid of me and yet she is *deferential*. You are becoming a woman, Anna. Someday you will have to choose a whole household. I will trust you in this, and woe to you both if she fails."

"Oh, Mama," laughed Anna. "You've been reading too many romances."

Mrs. Storace shook her head. "You may kiss me, my dear, and bring me that fan from the other room. I think I will dine with you tonight. You may not go out. You haven't practiced and you sounded weak in your low voice on Friday, although the last cadenza was well done. And you know I

70

never compliment. But you must not forget to practice."

Then she yawned and fanned herself and bade them a good afternoon.

Dear Stephen,

How I wish you could meet my Lidia. She is all virtue and sobriety but when she loves me she loves me wholly. I certainly have done nothing to deserve her. Really I'm such a silly girl! So silly! Last night we were out till four and today I look like death. But the gods are smiling and I don't have to sing tonight.

Mama and I are all amazement to read you've moved to the country. Next we know you'll be a monk! How can you be my only brother and so unlike me? How silly I am. I was very bad to stay out so late. Mama said so.

But here is Lidia with my tea! Dearest, sweetest, brown-eyed Lidia! Straight as a rod! How she cares for me — no matter that I'm a giggling creature. I would make her add a line to this letter so you could see her hand and meet her in that way, but she is so modest she'd run over the hills and dales.

Tonight we dine with Benucci and Michael Kelly. Benucci just got back and

71

we'll reprise our opera. I have missed my Titta, and he has missed his Dorina. Don't frown, I'm not in love with him, I mean with Benucci. Only Titta. Titta is my love. But Michael is my best friend, apart from Lidia and you. Don't be a monk, my Stephen. Do don't be. I should need you too much. Now tea!

Yours ever, Anna

COLUMBINA

The people of Venice sang as much as they talked, sang as they worked and wooed and slept, in gondolas and barges, on market squares, lubricated by drink and company and the place itself, a city in the water that waked by night and slept by day, that prized folly over sense, and saved itself for nothing, but spent all, risked all, for beauty's flowering and pleasure's gratification. A city that directed its people to go masked, that friends might meet as strangers and strangers as friends.

You might have found Anna, on nights she wasn't performing, playing faro at the Ridotto, with her darkly fringed eyes shadowed by a golden half-mask, a *columbina*. She sometimes sang at the table — everyone sang in Venice — and that was how one knew her, even masked, even in so crowded a place as the Ridotto. Anyone who considered himself anyone in Venice in December

1782 could identify the voice of Anna Storace, so warm and sweet it was, so personal and beguiling. Names for her hung in the air like the smells of the lagoon and the songs of the gondoliers: La Storace, L'inglesina . . .

She loved to play faro but never risked much. Her mother thought she was too young for it, but Anna insisted it was politically necessary. She must mingle with her patrons and benefactors and be known. She enjoyed the game for the way it made her feel as alive as she felt on the stage, with a racing heart and warm jovial bodies all around her and sensations of peril and security rolling in delicious contradiction in her belly. She loved, too, how everyone at the table knew and praised her, and blushed, some of them, to be in her presence. Young men grown bored of throwing away money in their own names placed bets in hers, leaning over her cards and urging her to bid another hundred, another thousand, until they had no more.

If not at the Ridotto she might be found at the private casino of a friend or patron, playing the same games with smaller and more select company. Sometimes she would be asked to sing. At three or four in the morning she would leave for home with

Lidia. Drowsily they'd float along the crowded torch-lit canals and disembark into the apartment where Anna's mother was waiting, there to take off their sweat-stained masks (Lidia's a hooded *bauta*), and then Lidia, suppressing her yawns, would undress Anna, and help her put on her nightgown, and comb her dark fragrant hair, and Anna, tired and intoxicated, would lean into Lidia's flat chest as if she could not stand, and so they would fall into bed like sisters and sleep into the afternoon.

In the weeks since she'd arrived in Venice, Anna had resolved to forget all about Francesco Benucci, to disdain and torment him, but the moment he walked into the theater and kissed her cheeks, surrounding her with his smell and his touch and his warmth, with his ringing voice, bright upon dark upon bright, wholly his own, wholly recognizable, thrilling to heart and bone, there was no hope for her.

He smiled broadly, his eyes playing over her face and torso. "Did you miss me?"

"I forgot all about you," she answered, turning up her nose at him. Then she darted away, laughing, before he could catch her.

Soon again they were performing their Salieri opera, but in this theater there was not the same machinery beneath the stage as had been at La Scala. At the end of the opera Anna and Benucci simply walked on from the side of the stage. They were never alone, and Anna's yearning increased to a point almost of madness. She feared he might love another. Venice was filled with beautiful ladies, far more beautiful than she. If she could never be alone with him, and if he did not like letters, she did not see how there could be a chance for him to declare his true meaning.

Yet even in her confusion she had never been so happy. Benucci understood her as no one else, because they worked so closely together. She strove for his admiration. Though he was almost as old as her mother, he treated her as his match. They were always laughing. She called him Signor Lazy-Fox. They were cheerful, good people, at the top of their form, and they looked pleasing together. She trusted him like the earth beneath her feet, the sun on her cheek. She traced his name in the air with her finger. *Francesco.*

"Now, Lidia," she said one night after the girl had been with her for a number of weeks. "You know I tell you everything, but I haven't yet told you all."

It was late; they had put out the candles

and could see each other only by the light coming through the shutters. Anna had sung tonight and was too thrilled to sleep. Every performance was with Benucci, and every night they burned for each other more. Was it any wonder they were the sensation of Venice? One could feel it in the air, she was certain; one could tell by the way she walked.

The girls sat on the bed in their night shifts, their hair hanging over their shoulders, Lidia's in a heavy braid and Anna's in loose curls. Sometimes she put it in wrappers, but tonight she had no patience. They sat facing each other on the bed with their knees touching and their hands loosely playing and interlacing across their laps. The moon through the half-open shutters cast bars of bluish light on the folds of their shifts. They were both so tired that their heads nodded together like flowers in the rain and yet they did not lie down; they did not wish to sleep.

Lidia had long, knobby fingers. They tended to Anna and were a comfort to her. Anna had not realized until Lidia's coming how lonely she had been for a girl her own age, a girl who would care for her and be her friend. It was not possible to be friends like that with the other sopranos. Anna had

77

never had a sister. If she was the gold leaf, Lidia was the wooden stuff that backed her.

Anna's shift had slid down over her shoulders; her dark curls slipped softly down as if to follow. Her face had been scrubbed clean of paint and powder and shone faintly with the fine oil Lidia had rubbed into it. She looked, in the dark, after this night's performance when she had been painted so gaudy and bright, younger and more naked than she might ever have imagined herself. Her downcast eyes seemed to throw shadows on the tops of her cheeks; her lips were smiling for Benucci.

She hooked her index fingers around Lidia's and pulled back until her grip threatened to break. "You know I'm in love with Signor Benucci," she whispered. "It burns my heart, Lidia. Whenever I think of him, whenever I hear his name — his voice! You've heard him. Does it not shiver deep inside you?"

"He has the most beautiful bass I ever heard," Lidia agreed. She let go of Anna's fingers and relaxed her hands so that they dropped open just outside the ring of their legs.

Anna fell to one side, pulling Lidia down beside her. "I can't bear it. I'll go mad." She took the other girl's hand and drew it under her chin. "You must help me," she said, staring into Lidia's eyes in the dark. "We must make up a rendezvous."

"Does he love you, too?"

"With all his heart. To have gone as far as we have — I haven't ever told you how far — it's more than any girl could stand. You must help me, you must, you *must.*" And she took Lidia's hand and kissed it repeatedly.

"Won't he marry you?"

"Oh yes, but there's no time for that now."

"Are you crying?" Lidia exclaimed.

"Ah! Just because I'm so weary, my dear one, and so tired." Anna rubbed her face into Lidia's shoulder. "I sang myself to death tonight."

"You were incomparable," said Lidia. Her fingers twined carefully in Anna's hair. "Do stop crying. You'll soak my shift."

"I'm a fool, I've gone crazy, everything is only Benucci. You must help me, you must."

Lidia was silent a moment. She smoothed Anna's hair back from her forehead. "I don't think it's right."

Anna lifted herself on her elbow and laughed. "Anything is right if it hurts nobody and makes one happy. Poor, sober Lidia! They ruined you in that orphanage. We'll have to find a gentleman for you, too."

79

"None would have me," Lidia murmured tiredly. Her hand rested flat on Anna's back.

"You would be beautiful," Anna said lightly, "if only you *believed* you were beautiful. That's all that's wrong with you, Lidia. You're such an alto. You should be more like *me.*"

"Impossible," said Lidia with a smile.

Anna gave her friend a loud kiss on the cheek. "Good night, my love. Tomorrow shall be the happiest day of my life."

They slept on their sides, *en face,* very close, their arms and legs touching. But Lidia remained awake for some time. Anna's breath was upon her and her legs twitched once or twice in dreaming. Lidia laughed to think herself with such a bedfellow, such a sweet, needful mistress, and to have fallen in love with her already, so wholly and simply, so that in the end she feared some pain would come of it. But she'd had a strange enough life that she could almost laugh at that, too.

THE LOVERS

Two hours Lidia sat with her book of French verse and her dictionary, listening to Anna and her lover. Sometimes it would grow very quiet and that was least bearable of all, for then the littlest sound, the softest sigh, or creak, or groan, became gigantic in her mind. She would be almost frozen to the spot lest she, too, might make some noise and be heard.

Francesco Benucci's flat in Venice was just what one would expect of a man like him: large, messy, filled with objects that were expensive but ill-placed; which had no sense or harmony. A pair of candles flickered at her elbow. She tried to read her book. *"Pour elle je cultive et j'enlace en festons . . ."* She would never go to Paris. The chair she sat in could have paid a man's room and board for two years. She took up some sewing but it was too dark and she could not move about to make more light. She was glad there were no other servants. She could not imagine what they would have conversed about.

She had seen Anna in all states of undress. She knew her body, her moods, her motions. The love she felt was not shallow or passing, though it was new, though it was not returned. It was love like Paris. She knew that figure, that breast, that touch. She knew the dark eyes laughing so closely to her own. It was easy to imagine them, Anna and Benucci. She could have wept for the ease of it.

"Pour elle je cultive et j'enlace en festons . . ."

She felt stiff and tall in Benucci's horrible chair. Her torso was like a bundle of sticks, bound and stuffed in a web of skin. Her neck was a slab of clay. Anna said Lidia would be beautiful if only she believed in it. But she did not.

After a long time she finally tapped on the door for fear they might have fallen asleep. Her legs were stiff and she was just about ready to cry. Out slipped Anna like the sunshine, all sleepy and giddy and covered in Benucci, who remained inside. She fell upon Lidia as though she had no strength, and she was dear and warm and one could not help wanting to forgive her even as one still wanted to cry. Her clothes piled to the floor. She was in nothing but her petticoat and barely even that. She spoke to Lidia but she was not there: she was still in the room with Benucci. Lidia had never hated any man more. He could have had any girl he wanted. That was how it was with men like him.

But Anna didn't know. With mute tenderness Lidia restored her beloved mistress to a state of dress, fastened her in, undid the disunion. One could express one's love like this, in lacing and securing, smoothing and molding.

"Your hands are so cold, Lidia. I left you too long. You poor puppy."

"I'm sorry — let me warm them."

"It doesn't matter. I'm so happy, the cold refreshes, only it shocks me just at first! But that's good, good to shock me. Oh, whatever would my brother say?"

THE MORNING POST

When Benucci woke, late the next morning, he did not at first think of Anna. He thought of his hunger and thirst. He hummed a few notes to check his throat and did some preliminary calisthenics. The weather was bright and good; he could open the window and taste a fine salty air. Vendors called in the street over the racket of wheels on stone. He sang a line from an aria, rinsed his mouth, stretched his arms, put on a pair of trousers. Tonight they were doing the Salieri again, rather a big sing. There would be a Count Durazzo in the audience, scouting them for the Emperor Joseph II of Vienna. The emperor wanted to create a new Italian company to sing in his Burgtheater. This Durazzo would be there tonight to hear the Salieri. Hell of a long sing, rather high. Too bad it wasn't the Paisiello. Vienna was the biggest and richest city in the world, next to Paris and London. Maybe even superior to

84

them. There was no better place to make music, Benucci had heard, than Vienna. And this Count Durazzo had come from there, on the Emperor Joseph's behalf, to form a new Italian company to sing there.

He screwed up his face and rubbed his chin, wondering if it had not been a mistake with Anna. But she was not the sort of girl one resisted easily — not by half. Still perhaps it would have been better not to have gone on like that. But she was a dear girl. She had been so ardent. He'd never met a soprano he liked better on stage or off. He did not want a lady in his life. His life was only singing, and he could not bear the threat of children — and yet he felt quite warm and relaxed, now, thinking of sweet Anna with her brown eyes and her perfect breasts, her studied devotion to her craft, her innocent infatuation with himself. It could not help but flatter and warm him, give him idle fancies of what could never be. Benucci had these goals in his life: to be prosperous, to reach the pinnacle of his fitness and ability as a singer, and to always remain a bachelor.

The housemaid brought in his breakfast on a tray, roast pork with apples from the inn next door. There were also two letters. He read them as he ate.

My Love,

For I may call you that, mayn't I? But you are, you are! I'm so happy I hardly know what I'm saying. My darling heart. I shall adore you for every eternity. Can you feel the kisses on the page? Here they are, a thousand times here and here and here — I adore you — I wish only you could see me blushing. Write me back. Write me before tonight. I'm dying for you — I could hardly sleep. Is this what Heaven is like? How have I never known such bliss? All my life, Francesco — ah, to write it, your own name! My pen blushes and seems almost to faint! — all my life, my Love, I have sung of this bliss and never known it, how it feels. I'm overcome, I've no strength left in my limbs. Write me this afternoon, for God's sake. If I have to see you not knowing — not knowing how you — ! But I don't care, I don't care! I adore you, my life is yours. I opened my eyes this morning and the world had become more beautiful. I'm too happy, and I love you, I love you, and am forever your,

Sweet and Dutiful,
Anna

Her hand was large and careless, the paper littered with ink blots. In some places the words had been underlined thrice. There were spelling errors in the Italian, but the grammar was proper. It was the only letter Benucci had received from her, next to the note of yesterday. He did not like letters.

His face changed, as he read it, and his chewing slowed. Then he set the first note aside and opened the second.

Sir,

Of all the men in the world I thought you noble. By all that's good I charge you to marry my mistress or else leave her in peace. Recollect her youth. She lacks discretion, she has little Judgment. I have failed in my duty. I shall do everything to restore and protect her innocence. If you do not either marry her, or let her alone, I shall relate the whole Story to her mother. I pray you are a better man than you appear.

A humble woman,
Lidia Martellati

He was an ass, and a weak-willed ass at that. He finished his breakfast and went out to read the papers in a café. He tried not to do much talking on days he had to sing.

THE CASCADING HEART

He had not returned her letter. She looked inquiringly and hopefully into his eyes, but he looked away. Then he looked back again, as if in apology. She noticed herself talking quickly, her tone high and thin.

It was as though her heart were cascading down a series of ledges into a pit. With each drop it paused a moment for her to hope again, then slipped away until it struck the next marker. And again and again unto the depths.

She knew him too well. He was off; he hardly knew what to do with himself; he could hardly speak like a normal person.

After the performance she knocked on his dressing room door. He shared it with Stefano Mandini and Michael Kelly, and all three were in semiundress.

"My dear," said Michael in surprise, "you were wonderful tonight. I'm sure I never saw you so fiery or so bright."

"Indeed," said Mandini. "That Durazzo will be pleased."

"*Hang* Durazzo," Anna said.

"I don't think he'd be pleased with that," said Michael anxiously. "Look here, Mandini, shall we step out for a moment and make sure he's not skulking at doorways?"

Mandini glanced around, took up his jacket, and ducked out after Michael.

Benucci had been removing his makeup. He wiped his forehead with a rag and drew it down the side of his cheek to reveal a stripe of his natural skin, then set the rag in a basin of water.

"I don't love you, Anna," he said. "I never will. I don't want to marry. I'm sorry."

"Ah," she said, staggering.

"I don't love you, Anna."

She fled him then. Someone said that Count Durazzo was looking for her but she would see no one. Poor Lidia did not know what to do. She was afraid her mistress would become ill.

"What's the matter with you?" Anna's mother demanded. "What have you done?"

Anna said she had a sore throat and only needed some rest. She spent a day in bed and the next evening was back at the theater. Every object, every corner, she had blessed with the name of Francesco Benucci. Every note of the opera had been sung and heard to the syllables of *Fran-ces-co*. The language she spoke and heard and in which she sang was the language that now stabbed her heart. Her hands, her legs, her breast, belly, neck, eyes, cheek — had been his. He had kissed her wrists, her feet, her hair. He had held her as though she belonged, tucked there, in his long arms. He had sung to her more beautifully and sincerely than any man on earth. Her body had been his, her mind, her voice, her heart. He had taken possession of her breath. She could not look at her hands without pain. She could not remember anything without pain and yet remembrances were everywhere. And still she must sing with him, must pretend to make love with him.

If she could have run away, if she had had anywhere to go, she would have done so on the instant.

"Are you all right?" he asked her. "They said you were ill."

She could not look at him. This would be a problem when they were on stage. "Please burn my letter," she said in a quiet voice.

He hesitated. "I already did."

This, strangely, was a fresh pain. He had probably burned it as soon as he'd read it.

90

She swallowed and gave a stilted kind of bow.

She saw, from his face, how unwell she must look. "I'm sorry," he said. "My God, I'm sorry."

He tried to take her arms, but she pulled away, her lips twisting. "We mustn't speak," she said. "We must only pretend."

The cast perceived there had been a rift — Anna, at the intermission, retired to her dressing room to weep. But the audience knew nothing. And there, at least, showed the extent of Anna and Benucci's skill, the depth of their training, the core of their strength and ambition. On stage they were still the happiest, the most blessed lovers who ever had been born. They bantered and chirped. They had amusing spats and made up with a kiss. They pined for and adored each other. Their voices were true and firm, their movements elegant and lively. They were not themselves, even as they were most themselves. They were Anna and Benucci — confused, rueful, hurt — safely enwrapped in the trials and rewards of Dorina and Titta.

But not so safely, no, for all that, for his hands were still upon her, his eyes still smiling into her own, his voice like beautiful thunder in her ear, and it was hard to

91

believe that he did not love her, that they were not still in perfect happiness. Then the moment of remembrance would come and she would have to steady herself so as to keep going.

She was shamed, she was chastened. She had believed in something that did not exist, trusted in what was daydreams and air.

LETTERS

My dear Mother and Sister,

The news that you are going soon to Vienna has filled me with pride. Fine stroke of luck that the emperor needs a buffa troupe just when you're the brightest star in their firmament. They say it's a better city for music than anywhere. You'll live like a queen, I don't doubt. I'm glad Mr. Kelly and Signor Benucci will go with you. May they protect and keep you well. You won't have to do much work at first, I expect . . . you can sing the operas you already know . . .

I wish I could convey to you how good my life is here, how peaceful and free. Freedom above all is the best of life's graces. Here the world has no urgency. Each day I rise and bathe in the near dark. If the weather is fine, I go outside with my brimmed hat and paint. If it rains, I study my scores and compose.

In the afternoon I ride around on my little horse to visit my students. Is it not an envious life? Is it not the life of a perfect monk?

Vienna! Anna, you know Mozart is there. You must meet him and tell me what he is like.

There's a robin in the birdbath. For ten minutes together it has been standing ankle-deep in the water and making no motion. Does it care about ambition? Does it wish to be more beautiful than it is? No, it is beautiful as it is, because it is. I will fix it in my mind and paint it in the afternoon.

I wish you a safe and comfortable journey. Tell me about that world. I hope my mother is in exemplary health, and I remain,

Your Loving and Dutiful,
Son and Brother,
Stephen

Dearest Stephen,

Mama fears you've lost your senses but I like all this talk of freedom. Of course I will meet Mozart. It will be such a lark. We arrive in April. The contract is for a year. But we talk already of staying longer. You must come to Vienna as soon

94

as you can. We are to live in palaces and have all our firewood and candles provided for, etc. They say the emperor is just a regular gentleman: he wears plain clothes and doesn't stand on ceremony. Doesn't that sound like something you'd like? I shall talk to him and get you a commission. I miss you terribly.

Your ever affectionate,
And extremely fortunate,
Anna

My dear Anna,

What a proud singing teacher I am! When I read about Vienna I had to put down your letter. I went onto the street. I wanted to order a carriage and come to you. I don't know why I didn't, except you'd have nowhere to put me in your luggage. I suppose this pride is what a father feels. Forgive me. And yet you should know that you have my thanks. You give me joy, even from afar. Sing well. Remember what I taught you. Keep your heart safe, your heart's core. Keep it strong and safe.

Ah! — a fine father I would make!

I remain, etc.,
V. Rauzzini

ANNA AND THE THIEF

Joseph II, emperor over most of the civilized world, had to be kept rich in chocolate drops or he lost his optimism. Lost his cheery yet exacting personal fortitude, his relaxed and progressive outlook of can-do and savoir faire. Vienna had some of the finest chocolate anywhere, and Joseph, despite his disdain for extravagance, wished it no other way. He had hot, melted chocolate every morning for breakfast, brought to him in a teacup so thin that when placed, trembling, on his broad mahogany desktop, the chocolate inside showed like yolk through a shell. By that time Joseph would have been up for hours, writing, pondering, and the rich, extravagant liquid, like an embodiment of heaven, would warm and revive him.

In a way chocolates counterbalanced the other austerities of his life. The emperor wore the brown clothes of a layman, worked long hours, and aspired to reform all the excesses of his relatives and ancestors. He shut down churches and opened hospitals. He fired useless members of his court, no matter their birth or heritage. He bolstered all kinds of music-making. Even his new opera company was for the people. Anyone, after all, could buy tickets. When the hall wasn't in use he let it out for pennies to the musicians and composers he favored. In music, he felt, lived the soul of humanity. He played chamber music every day, and frequently and unaffectedly visited musical salons. He often said that if people around him forgot he was the emperor, he had done his duty.

He carried chocolate drops in his waistcoat pockets, wrapped like jewels in brightly colored tissue paper, and ate them at all moments — when taking exercise among his subjects in the Prater, when consulting with his ministers, when pacing with his pet beagle down the lawn or attending Shakespearean tragedies at the theater.

The audience at his royal opera house were nothing near as raucous nor demonstrative as those in the theaters of the Italian states. Beneath the music, beneath the soft murmur of gossip, beneath the pad of slippers on bare wood and the sigh and rustle of silk frock coats and full muslin underskirts, one might have heard the neat unwrapping of the emperor's chocolates, the smacking of his full, placid lips, as pink as if they'd been painted, as he sucked and chewed. His appetite for chocolate reflected his interest in the performance. Anything over twenty drops meant the opera was a winner. On April 22, 1783, a Tuesday, on the occasion of the debut of the new Italian opera troupe with a comedy by Salieri, the emperor consumed twenty-six chocolates before the end of the first act.

Anna, on stage, heard none of the sighing of muslin, so discreet and well mannered were these operagoers. After Italy, it was like being in a deserted church. Nobody called out to her, nor applauded in the middle of her aria, nor threw food nor spat on the floor. Even the theater was austere, a white box with understated decorations, no gilt or frescoes anywhere, and so small and intimate that it was like performing in the emperor's private salon.

The Italian company had been brought intact from Venice to Vienna: Bussani, Mandini, and their wives; and Benucci, Michael Kelly, and Anna. They were to replace the disbanded German-language singspiel company, which had flourished briefly and then fallen into disregard.

In Vienna there were no street singers. There was no shouting. The side streets were paved with stones that seemed hewn, on purpose, to cause one to fall; the main roads were laid with white gravel that lifted up clouds of dust whenever anyone walked or rode on them. In summer the air became thick with dust and everyone had to cover their mouths with handkerchiefs. Outside of town, though, the air was fresh and clean. The inner city was flanked by a swath of green commons, the Prater, where Viennese of every class would go to recreate, listen to concerts, picnic, and dance. The Viennese loved to dance as much the Venetians had loved to sing.

It was good, Anna told herself, to be in Vienna. Everything was so brisk and orderly. Venice had been a city of passion. Vienna would school and restore her. Though she would be seeing Francesco Benucci nearly every day, at least she would be somewhere new; at least she would be learning German. She had already been complimented on her pronunciation.

Following the opening night's performance there was a party in one of Joseph II's ballrooms. Everyone of consequence was

99

invited, and the emperor himself could be seen pouring out wine to his guests.

Anna had slept poorly the night before, from her nervousness. She had been afraid she would not be in good voice, but she supposed everything had gone well. In a corner of the ballroom Benucci flirted with some chorus girls. His face was damp and flushed and he let out great booming laughs. One of the girls had her arms around his neck.

Anna had sent Lidia to find a glass of punch but she could not bear to stand there waiting while Benucci made love to chorus girls. She bowed to the gentleman whom she had been talking to and fled past the tables of faro and whist, past the diligent chamber orchestra, through some glass doors, and onto a terrace.

There was a garden arranged in geometrical shapes with a small orchard. It was a clear evening, although cooler than she was used to. She felt herself reviving to the coolness. With light steps she ran down the path to the end of the garden, where she found a bench and a statue by a tree. She would just sit here a moment, hidden away, she thought, and rest her feet. Then she might return to all of those strangers with a calm spirit and genuine smiles.

She had actually removed her shoes and

was stretching her toes in the air when she noticed a gentleman standing in the shadow by the statue. He had been so still, and she so self-pitying, she had not noticed him. She let out a small exclamation.

He darted forward, caught up her shoes, and ran off with them.

"Oh, you wretch!" she cried.

He'd gone behind some bushes. She glanced back at the lights of the palace and bit her lip. Perhaps he was a murderer. But she could not appear before the emperor without shoes on.

Her stockings were new and they were silk. With a whispered curse she slipped them off and stuffed them down her bodice, and went after the villain.

The ground was wet and soft, cool to her feet. She lifted her skirts so as not to get them damp. He was waiting by a fountain, grinning, his hands behind his back.

"My boots!" she said in German, not remembering, in her agitation, the precise word for "slipper" or "shoe."

"What boots?" he asked softly.

"Mine!" she cried. She opened her mouth to say more, but the horrible language betrayed her. "Oh, you wretch!" she exclaimed again in English, and stomped her foot.

He was a slight man, perhaps thirty, with a profusion of hair and a big, sharp nose. His clothes were fine — she could tell even in the dark: a nobleman making heartless sport with her.

"I know Italian," he offered in that language. He had an elegant, well-produced tenor voice. She lunged after him and he took off around the fountain, a shoe in each hand, laughing. But the pebbles were painful beneath her feet and she did not have enough breath to continue. He backed his way toward the high bushes, laughing at her. With her eyes fixed on the slippers she followed slowly, relieved to be moving out of sight of the palace.

"Why do you know Italian?"

"I spent some time there."

"Your accent is impeccable."

"So's yours."

"Thank you."

She darted at him again and he lifted the shoes out of her reach. He was just that much taller.

"I'll scream," she said.

"Please don't, mademoiselle. Everyone would think we'd been having a liaison."

"You're a brute and a thief."

He seemed startled at that. "I'm not a brute. I haven't touched you."

"You spied on me and stole my shoes."

"I did not *spy*. I was *there* and you intruded."

"Please give them back."

He looked down. They were pretty slippers with a gold trim and pointed toes and had cost a fortune. "I'd give them back for a kiss," he said thoughtfully.

Now she really should scream. Her heart pounded enough to break.

"All right," she said.

He looked up quickly. They were standing quite close now.

"For the shoes," she added, blushing.

He gave her a wondering smile. "Is that so?" he said, in a low voice. "For the shoes?"

Then, with extreme care, as if afraid she would panic, he set the slippers on the ground beside her. She was breathing quite fast. He straightened and glanced around. "Just one?"

"Well," she murmured, amazed at her boldness. "The rest depends on if I like the first."

He laughed again. "My God," he said. "I've been longing for this all evening. And here it is."

He put a hand to her waist and touched her cheek and looked closely into her eyes, though it was very dark, and then he kissed her lips, gently and softly and long.

It made Benucci's kisses seem like hard, hasty fumblings.

"Oh," she breathed.

"One more?"

"You're a brute."

"All evening," he said. "And then you come running after me." And he kissed her again.

She didn't want to know who he was. She didn't want to go inside. But everyone would be wondering. She pulled her stockings from her bodice and he helped her put them on and fasten them with her garters, then helped her with her shoes. His fingers circled her knees and wanted to go higher. She laughed and wriggled away.

"Go on," he whispered, and gave her a light push.

With cautious steps she eased back into the bustling hall. The crowd seemed larger than when she'd left it. She could not contain her smile. At length she found Lidia with the punch. Lidia gave Anna a reproachful look. "I'm parched," Anna exclaimed, and drank down half the glass. Her eyes searched the crowd for the gentleman from the garden. She did not know what she would do when she saw him. But he must surely have come in after her.

104

"There you are," said Benucci, approaching with a lady on each arm. "We've been looking all over. This is Madame Aloysia Lange. She's a marvelous soprano. She doesn't have much Italian so we'll have to make do as best we can with our German."

"How do you do," Aloysia said daintily. "You sang very prettily tonight, everyone thought so." Her voice was sweet and high as a child's. "This is my sister, Madame Constanze Mozart; I don't believe you've met."

"Hello," said Constanze. "How nice to meet you. I enjoyed your singing very much. My husband was in ecstasies. He's a composer. We can't find him, but he was so impatient to meet you and Signor Benucci and he has such excellent Italian — he'd be able to translate for us."

"You're the wife of Herr Mozart?" Anna asked. She felt a hint of apprehension. But there must be many gentlemen among the party who spoke excellent Italian.

"That is my fortune," Constanze observed placidly. She was taller and plumper than her sister — perhaps with child. Her face had a certain lack of expression, as though she were either shy or dispassionate. Her form and complexion were good, but hers was an ordinary sort of prettiness — she

105

did not have Aloysia's lips or cheekbones or waist.

"I would love to meet your husband," Anna said, still in German, though she hardly knew if she was being intelligible. But Constanze smiled encouragingly. "I've heard so much about him."

"He's like nobody else," Aloysia said. "Here he comes now."

Anna turned, and begged heaven to help her. It was he. Indeed it was he. Wolfgang Mozart had stolen her shoes.

"Where have you been?" Aloysia asked. "You abandoned us completely. We were forsaken utterly."

A hint of irritation crossed his face. "You were talking to that Herr Gosta. I can't stand Herr Gosta."

"But where did you *go*?"

"Oh, here and there. I have to spread myself about and remind them all I'm still alive. I talked with this person and that person and then I went for some air out on that terrace. I think I may have seen this lady there," and he nodded kindly to Anna. "Though she went in before I had a chance to introduce myself."

"You weren't out all alone?" Aloysia asked Anna. "But how very modern of you. I suppose you don't care what people think."

106

"Not really, no," Anna said pleasantly. Aloysia smiled.

"You all sang splendidly tonight," Mozart said to Benucci in Italian. He turned to Anna and gave her a determined smile. "Are you enjoying Vienna, mademoiselle?"

"Yes, quite well, thank you."

He was certainly not thirty. Later she would learn he was twenty-seven. He carried himself proudly and easily, like a magician or a dancer. There was a mixture of lightness and strength about him; how he spoke, how he held himself, how he used his hands. His face was softly rounded and quite pale. He had a strong nose and full lips. His smile was ready and catching. Most of all she noticed his eyes, unusually large and slightly protruding, a pale hazel which in some lights looked blue-green and in others almost dark. He wore his natural hair — a light brown that hinted at red, abundant and somewhat untidy — tied back in a pigtail.

Aloysia and Constanze, bored by the Italian, moved to a different party of friends along with Benucci, who still had Aloysia's arm. Lidia, who disliked large crowds and was embarrassed, retired to the side of the room and sat on a chair.

"You *wretch,*" Anna whispered to Mozart.

"I was beside myself, hearing you tonight," he said, stepping closer. "I nearly went out of my mind. I don't want you to think — you see, these things mean so much to me, obviously they do, I mean they are things I think about and that have direct bearing on my life and all my dreams — and by things I mean I heard and saw you and went out of my mind — with excitement, you know, and joy. A man spends all his life dreaming about a certain kind of singer — but then to see you, to almost be able to touch you!"

Then he looked at her with wide eyes and she knew they were both remembering about the stockings. "Oh, God!" he cried. "What I wouldn't *give* to write an opera buffa for a singer like you. I'd cut off my own foot. Not my hands. My hands I need."

"You knew Thomas Linley," she said. "I was in love with Thomas Linley when I was a girl."

Linley, a brilliant young English composer, had met Mozart on tour in Italy when they were boys of the same age. He had drowned a few years ago on a lake at Grimsthorpe Castle, all his finest music unwritten.

"Were you?" Mozart asked, with a soft look. "He was my friend. He was a true genius."

She was sober, suddenly, and sad. "It was very wrong of you, signor. You shouldn't do such careless things. If it were a play you could have marked me for life."

He raised his brows, interested. "I wish it were a play."

"Plays only ever end badly."

"Not if they're comedies."

She frowned and looked away. "It's not a comedy when Thomas Linley drowns."

"But that was the last play. Now you're in Vienna."

"I'm in Vienna and you're married," she said.

"Indeed," he said. "I'm sorry. I'm, ah — I can be impulsive, especially when I've been working hard." He glanced around the party, smoothing his hand on his thigh. His clothes were the finest cut and material; they made him handsomer than he was.

The emperor has been to visit us at home, Anna wrote to her brother. *He stayed half an hour and played with the dogs. Mama was beside herself. When he left he kissed my hand! This should tell you something of how I am esteemed here.*

Stephen replied: *I can't think but you exaggerate about the hand kissing. Have you met Wolfgang Mozart?*

Yes, she wrote, *I met Mozart. He's rather*

*arrogant for someone who's not done much.
Anna,* Stephen answered, *he has reason.*

At Café Hugelmann

In June, the Italian company gave its last performances before the emperor retired to his summer palace. Since coming to Vienna they had put on four new operas. They had been joined most recently by Mozart's sister-in-law, Aloysia, who had sung with the old German singspiel company and now took second lady to Anna's first.

She was five years Anna's senior, with striking cheekbones and rosebud lips. The men of the company loved her hesitant, broken Italian, which they declared the sweetest attempts at their language to ever have endeared them. They all endeavored to give her Italian lessons and declared she would be one of them in no time at all. She was married to a well-regarded actor and painter, Joseph Lange.

"I never felt more secure," she told Anna prettily, "than in the cherished moment when my dear handsome husband made me his wife."

They were sitting at an outdoor garden café, Café Hugelmann, on an island in the middle of the Danube. One bridge led to the festivities of the Prater, another back into the city. Boats floated at speed down the deep-running river. The garden was filled with flowers and birds. The two sopranos sat in the shade of a wide parasol, eating cream cakes and drinking from small cups of coffee. They spoke in German, and Anna, still far from comfortable in that language, fit in a word or two where she could. It put her in the position of a child.

"He is extraordinarily jealous and possessive," Aloysia continued, "as all the world knows, so no one questions my honor. I used to have all sorts of fellows in love with me — though, mind you, I never encouraged them. I just couldn't help it. There is no stopping a young man once he gets his mind set on an object, and then people *will* talk. You must know all about that already, how cruelly people talk of us female singers. But my dear husband put a stop to all of that, and I never felt more chaste and safe than on the day he took me for his own. I declare it was the best feeling I have ever known, to surrender myself to his power." She smoothed a curl from her eyes. "I'm surprised you're not wed yet yourself, a girl so fetching. You're quite the thing now, aren't you? I am not so vain to claim to comprehend your degree of occupation. Even at my height," she said, snapping open her fan and looking to the side, "I was not singing nearly half so much as you are. Do not you find it wearying? La! I should worry for the health of my vocal apparatus. I just don't know *how* I would manage so much singing. But I suppose my own arias are much more taxing than yours."

She sighed and nibbled her pastry. Yellow cream bulged out the side and she licked it up with her tongue. "You quite put me to shame with all your theatrics. I mean to copy your every motion, though I expect to fall flat. My beloved husband is quite an admired thespian, you know, and is always making fun of me for my unnaturalness. But you shall be the cure of me."

"Oh," said Anna, "you don't need a cure."

"I do if I want to keep singing in Vienna." Aloysia sipped her coffee and smiled seriously. "Let's not be circumspect — we are too wise and practical for that. You have usurped me — no, I do not blame you, only myself! — and if I am to survive and live again I must try — let us be totally honest — to outshine you. Pray then do not see my

113

efforts as a personal attack. I like you — admire you — very much, mademoiselle. I do not know, even, that I will be able to outshine you at all, though I have a few resources of my own and I believe myself to have the superior *voce.* But of course so much depends upon fashion and favor, and you, at the moment, are in the favor of everyone!" She gave a light laugh. "But though we may be fierce competitors on the stage, as plain women we may still be the best of friends." She pressed Anna's hand. "My dear — *may* I confide in you? I have so *few* confidantes."

"Of course," answered Anna with trepidation.

Aloysia bit her lip and said in a small, portentous voice, "Francesco Benucci has seduced me." She put a hand to her breast. "Ah! I see you are speechless. But you must have seen how perfectly smitten he was with me from the first moment. Of course I never dreamed anything should come of it, but then he was so handsome and his voice, you know, would corrupt a saint, and then my husband and I had the most dreadful fight . . ." She shook her head again, as if in amazement. "Well, now I'm in such a constant flutter! My husband doesn't suspect, but if he did he would kill us both. Of

114

course it must never happen again, but oh!" She sighed. "I don't know if I can resist him. He sends me heaps of love letters, by way of my maid. It is quite diverting. Once my husband came in while I was reading one of the letters, and I had to stuff it away. Oh, I am so relieved to confide in you, my dear — you are so sweet and good! You lift away all my burdens! I have been bursting for want of anyone to tell and you listen like an angel as I knew you would. We shall be *such* friends. I'll see you tomorrow. I've got a wonderful surprise but I don't suppose there's any harm in telling you now. My arias in our opera were so tedious, you know, and so entirely unsuited to my voice and talents, that I commissioned my brother-in-law Wolfgang to write a pair of substitutes for me. And he has done it, most superbly! I will sing them tomorrow. He used to be passionately in love with me, when we were young. I do believe he fell in love with my voice. Musicians will do that. But I wouldn't have him no matter how he pleaded, and so he married my sister! Would you believe? I always thought him quite odd-looking but of course Constanze has fewer advantages. But I think he still loves me. One can hear it in the way he writes for me. Wolfgang's heart is transparent in his music."

THE SECRET TRYST

In love with her or not, Mozart knew Aloysia Lange's voice. The substitute arias he'd composed for her received the biggest ovations of the night. One could hardly even feel resentful of them, because one was simply glad they had been written. There was more interest in Aloysia's first aria than in the entirety of Anna's role. Aloysia was all in ecstasy. But she still couldn't act, nor sing convincingly in Italian, and when she sang in her lower register it was nearly impossible to hear her over the orchestra. So, at least, thought Anna. But perhaps that was the kind of voice Mozart preferred, silvery and high. There was undoubtedly a rift between the German and Italian schools of singing and composition. The Italians had all the power and the weight of tradition. Mozart was a bit wild, a bit new, for current taste, and he was certainly not Italian.

Watching Aloysia and Benucci jest and play that night — Benucci practicing his German — Anna felt the kind of agony of jealousy she had often sung of but rarely felt. She pressed her lips together and resolved to be more hard-hearted. She need not compound her shame. He did not love her and never had. Though he was handsome and strong, though the sight of him made her heart dip and leap, she was not the one he treasured. He treasured a woman opposite her in every aspect. And should not that, then, diminish him in her estimation? Did it not show a fickle, a careless and an unworthy character in a gentleman? Her mother often lectured Anna about matters of character and fidelity. It was not a question, her mother said, of *love,* or *flattery,* or *liking the look of someone.* That would all reduce to dust. What counted was character and honor, the man's birth, his family, how he held himself and how he spoke and how he formed his letters. These were the qualities that might last.

It hurt Anna to watch Aloysia with Benucci. She knew it was vanity and yet it did hurt her. Never before had there been an Aloysia. If the other soprano had not been so simpering, so striving, so apparently lacking in decency, it might have been easier to

118

see her with Benucci. But that he should love *that* lady — that he should actually have written her *love letters,* he who disliked letters! That Anna had trusted in a man like him!

And yet it was of no use. She loved him, and likely would do so till the end of her days. There was no hope. She thought of him always and could not even confide in Lidia, because Lidia wouldn't hear of it.

Her life acquired a kind of grayness. She could be happy with nothing, she who had always cheered others. She felt an ever-pressing itch of displeasure and dissatisfaction. Then she found out he was leaving soon, temporarily, to fulfill a previous contract in Florence, and somehow she felt she must act.

She brought him to her dressing room, between the acts, and pleaded with him to make love with her. She had never before been so bold, not since the time Lidia had escorted her to see him in Venice.

He didn't want to. He kept saying he didn't love her and couldn't wed her, but she begged, and kissed him, and after all they were more comfortable with each other than with almost anyone else. Still it was something of a shock. He kept denying and denying her and then suddenly he was backing her onto the table and almost violently pushing up her skirts. She had to use all her strength not to make a sound, not to let him realize how much he was hurting her. His face, usually so cheerful, was as if possessed: he scarcely looked at her, and she almost wept, not only from the pain but because she felt she would never be this close to him again. Neither of them, she knew now, would ever again be this foolish. She tried to feel as deeply as she could, to fix in her memory every touch and feeling and breath.

He left without a word. She restored and steadied herself, too shocked for reflection or regret, and went outside for the singing that remained.

On stage he was Titta, jovial and unchanged, but he met her eyes less readily than usual. Her own Dorina was distracted and lackluster, with a weakened voice. The stage manager remarked upon the change and bade her to get more rest.

The opera company broke for the summer, the aristocrats went to their pleasure houses in the country, and Benucci departed for Italy, where he would be gone a month or two, and though she thought of him every moment, she sent him no letters. That was her only pride, that this time she did not write to him. There were not many young ladies, she thought, who would have been so strong. Now and then, in dark moments, she wished to harm herself. But she did nothing. She reminded herself that her sorrows were not so much.

A Visit

She visited Mozart one afternoon so that he could try out an aria on her. He was writing an opera called *The Disappointed Husband,* which he hoped would be accepted by the emperor for the Burgtheater. Anna was happy to oblige him. She had been feeling unwell and hoped he might cheer her.

Mozart and his wife lived on the second floor, above some shops. The household was a chaos of people and noise — servants and student boarders, various instruments, heaped-up scores being copied by Constanze and his assistants. Anna felt she was almost entering a marketplace rather than a home. The gracious front room, which had a high ceiling painted with stars and cherubs, was large enough to dance in and held thirty chairs, it seemed, and four sofas, to provide seats for the audience when he held concerts at home. The air smelled of coffee and smoke. Someone was playing a violin.

"He's just through there," Constanze said. She brushed her hair from her forehead and left a daub of ink. "Sorry I don't get up. We've got to get these all done by tomorrow."

Anna threaded her way through the furniture. The door to his study was shut. She knocked too lightly and then had to stand wondering if he'd heard. "Just go in," called Constanze from the other room. "He knows you're coming."

Mozart was scowling at the piano. "I can't play today," he said. "It's all rubbish. Listen." He played a few bars and finished with a crash.

She smiled, feeling nervous. "You can't play badly even when you try."

"I'm not trying. God in heaven! I don't know my own hands." He got up with a restless start and kissed her cheek. His hands touched her arms. Then he looked away as if distracted. "I've got a big concert in a few days. You should come." He frowned. "It's good to see you. You're looking well. Here's what I've got of the aria. Just a sketch really."

But he was contented with nothing, no matter how many times she sang it. He scratched notes out and then wrote them in again. He kept saying how he detested

123

the libretto.

At last she asked tentatively, "Are you unhappy with me? Have I not sung well?" And though she smiled, and spoke lightly, there was a tremulousness inside her, because to be at all displeasing was something Anna could not bear.

He shook his head. "I'm not even thinking of you."

She winced. "Oh."

Rising again he gave her a quick smile. His large, changeable eyes went everywhere but to her face. He moved to and from the piano. "Well. I'll see you out."

They stood for a moment not looking at each other. It was up to him to open the door. She would not open it herself. He was standing close to her and she felt very unwell. It had been wrong to come and yet she did not want to leave.

"Signorina," he said hesitantly. He had a warm, gentle voice. "When we — when I first met you. You know I was half drunk. Can't think what came over me. When I was young, it was one thing — but I've been married two years."

She felt a kind of burning, high in her chest. Everything was wrong. "I hardly remember that," she said with a gracious smile. "We were not ourselves."

ALL HER JOYS

Anna floated in for breakfast one morning, looking pale, while Mrs. Storace was staring out the window with an open book in her lap. Her daughter fiddled with the breakfast things.

"You look ill, Anna," Mrs. Storace observed. "And you don't eat."

"Mama," Anna said. There was a moment's silence. Then her face crumpled. "Mama, I have something I must tell you."

Quietly and slowly she related her story. She would not identify the father. She would only say that he must not know and that he would never have married her. But it was easy enough to guess. The buffo. The Italian snake.

"You've ruined us," Mrs. Storace whispered.

She stared at her daughter. Then she got up and began to pace, each word like the lash of a whip. "Either we must flee, throw ourselves at the mercy of some sisters of charity, or you must marry. If the world finds you for the whore you are," she said steadily and sharply, "it will be the end of everything. All your joys, your balls and princes, your pretty jewels. You stupid child. Either we must conceal you or *you must marry.*" She slammed the book on the table, the noise like a thunder crack. Anna sobbed loudly and covered her face in her hands.

"Listen to me," said Mrs. Storace, pacing. "There is a gentleman in town who knew your father. An Irish violinist, a virtuoso. He wrote me last week. He mentioned you. A virtuoso and a widower. We shall ask him to tea and you shall be your most charming and pray God he saves you. Do you hear me? And you will send that Lidia away tonight. I won't have a woman who has sold your honor living under my roof."

"But Lidia did nothing —"

"Whatever she did," snarled Mrs. Storace, "or did not do, she did not do her duty." And taking up her book, which she clutched like an armor, she returned to her seat, while her daughter wept, and began to read again.

Dear F, my mother has had a fit and turned Lidia out — I can't explain why.

126

It's nothing to do with Lidia. Won't you take her in till it blows over? I know you have too many rooms already. She's a hard worker and will serve you better than anyone. I wanted to send her to Michael but she insisted on you. Please? I love her like a sister and am your heartbroken, A.

Benucci had recently returned from his engagement in Florence. He peered at the woman — nearly as tall as he, with a baleful look in her eye.

"You," he said. "I remember you from Venice. I thought you didn't like me."

Lidia sniffed. "You were correct."

He thought of Anna. He felt guilty over her but could not decide how to fix it. Whenever he saw her, there seemed nothing to be done.

"You are welcome here," he said at last. "For a time. For the sake of your mistress."

"Kind of you, sir," said Lidia tightly, and pushed past him. It was not her intention to poison Benucci but it gave her satisfaction to know the possibility was there.

THE COURTSHIP

My dear Madame,

You do not remember me, I am sure, but yet I hope you will forgive my presumption in writing when I say that I knew your husband in London and heard your daughter sing there when she was just a girl. Yet how finely I knew she would turn out! You surely do not recall, and so I will inform you again, that I am something of a virtuoso violinist. Having spent the past year traveling the Continent and being lately arrived in Vienna with no friends or contacts here, I find myself yearning for good English company. Even writing this letter now in our own perfect language is a great refreshment to me! Since the death of my wife I have been alone in the world. Please write to me at the Harp and Boar if you would not find yourself opposed to my calling on you and your daughter some afternoon for a little English conversation. I remember Miss Storace with admiring fondness and it would be a treasure to me to see how she is grown.

But you, dear madam, I am sure, have neither grown nor changed nor aged since last I saw you selling plum cakes in Marylebone Gardens with powder on your chin.

Do you remember?

Your most humble servant,
John Abraham Fisher

Sunday afternoon found Mrs. Storace reading Richardson's *Pamela* in the downstairs suite of the three-story house the emperor had provided for them. It was the beginning of August, a rainy day and cold. The lapdogs, Bonbon and Fichout, snored before a fire. The room was dark. Anna had no performances at the Burgtheater for the next several weeks, not until they revived *The Barber of Seville* in September.

The maid came and announced a John Abraham Fisher. Anna's dogs, rousing themselves for the stranger, paced over to sniff at his dusty shoes. "Good afternoon," he announced in a mild Irish accent. "This is an honor beyond my deserts, a sight for sore eyes, to be in the presence of good

English ladies who are also lovers of music." He looked in a lively way between them.

"Good sir," Mrs. Storace interposed. "You are most welcome. Please let me introduce you to my daughter."

"Charmed, Miss Storace."

He was a tall man, heavyset, with a mass of wavy blondish hair that collected in side-whiskers on his wide, blunt cheeks and gave his face the broad, formidable aspect of a lion. The impression was not of elegance but of power. Anna felt acutely the pressure of his gaze and glanced nervously at the fireplace.

"Ah," he said with a smile, "forgive me if I am staring — I never have been justified in calling myself a gentleman — but the last I saw you, Miss Storace, you were a little girl. You won't remember me. I only sat in the audience that night, though I knew your mother and your father from my days with the orchestra at Marylebone."

"You have a prodigiously clear memory, sir," Mrs. Storace said primly. "When I read your line about my old plum cakes I thought, 'Now here is a true friend from those long-ago days.' "

Fisher, who had continued to let his eyes linger on Anna, suddenly turned all his forcefulness upon Mrs. Storace to say in his bright, lilting voice, "*Remember* your plum cakes, Mistress Storace? How could I forget them? I swear to you I never tasted better in all my worldly travels."

"Mr. Fisher. You are too kind. So many memories you bring back to me."

"Madam," he said gravely, "would it not be now so evidently beneath your station and did I not suspect this good city of having a shortage of plums, I should ask you to bake me some of those cakes this instant, that I might experience once more that peerless, plummy, buttery-sweet rapture."

"Thank you, sir. You are poetical."

"It really is quite extraordinary," Fisher murmured, turning to Anna, "how quickly the girl has become a lady. When I saw you sing all those years ago, I said to myself I should never forget it, and forget it have I not. I said to myself here was a young girl who was yet a kindred spirit — I felt it, I knew it, because of the way you made music. We have an affinity, I thought. We are kindred in song."

His eyes were an arrestingly pale blue; one felt caught in them as if held by a knife's point. His cheeks were reddened as if by wind or frost. His dress was fine, his age perhaps forty or forty-five. "You don't believe me," he continued with a rueful

131

smile. He looked down at his interlacing hands. They didn't look like violinist's hands. They were broad and thick. "And I'm afraid I'm being too forward. But it is the truth, and I must speak it when I see you so grown, Miss Storace, so beyond what I remember, and become so fulfilled in your music, as I knew you would be!"

It was the baby, perhaps, that made her feel sick. But she could never tell Benucci about the baby. She would rather die. If she told him, he might want to marry her, and then for the rest of his life he would hate and resent her, as her mother had hated and resented her father. But if he did not want to marry her, if he scorned her, her shame would reach to the very depths. So she could not tell him. That way was closed. She was too afraid, and too proud. The secret was like a rotten quail's egg, webbed with cracks, which she must carry inside her mouth. Her tongue pressed it against the back of her throat and saliva collected around it, and at every motion the shell threatened to burst all its putrefying liquids. She must paste her lips in bandages.

"I was going to congratulate you that night," continued Fisher, "after you sang Cupid, but you were surrounded with friends and my late wife was tired and wished us to go directly home. So it's her fault, you see, that you've now no memory of me and must take only my word that I have recalled and admired you ever since that day. Such a felicity, to find the Storace ladies here in a city where I expected to find nobody!"

"Why did you come, then?" asked Anna.

He sipped his tea. "I've been seeking something."

"And you think you'll find it here in Vienna?"

"Perhaps I already have."

Anna set down her teacup abruptly and called to the two dogs, who lifted their heads and came to her. "There," she said to them, "aren't you my only darlings?" The dogs, their faces rubbed this way and that in her hands, wagged their tails and looked at her with vague curiosity. "Are you fond of dogs, Mr. Fisher? I love them." She dragged one of the poor creatures into her lap. "My singing teacher had wonderful puppies like these. Sometimes I do think they are better than people. They're simpler than we are. They give their love wholeheartedly. They are never inconstant or changeable."

"Admirable qualities in beast or man," said Fisher.

"They're just like babies — they are wholly dependent on their master. As are we poor females, some might say!"

"Oh, no, indeed," laughed Fisher. "You will not draw me there, Miss Storace, comparing dogs to ladies."

"I had a cat once in Naples," Anna said. "Do you remember, Mama? It was a stray. One day it ran away. It never cared for me — I knew it then. So I didn't grieve for it — didn't even look for where it had gone."

"It must have been crushed to death under some carriage wheels," said Mrs. Storace. "Or been eaten by a wild beast."

"I hope it was," said Anna. "The wretched creature."

"But you're mistaken, my dear, that you didn't grieve," said her mother. "I don't know why you say such things. You were brokenhearted. You wouldn't eat, you wouldn't sing."

"Well," said Anna softly and sternly, "it is a hard thing when an object of tender affection does not come back to you."

Fisher cleared his throat and leaned forward. "I hope to have the honor of playing for you, Miss Storace, so that you may see my real strengths. I'm not a man of words. Do you like the violin?"

She forced herself to meet his eyes, and

134

saw him smile. "It's my favorite instrument."

He nodded. "I knew it would be."

"Did you? And how? From seeing me when I was a child? Did you hear me sing and see clear into my soul?"

He raised his brows and nodded evenly. "I believed I did. You were just a girl. But I felt I knew you, almost as I knew myself."

"Nonsense," Anna said briskly. "You never did anything of the kind. You're making it all up."

But he would not relent. "I thought you were like me, yes. In your *musical* soul."

She sighed. "Then you were mistaken. I do sometimes think my soul the most tuneless in all the universe. Please don't offend yours with comparisons to mine."

"I think the opposite is true," said Fisher. "You are too modest."

Anna pushed her dog away. "You haven't heard me sing yet, Mr. Fisher. For all either of us knows I may have reached my height when last you saw me."

"I've heard marvelous accounts of your singing," Fisher said. "I don't doubt them. I can hear your singing even now, behind your most musical speech."

"I'm not that child," she said severely. She brushed at her skirts. "You shall make me

135

angry in a moment."

"Anna," said her mother.

"But you are," said Fisher.

"Sir, I am not."

She stood and he rose with her. He was tall.

"Good-bye, Mr. Fisher. We wish you joy of Vienna."

He seemed surprised. "I see. You're angry." He glanced at Mrs. Storace and gave her a reassuring smile. "Well, we shall meet again, I hope, when you are more agreeable. Farewell, for now, Miss Storace."

"If you lose him," her mother remarked bitterly, later, "there will be no help for you."

Anna stared into the middle distance. She felt so ill she wanted to lie down. "Oh, Mama. He has no wish to be lost."

ROSINA

The next day, John Fisher invited Anna to see *Hamlet* with him that evening at the Burgtheater. She accepted. The performance was in German. Joseph Lange, Aloysia's husband, played the title role. Fisher sat next to Anna and the heat of him and the smell of his breath made her want to put herself away, but she remained calm and cordial.

"May I see you again?" he asked. "Tomorrow?"

She shook her head. "Tomorrow I'm singing for the Thun und Hohensteins."

"Then I'll join you."

She flushed. Mozart would be at the Thun-Hohensteins', and she had never heard him play. "It's a private salon, Mr. Fisher."

"I'll be your guest. I can play my fiddle. I've played for the empress of Russia, I'm good enough for Thun-Hohenstein, whoever he is."

He was annoyed. She pressed a hand to his arm and gave him a tender, beseeching look. "Another day, Mr. Fisher. The day after next. I shall be all yours, the day after next."

He narrowed his eyes. "But not tomorrow."

"Not tomorrow."

"You're ashamed to be seen with me."

She swallowed and said, "My dear Mr. Fisher, nothing could be further from the truth."

The next evening, at the salon hosted by the Countess Thun, a woman whose beauty, taste, and elegance would have inspired poets of any age, Anna arrived alone. She had been invited there to sing, but it was as much a social occasion as a professional engagement, and she had been looking forward to it for a long time, even amid her personal turmoil. Mozart was already there when she arrived. He greeted her and then was pulled to another corner of the room. Anna was glad. She would not have known what to say to him. She looked forward to seeing him play because then she would be able to stare frankly. She had forgotten about his eyes and his paleness and slightness, forgotten the variety of his expressions, how they crossed so easily from cheerfulness to concentration. And then it was time for her to sing.

Aglow in her daffodil gown, the countess, an expert player, accompanied Anna in arias from Paisiello's wildly popular adaptation of Beaumarchais's play *The Barber of Seville.* Anna, somewhat to her chagrin, was conscious of trying to please and impress Mozart above all the rest. She *thought* he was attentive. She thought he must be pleased. And in these idle musings she forgot, for a moment, John Fisher's breath. The room was large and had a pleasant acoustic. The countess played as well as any concert artist and the piano was a beautiful Stein.

After she sang, Anna returned to her seat in the gathering and with a shaking hand accepted a glass of sherry. Count Thun, the countess's lucky mate, beamed at his wife, who moved so gracefully among her guests, every gesture simplicity, no more than it should be and no less, her face open and kind, accepting the compliments of her listeners and remarking in low, lilting French (she spoke in French almost as well as German) how blessed they were to have a singer like Mademoiselle Storace among them. One could not help but recollect, seeing Anna and this gracious lady together, how the pert Rosina of *The Barber of Seville* became the melancholy, neglected Countess Almaviva of the second Beaumarchais play, *The Marriage of Figaro.* The Countess Thun, however, had no such impediments. There was not a better heart in all of Vienna, nor one more beloved, and thank God for her love of music.

Mozart arranged himself before the pianoforte and waited while the guests settled and seated themselves. He wore a red frock coat trimmed with gold thread. A froth of lace cascaded from his throat. He had brought no music. He would play a sonata from memory and then improvise for a time on any theme given to him.

The room seemed to grow smaller around him, the light in all corners to flicker and dim. He played almost without appearing to move, sitting at the piano with a quality of straightness born more from attention and relaxation than from any excitement or anxiety.

Anna had seen many virtuosi play. Wolfgang Mozart surpassed them all. He exhaled, and so many breathing notes unfurled from his unhesitating hands. He played as she had always wished to sing — how she imagined she might sing if she were not so excitable and striving, but selfless and assured, bound to music alone. His expression hardly altered. He looked as if he were listening to a soothing prophecy about the felicity of his children. His eyes, relaxed and open, took in the room and yet looked at nothing. The smile on his lips was scarcely there — a smile for himself, alone, because he felt no need to parade his emotions for their benefit. He would not distract them from his music, nor undermine the balance of its perfection with aping or sighs. He looked as noble and quiet as a physician tending a miraculously reviving child, and no one seemed to take more pleasure in his art, for all his equanimity of expression, than he himself.

When the sonata was over he turned to them all with lively good humor and asked for a tune on which to improvise. Count Thun, winking at Anna, proposed the theme from her most famous *Barber* aria.

"Too obvious!" cried Mozart. "Everyone will think I've planned it out beforehand." But no superior alternative being found, he at last consented to the *Barber* theme.

There could be no question that he was making up the variations on the spot, finding novel and ever wilder ways of exploring and distorting the theme, every turn unexpected and yet wholly right-seeming, without pause or misstep. His resources of creation were as if bottomless. The theme was always there and always changing. Just when it seemed he had ventured too far, beyond recovery, there was the original melody again, Anna's melody, waiting for him patiently at the end of the next corner, nearly the same as he had left it — nearly exactly the same — and yet deepened, made somehow more complex and reassuring, by the twists and convolutions, the permutations of key and rhythm and mode, to which he subjected it. Anna was wholly rapt. When he had finished she felt almost hollow with the transformation. Here was an intelligence, a perception, quite beyond her scope. It humbled and inspired, and made her want to sing her aria again, right now, so that she might show him what he had taught her — or else to never sing it again, because she could never be as good as he had suggested.

"Isn't he marvelous?" asked the Countess Thun. She offered Anna a few savory pastries. "I told him he would have to go last, or my fingers would be paralyzed when I went to play with you." She gazed around the room with benevolent approval. "He outdid himself tonight. Did you ever hear such an extensive improvisation in your life? At every change I felt my eyes gape wider and my heart rise still farther with I don't know what — nervous excitement, joy, gratitude — sincere astonished gratitude."

"I'm quite speechless," Anna confided to the good lady. She smiled, feeling restored and happy. It really was easy in this moment to imagine there was no baby and no John Fisher. They were all quite removed. Everything was whole again, restored, as it should be. Mozart's playing had soothed her hot brain like sweet water. Where once there had been panic and confusion, there was now clarity, a peculiar, tingling calm. All would be well. She was almost sure it would be well. "I'd never heard him before."

"What, my dear? Not in all these weeks? I'm surprised. I suppose you are prohibitively engaged. Well, you're lucky you saw him tonight, because he's leaving Vienna the day after next."

"Leaving?" Anna looked around quickly and saw him by the whist table, conversing patiently with a dowager.

"Tragically so," said the countess, following Anna's gaze, "and the more loss for the rest of us. He and his wife will visit his family in Salzburg."

"For how long?"

"Oh, some weeks, I'd think." The countess's smile deepened. "I see you're disappointed. I felt quite the same when he told me. I am one of Herr Mozart's greatest admirers and because of that, I get foolish notions that I can claim him for my own. But he is a free man and may do as he likes. You're lucky to have heard him tonight, at his best!"

A little later Mozart came nearer and Anna could speak to him at last. She congratulated him and saw how happy and proud he was, how well he spoke of his wife. She tried to explain how moved she had been by his playing, and how he had changed her perception of an aria she knew so well. She felt suddenly shy, yet also as though he understood her. Last night she'd seen *Hamlet* with John Fisher's breath upon her. Now that was forgotten. She was herself again, at peace.

"Do you," she asked hesitantly, "did you hear it all at once? I mean, when you heard me sing, were all the other variants already in your mind?"

He laughed and shook his head. "I make it up as I go. That's the fun. Can I do this thing? Is it too far? Oh, *now* it's too far and I'll have to scramble to find my way back. And now is anyone bored, anyone nodding off? Yes? Better speed up, better get louder, range round the highs and lows, modulate, go backward and upside down and stick the ass on its head, and then isn't this a sad little thing now, let's do that again, and then add it to this one, like so, and softly softly softly, and here we are back to the theme again in minor and the tune is like a thread through all of it, guiding me through it like a maze, you know. If I lose it I'm finished! It must be at the heart, my heart. Everything spins around it. You see? But there's no plan. If there were a plan it'd be a travesty. I'd have to call it something else."

His face was rosy with pleasure and his hands, as he tried to let her see into his mind, drew vague excited pictures in the air. He looked into her eyes with such brightness and unreserve it was like watching a breaking sun along the sea. Anna nodded and nodded again and told him she did the same sort of thing when she was singing, or at least tried to. They were comrades, then. It relieved her that he had not been thinking of her directly when he played — it had been vain of her to hope for that, his thinking of her. No, it was all much simpler than that. He had been at play. He had allowed the rest of them to see into his amusement. And it was this play, this risk, that made him so extraordinary.

WITH JOHN

The first time Anna saw John Fisher perform, at a private concert, he sought her out with his eyes at every pause or interval. He was as fine a violinist as any she'd heard, next to her brother and poor drowned Thomas Linley. His face in meditative concentration became softer, younger, and more open, and his arrogance, his slight tendency to swagger, became, in performance, natural and called for. His hands as they worked the burnished instrument were graceful and gentle and light. Had they been otherwise they would have elicited no music.

By Lidia's calculations Anna was two months gone with the baby, but it stayed quiet and small, as if it was aware that it must not be known.

John Fisher was a well-spoken gentleman and a fine musician. He had been friends with Anna's father in their youth. Her mother had always wished for Anna to marry a man from the British Isles and it would not perhaps be surprising to others that Anna was obedient in this wish.

She saw Lidia when she could, in parks or cafés. Lidia wanted Anna to run away but Anna said it was impossible. Lidia blamed herself for the pregnancy.

Anna and Fisher read plays and made music together, and went to concerts and had picnics. In mid-August Mrs. Storace had tea with Fisher and told him that her daughter was willing and there must be no delay, lest her honor be compromised. He, although somewhat surprised, admitted that a brief engagement would be agreeable to himself as well.

"Miss Storace," he said abruptly one afternoon shortly thereafter while they were strolling in the Prater. "I think you the sweetest lady I've ever set eyes on." He drew to a halt and clasped Anna's hands.

She did not like him. She wished she were anywhere else. His cheeks were fat and his eyes so sharp and blue. He spoke quickly, as if afraid she would flee before he had finished. The sun in his face gave him an unattractive scowl. His hands, from either nervousness or heat, were bathed in sweat. She held them as lightly as she could and hardly took breath.

"You enchant me," he said. "I have remembered you, all these years. I loved your father." His eyes flooded with tears, and she thought distantly that he was more emotional a man than had first appeared. "I know I'm almost a stranger to you," he continued. "I know you could have any man you liked. By God, I know." This was hardly the case — no true gentleman would ever wed a girl who went on the stage. "But I love you," Fisher went on. "I would do anything, anything, dear Miss Storace, to have you." His damp hands squeezed her own. He scowled into the sun. "But why don't you speak?" he cried. "Miss Storace, why do you turn such a look of blandness on my heart? Won't you consent? Won't you make me the happiest of men and be my bride?"

The blood had drained from her face. She waited a moment for someone to rescue her. But there was no one.

"Yes," she whispered. "Yes, Mr. Fisher, I will."

"My darling," he said, seizing her tightly. "*John.* You must call me *John.* My darling!"

And she, smiling up at him and accepting his pressing kisses, thought of herself as one of the flat, pieced-together cargo barges that floated headlong down the deep, swift

Danube to the waiting towns below, but that would never have the strength, or the means, or the will, to return.

Stephen wrote:

I confess I'm surprised. But though I have never met the gentleman, I trust in the judgment of my mother and yourself, and wish you, dearest sister, incomparable, darling Anna, all the happiness and joy the heavens and this gentleman Mr. Fisher can offer you. Tell him, for me, that he takes possession of one of the most precious female creatures in my life. Let him treat her like a goddess and a queen.

Benucci frowned and looked confused. "But why such haste?"

Anna laughed gaily. "Yes, it's rather racing, isn't it, but it's what we want. He's a good man and shall make me happy, and everyone is always telling me I should marry."

He was silent for what seemed a long time, and in spite of everything some part of her began wildly to hope. *Please,* she thought, smiling at him. *Please, Francesco.* But then he gave a small start, as if returning to his senses, and beamed at her and kissed her cheek. "Forgive me. I'm only surprised. Let me congratulate you. This is happy news. You'd make any man the luckiest in the world."

"Well," she said, renewing her smile. "Not *any* man."

He squeezed her shoulder, as if she'd said nothing. "And we're still friends. That's the main thing."

She turned from him and said, "Yes."

Courage

They were married in the Dutch Embassy. Anna wore her best silk and looked, her mother said, the loveliest of her life. Mrs. Storace, in a high, white wig, did not say much to anyone, but it was clear she relished in this kind of ceremony, with its rule and straightness and sanctity. She was more than satisfied with John Fisher. He had a strong carriage and a Christian heart; a steadiness and a sense that would regulate her daughter. Much good, she observed, could come even of misfortune.

They were married in the morning, a Friday. Light touched their shoulders. Anna's friends were there and some of her patrons. Benucci sat on the left, a dark-haired figure at the edge of her vision.

Fisher's face was schooled and stern, as if feeling the weight of history upon him. They said their vows and signed in the book and everyone prayed. There was music from a wind quintet, friends of Anna's from the orchestra, and then some small refreshments. Her mother would not speak to Benucci. Anna, too, could hardly speak to him. He muttered a low congratulation and moved away. He had brought Lidia, who hugged Anna tightly and whispered, "Courage, courage, he is a good man, all will be well," because there was nothing else now that could be said.

What a terrible thing to go to bed with a stranger. A bedroom was meant to be a place of comfort and repose, a place for love and rest and the vulnerability of sleep, where even the darkness of night was yet safe and enveloping. To welcome this man, accept his demands and his professions of tenderness, and try to fall asleep in his heavy arms, indeed took all the courage Anna possessed. She thought of the future, of "forever," and it seemed a horror beyond imagination or dream. She could not bring herself to wish for his death, not even if it meant her release. But he would grow old, someday he would surely grow old, and with age would come blessed neglect. She laughed to think that this was the best she could hope for, she who had been used to having every favor in the world. And now more than ever, when it was too late, did she wish she had told Benucci, and asked him to save her. Her pride, wrapped in the heavy arms of John Abraham Fisher, crumbled to nothing.

"Now you're mine," he said, as if that were all he had ever wanted in life. How small her hand was in his. There were calluses on his fingers from pressing the strings of his violin, just as there had been on her father's fingers, and her brother's, and a red mark on the left side of his neck, almost like a blister, red and rough, where the violin rubbed against him. When he said, "You're mine," Anna touched the red spot with her finger. Fisher pressed her hand away. In the morning he made love to her again. She had slept restlessly and felt unwell, but she tried to be docile. Good, she thought, that she hated him, that she was disgusted and tightly wound: it would make him think she was a virgin. He did not know her secret and never would. The baby stayed quiet and small.

Sometime mid-morning Fichout and Bonbon, her pet dogs, came whining and scratching at the door, and she got up to let them in. This for some reason put Fisher into such a repressed fury that he stormed out in his nightshirt and bare legs to dress himself in his own room, where he called for coffee and breakfast. After some time he told her it was because she had let the dogs in without first asking for his permission.

The next morning she did ask for permission, and he told her to let them be. She lay in bed listening to them whimper and then rose and put on her dressing gown and slippers. "What are you doing?" Fisher asked from behind the heavy canopy.

"I'm going," she said, a little petulantly, "to tell them they can't come in. They don't understand."

"Because they are senseless animals, my love." But he lay back in bed and didn't stop her.

Fisher liked to keep hold of her when they walked. He clasped her hand on his arm, or else touched her back or waist or shoulder, never losing contact, with an insistence, it seemed, born out of his love, his joy at their finally being consecrated together and at his future being secured. It was not lost on Anna, nor had it ever been, that John Fisher had been almost penniless when he first came to them — not being the sort of stooping ingratiating idiot, he said, who for his bread gave lessons to children or played in chamber orchestras. Now, with Anna's income, so large she herself didn't know what to do with it, he would want for noth-

155

ing, would never be asked to stoop. No very great wonder he wanted to keep a hand on her always. She was in this respect like his violin, an instrument of his prestige and livelihood.

He hated to see her sing, being a jealous sort of husband, exactly the sort Aloysia Lange had recommended so long ago at Café Hugelmann. Could he not tell the difference between truth and a play? she asked him. He answered that he could not. Not since he'd met her.

His hand upon her came to feel like a mark — not native to her but imposed, applied, until it became part of her by attrition. It was his left hand, most often — the hand that made the melody. "If it were a play," she'd once said to Mozart, the night he'd kissed her on the terrace, "you could have marked me for life." But kisses did not mark, she knew that now. Kisses left no trace. Hands marked. And it was no play. The story was done, or it had never been. The first time Fisher hurt her was in bed. He had wanted to punish her, he said, for making eyes at Benucci that evening in the opera. He seemed to take much pleasure in it. He was different, in that moment, than he often appeared during the day, when he could be exceedingly polite. He was the youngest of five children, he said, and had grown up with excesses of punishment.

Anna went down to her mother the next morning and told her she could not go on living with John Fisher. But her mother did not understand. She said that Anna must endeavor to make herself more pleasing and modest and good, and not be so fussy and delicate. If she turned Fisher out now, she said, it would be as much of a scandal as if she'd given birth to a bastard.

She listened to her mother. She tried to be pleasing. And the baby remained, stuck like a root, tenacious, quiet. If she had told Fisher about the baby, perhaps he would have been more gentle, but she could not tell him yet or he would know it was not his, because not enough time had passed. And then he might kill her. Every night she closed her eyes and prayed for the baby to stay small for as long as it could.

She tried to keep some lightness in her life and that was in music and singing. She attended parties and salons. She pretended she was the Anna of before, of Milan and Venice, La Storace, L'inglesina. She sought out moments of peace, treasured them more for how they had become so rare. She loved her dogs with all her heart. She went up to a tree by the main square and touched its trunk with her hands. Once she actually leaned her forehead upon it. The tree did not care about husbands and babies and scandals. It was just a tree. It stayed in the ground and did not care. The leaves played in the sky. The tree did not mind that she leaned her forehead upon its cool, solid trunk and pretended that it loved her. And when she was on stage, with the orchestra beneath her like a great ocean, her voice still her voice, her breath stretching every corner of her lungs, the poor baby safe and snug inside her, she could forget everything else, and only be where she was, relaxed and alive. And though she was not quite herself, though she sometimes made mistakes, still the audiences laughed, still they clapped, because they expected her to sing well and could hardly tell the difference. And though, outside, with John, there must still be the "forever," the oppression, and the terrible absurdity, here, in her music, in her life's refuge, she had everything that was beautiful.

Benucci worried for her. She felt him watching her with a brooding frown. But she tried to tell him, with her actions and smiles, that she had taken courage, and he should not fear for her unhappiness. It would not do, she told herself firmly, to impose her griefs on him. She had not been raised to complain.

Each Taste a Kiss

Joseph II assented with interest to Anna Fisher's request for an audience. He had not spoken to her since before her wedding, and he congratulated her, upon her entrance into his study, on the happy occasion.

She seemed to have grown softer in the face since last he had seen her, and her eyes were darkened, as if with preoccupation. She had come to speak of her brother, a composer now living in England who wished to write an opera for her in Vienna. She seemed uncharacteristically nervous. Joseph leaned back on the rigid sofa — he preferred furniture of a certain hardness, to keep him awake during affairs of state — and crossed his long legs at the ankles. "It might look odd," he told her, "to order an opera from a man I've not met and whose music I've never heard in my life."

"I have an aria here," said Anna gently. "I can play it for you."

She crossed to the harpsichord. Concentrating too much, perhaps, on appearing composed, she swallowed to clear her throat. Her arms were soft, her head tilted slightly to one side, as if overbalanced by the weight of her piled hair. He watched her breast expand and contract as she sang. An expression of pleasure, or repose, settled over her features, as though the act of singing were a comfort and relief to her. The voice was still lovely, but betrayed an edge of roughness or tiredness he had not often heard from her. He may only have noticed it because of her proximity. He found himself reflecting that this new catch or burr in the sound gave her voice somewhat more pathos.

He rose in an impulsive movement to turn the pages for her, and standing then beside her could not suppress the impulse, as if in a dream, to let his long, heavily ringed hand drift lightly down to rest on the top of her back. His index finger lay along the soft skin above her neckline, while his thumb curved up to touch the inclining nape of her neck. She stiffened, almost imperceptibly, and then he felt her relax again; seeming, as she did so, to press back against his palm. Letting go his breath he leaned over her to turn the next page, catching a whiff of her perfume — a Spanish sort of scent — and remaining close enough, ostensibly to examine the music, that her arm as it ranged the keyboard brushed once or twice against the pearly front of his trousers.

"Pretty," he said when she was done, and leaned over her again to flip back through the pages. "Your brother writes well for you."

"I'm not in good voice today," she said. "I apologize."

"May I?"

The girl made room and he sat beside her. He spread the manuscript before him, peering at its neatly lettered notation. "Yes, very pretty." He hummed a few bars to his own accompaniment. "Skillfully done. Very tasteful. One can hardly detect his Britishness."

It was not a wide bench, more like a broad stool. The fullness of her skirt overbounded it and puffed into his lap. They sat shoulder to shoulder. Now and then his roving foot, as he played, brushed against her own. She made no move to stand — seemed, indeed, unusually still. She was a girl who was always turning and shimmering and sashaying. But her expression now held the same bland emptiness that was so often presented to him by his courtiers and servants.

He had spent many hours now observing Anna in the opera theater; allowing her performances, as it were, to seduce and conquer him from the stage. No wonder a certain portion of that feeling might carry into this room. His foot found hers once more, slid against it, and this time she did not move away. So simple a change and yet what a stirring it gave him, what a feeling of anticipation, of suspension in time.

He lifted his hands from the keys and dropped them into his lap. The rings — a signet for his office, a ruby from his mother, a few others whose provenance he could not recall — felt heavy and languishing on his fingers. Her skirts, overflowing, caught beneath his hands in his lap and he pretended not to notice. Her small foot remained flush and coconspiring with his own. The sensation of touch traveled in small pleasant shocks up his leg and into his gut and brain. The fabric of her dress was pleasing, a green satin, like forest leaves, and he smoothed it absently against his thigh.

"You are happy with your husband?" he asked in a quiet voice.

She stirred and turned her head; her foot did not move. "You flatter me too much, Your Excellency, to worry about my happiness."

"I've heard he has a temper."

"He is Irish, Your Excellency. And I have a temper of my own."

"Do you?" Joseph countered with amusement, twisting a little to face her — a movement that increased, rather than diminished, the seeking pressure of his foot. "Then I've never seen it. You have always seemed the picture of tractability."

"I would not dare to show my temper before the emperor."

"Dear God!" Joseph exclaimed. "And do I not try to make everyone treat me just as any other man?"

"That would succeed only if you were like any other man."

Joseph frowned. "I am, I swear to you — more than you realize."

She gazed long at him. "My brother would do your court much honor, sir."

Joseph sniffed and turned back to the music with a feeling of irritation. "I have too many composers wanting my attention already. There are only so many operas one can sponsor in a year."

"As a favor to me," she said.

Her hands had been folded in her lap. Now, as if of its own accord, one of them moved to rest on his knee, his knee that was covered by her own skirts.

"A favor?" he laughed. "I see marriage has

made you grow bold, Madam Fisher. What have I done to owe you a favor?"

She retrieved her hand, still with the same steady smile. "Nothing, sir. It would be a personal favor, a kindness I could never repay, greater than anything I could hope for."

"You love your brother so much?" he asked.

"Yes," she said, unhesitating.

"Can't he come here himself to court my favors?"

"He can't leave England without a commission." And suddenly she seemed close to tears. Perhaps the man was harsh with her, Joseph thought — her husband, the big Irishman. Why she'd married the fellow was impossible to say. She was a charming girl and bright.

A knock at the door announced the emperor's mid-morning cup of chocolate. He extricated himself from Anna to sit and drink it at his desk. There was only one cup on the tray, the attendant not having been told that the emperor had a guest. Joseph sipped the thick, bitter liquid and sighed with pleasure. "Would you like a taste?" he asked. "Rude of me to partake without you. Come here and have a drop."

"Oh, I couldn't possibly," she murmured.

But her face, he thought, held a kind of longing.

"Think of it as an imperial decree," he said with a poised smile, "to give me peace of mind as your host. You wouldn't want to compromise my peace of mind."

With a blush of modesty she rose and came to stand before him, her swelling bosom level with his formidable Hapsburg nose. "Come sit," he said.

She might have drawn up another chair — might indeed have left the room — but with a simple acquiescent movement she knelt before him, her skirts spreading about her, one hand balanced lightly on the arm of his chair. Joseph, who under normal circumstances would have disliked sharing his chocolate with anyone, found himself moved to a most unusual degree by this new view and prospect. He took up the teacup with its precious cargo and offered it to her parted lips. She steadied and guided the cup with her hand. He did not let go. His finger, just below the rim of the vessel, touched her lip and chin.

"Is it not exquisite?" he asked.

"Heaven on earth," she said. She did not move to recover from her supplicating posture, and he was glad of that. He had been lonely, truly, almost his entire life.

Both his marriages — arranged, of course — had been deeply unhappy and blessedly short. His only child, a daughter, had perished before her eighth birthday. He was not the great breeder that his mother had been; not anything like her, in fact.

He stirred the chocolate with the tiny spoon and sipped again. He could sense the touch of her lips on the fragile cup, reverberating there like the sympathetic vibrations of a stringed instrument.

"Your brother may write an opera for my people," he said. "Tell him to come in the spring. One does not want one's prima buffa in a melancholy humor."

She smiled and dropped her eyes. "Thank you, Your Excellency. He will do you much honor, I swear it."

"Then let him not arrive too soon."

She waited a moment, as if expecting him to request something more of her, but he sent her away. He wished to finish his chocolate in peace, each taste a kiss, while the pleasant residual warmth of toying with her still sighed and faded in his belly. As for making Madame Fisher debase herself, even so slightly, to achieve her purpose — well, he wouldn't have wanted her to think she had him at her beck and call, considering how much he paid her.

CONSTANZE'S LOCKET

Mozart and his wife had returned from Salzburg shortly after Anna's wedding, but she had not seen much of him since then. A few days after the meeting with the emperor, she wrote to ask if she could visit him. She said she wanted to sing her aria from *The Disappointed Husband*. A frail excuse: they had done the aria enough already. But she loved singing with Mozart — she felt, sometimes, it was the best part of her life. He propelled her along in the most natural way, while still listening and responding to her. He made her feel a better singer than she was.

He wrote back immediately and asked her to come over that afternoon.

After they had finished the aria he asked, "You're well? In good health?"

She bit her lip. Perhaps she looked unwell. It was true that she had slept poorly. The baby made her feel sick. But she was only three months gone, certainly not four; it did not show. "Quite well, though this dusty air, you know — gives me some low humors."

"My wife sometimes takes the air at Baden-Baden; perhaps you would like it. Perhaps it would be a respite from town. Refreshing."

"I couldn't get away," she exclaimed. "I'm positively trapped here with all these concerts and parties and obligations. When I was a little girl and very taken with myself, my mother — who is strict and always has been — used to spank me and remind me that the world didn't revolve around my rear end. But now if I were to step out of it everything would fall apart — the operas, my husband —"

Mozart fidgeted with his foot. "Perhaps you could give them a chance to try getting on without you. Husbands need very little when it comes down to it."

"I love my husband too much," she said.

With a grimace that was almost a smile he rubbed vigorously at the top of his keyboard. "That's not what I've heard."

Her breath caught. "No?" she said. "What have you heard?"

"That he's a boor."

She stared at him a moment and then twirled away to coo at his pet starling, which he'd raised from a chick. It could sing like an angel. "What nonsense. I swear I've never been so happy in my life. Really I quite like boors. They show one off so well."

"For God's sake!" he cried.

She flinched, then schooled her expression into a kind of determined mildness. "My dear Herr Mozart," she said, turning to him, "I believe you are jealous of my husband."

He shook his head in frustration. "You're acting as though you're on a stage."

"If I didn't put on airs," she said, in a light, high voice, "you wouldn't like me."

"I liked you the moment I saw you," he said. "Do not pretend, madame, to know what I do and do not like."

"You were half drunk. Remember?" She leaned playfully at the window and said in a blithe voice, "It's true my husband has a temper, I mean with others, but he's quite tame, really. He adores me as no one else."

"Why are you talking like this?" he asked. He frowned like a schoolboy being subjected to a great injustice. "Don't you know I'm the only one here and I don't care? Talk like yourself, for God's sake — as you are, as you are. You're talking in buckets of piss, is what you're doing. My God, you're the most adorable girl I ever laid eyes on. You're the smartest, next to my sister. You've the world at your feet. You have my friendship and high esteem. We live in a civil society with rights and laws."

"Furthermore," she said, "I'm perfectly fine."

"They say he treats you roughly."

"Then they're vicious liars." She stared at him, and then, still smiling, looked at her hands. She saw that her fingers were shaking, and pressed them together. It did not do to let one's fingers shake in public. "Once," she amended, "he slapped me — once in some silly argument. It was my fault as much as his. But after it happened he was wracked, you see. He could not forgive himself. So that's all over now. Now we're very dull. Really it's extraordinary how these rumors blow up."

Mozart turned red. "I'd kill him."

"Oh, don't say that!" she exclaimed. "Please don't. Then you'd have to kill yourself, too, and I'd have to drink some poison and collapse on both your bodies. Then what would become of your wife and child? Believe me. You must believe me. If you don't, I shan't be able to see you ever again, and wouldn't that be sad?"

She remembered that night, only a few weeks ago, before he'd left for Salzburg, when he had played variations on her aria. How he had upturned the pattern of his mind across the keys. She remembered how he had kissed her in the garden, as though her kiss had been all he desired. "If you had wanted to save me," she continued, "you should have said so before. It's quite too late now. The best thing is for us all to be as happy as we can."

Just then Constanze came into the room in a happy flurry. Her cheeks glowed. For a moment it seemed she did not see them there. "Oh dear! Are you not finished?"

Mozart gave Anna a sober look. "Done just this instant, my dear," he said. "This lady sings like an angel and is so obliging she won't have me change a note."

"You can't imagine, Madame Fisher," declared Constanze, "what this man puts me through. It's like living with a child! I don't know how he managed before he met me."

"Grievously," said Mozart, laughing. "On death's door from the time I was a boy."

"What do you think?" Constanze asked Anna. "When I got out my key ring to open the safe box, to pay the chandler, what do you think I found?"

She held the ring up for Anna to see. Five or six keys of varying weights and sizes hung from a chain around her neck. One was tied with a red ribbon. Constanze brandished it at her husband. "*This* key, ribboned thus, I have never seen in my life — I would have recognized it as a trespasser even if some stealthy elf-in-the-night hadn't marked it with one of my own hair ribbons."

Mozart regarded his wife with amusement.

"And *then,*" she said, "I go into the nursery and what do I find in the bassinet? A locked chest like a pirate's treasure. But I haven't opened it yet because I wanted my scoundrel of a husband to be with me."

"Haven't opened it?" exclaimed Mozart. "My curious Constanze? As you like. It might not even fit the lock. It might be a key to something else entirely."

Constanze looked at him a second, her mouth open, then took up her skirts and darted out of the room. Mozart went after her. Anna, after collecting her belongings, followed some distance behind.

A sweet domestic scene greeted her: Constanze on her knees by the bassinet; Mozart behind her, leaning down to see again the objects he had placed inside the trunk for her to find. They had lately welcomed into their family a baby boy, Karl, not a year after the sad death of their first infant. The

173

wet nurse held Karl in a chair. Inside the box was a child's rattle with tinkling bells and a large silver locket inscribed with some private love sentiment that made Constanze dissolve. "It contains locks of our hair," she told Anna. "Mine and Wolfgang's, and both the babies'." She wiped her cheeks and looked at her husband. "You crazy boy," she said. "Did you cut my hair while I was sleeping?"

And Anna, thinking of her own poor baby, and her husband, and her life, wished in that moment to be anywhere else.

A Corner of Her Heart

One would not have thought, given the sweet prize Fisher had won, that he would have done anything to sabotage the situation, but it was common knowledge, by November 1784, that he beat his wife.

Since their wedding he had almost ceased to concertize. When asked, he refused, considering either the venue or the fee beneath him. He practiced in fits and starts, going for days and weeks without playing, then shutting himself in his study for hours, playing music he already knew, with a kind of obsession. He struck Anna's dogs with booted feet. He raised his voice. He wouldn't speak to her for days. He called her coarse and fat, a whore. He forced himself on her in the middle of the night when she had been soundly asleep, and made motions, on a few occasions, of strangling her. She could never know when he might elect to hurt her, and that was part of the torture. Often it was when he had drunk too much — but not always. Sometimes it was when he had slept poorly — or too well — sometimes when he had eaten too much meat, or too little. In short he contradicted all logic.

The servants quit their posts. New ones, more deaf to marital discord, had to be found. Fisher was calculating enough to spare his wife's face and arms from welts or bruises, although one or two slipped past his guard to come under the notice of her colleagues at the Burgtheater, as did a new stiffness in her movements, always before so graceful and easy.

By mid-November she was about five months pregnant and could not hide it longer. She decided to tell him. She would say it was three months. She would say she'd wanted to wait until she was sure.

They had just had their supper and he was in a good mood. Anna had sung tonight and Mrs. Storace had eaten early, as was her habit, so Anna and Fisher had dined privately together in Anna's large, gracious bedroom, where there was a small dining and sitting area. He smiled and let go a contented sigh. He told her she looked well and that she had been behaving better these days. He took frequent issue with her behavior. He believed she flirted and degraded herself. She told him a buffa soprano was required to flirt — it meant nothing — but he would not listen. He said he feared for her intellect, for the safety of her soul. She hated when he came to the opera because he would loom over her in her dressing room, not talking to any of the others, telling her she had sung better last night, or that the orchestra had played like rubbish.

But tonight he was happy. He gave her soft looks. He touched her gently and said she was beautiful, that he could find nothing today, no matter how he looked, to reproach in her. And she, too, was almost content. The food had been good and she'd drunk a glass of wine. The baby was quiet and did not kick her. When John visited her bed it was always dark and she wore a loose shift and she was almost sure he could not tell. Really no one could tell, not for certain. She was still small and she dressed carefully. She only seemed plumper, that was all; it only made her more fetching. He looked pleasant in the candlelight. He was a handsome man when he was happy, and darkly lit.

She would say she was three months gone. There might not be a better chance than

177

now. She only had to find the courage to tell him. She poured them both more wine.

"I love you," he said, stroking the back of her neck.

The touch repulsed her. She could not stop herself from turning away. She said, "Not *me,* John. You never loved *me.*"

His eyes hardened and his hand grew heavy. The moment was gone. She held her neck steady and gave him a wide, mocking smile. "Not *me!*" she trilled again.

He let her go and in the instant she was dancing away from him. She made it halfway across the room before he caught her. She should have told him before. Now it was too late. "I love you," he cried. She laughed and said he did not.

He encompassed her world. She was always thinking about him, always being touched or not touched by him, always hearing or not hearing his music. It moved her, almost, to hear the sound of his violin through the walls and know that he was shaping the tone with his mind and hands, because that indicated tenderness and understanding. His embraces still stunned and bewildered her, made her feel unhinged and abandoned, and yet she could not tell sometimes whether she desired or loathed them — or whether she was beyond even

178

that, now, and had simply fallen into an attitude of submissiveness. But when the lights were still up, and she still clothed, armored with insignias of rank and success, her puffed coiffure, her stays and petticoats, her velvet choker with the single drop pearl, and while her ears were still hot with the music of the evening, the chaos of the applause — she became reckless, heedless, and thought her husband the most laughable fop in all the world.

"Not *me*!" she sang, over and over. "You've never loved *me*! Nobody's ever loved *me*!"

She meant, or thought she meant, that the girl whom Fisher and everybody else purported to love was not her. The logic was clear and amusing, in the state she was in. Whoever she was, she couldn't have said, but it wasn't the girl everyone purported to love.

She escaped him again, or he let her escape, she could not tell, and he started chasing her around the room, saying in French that he loved her — *"Je t'aime, je t'aime"* — until it became a chant in itself, a threat, a rhythm for the hunt, while she shrieked and giggled and ran away, feeling dizzy and heedless. A small corner of her heart, perhaps, was frightened, but she shut it down, slammed it away, was all sharpness and gaiety, teasing and fleeing him. He would wake her mother, who was sleeping downstairs with cotton in her ears.

And then somehow he captured her, though she had thought this time she would win free. It must have been the wine that confused her dancing, slippered feet and made her dizzy and slow and sick to her stomach. With a satisfied grunt he lifted her in his arms. Her hands went around his neck, her feet kicked the air. Breathing heavily he bent to kiss her mouth.

"No!" she squealed, half laughing, batting at his face with her hand, conscious of speaking and behaving like a child, with a child's voice and gestures. "Let me down," she cried, pounding his shoulders and squirming this way and that. "You *brute,* you ugly brute, everyone hates you — let me down — let me out of this house —"

She had slipped into Italian, the language of Dante and of her father. She kicked and twisted but Fisher only gripped her closer, so hard she felt he was gripping her bones. She turned her head and bit his shoulder; she scratched her nails down the back of his neck sobbing for him to let her go.

He must have meant to do it. He walked up to the table, as she thrashed and struggled, and lifting her over it — lifting her as though over an altar — he tossed her up and let her fall. He might have put her down on the sofa or the bed, as he had done before. But something now must have inclined him to let her fall, as if from heaven, on the wastes of their meal: the little table with the half-eaten pheasant, the wineglasses and pitchers, forks and knives, fruit peelings, bread crusts, blood pudding, roast beef, potato remnants, syrup and pastry crumbs, milk jugs, coffee cups. Her scream was real, then. He had given no warning, except for that slight toss at the end. Glass broke under her. The copper pitcher bruised her back. Her head jerked over the lip of the table and struck the arm of the chair as she bumped to the floor, her gown of armor stained with wine and grease.

So great was her shock that at first she didn't move and barely made a sound. Fisher stood over her. "There," he said. "There."

He sat in an armchair and rubbed his mouth, frowning. Anna put her palms on the floor and pressed herself into a seated position. She touched a hand to her head to see if it was bleeding. It was not. Then she remembered about her baby and began to cry. Surely he had killed it. She could feel it

181

already dying inside her. The poor, sweet, good baby, which had stayed so quiet and small, that it might remain safe and be her own baby, to love and need her and bring her joy. She had done it to herself. If she had told him about the baby he would not have dropped her on the table. But she had not told him.

The door opened and there stood Mrs. Storace in her nightcap and dressing gown. Her face went white and she rushed to Anna and told Fisher to call a doctor.

"I'm all right, Mama," said Anna. "No doctor, no, no." A doctor would tell Fisher it was five months and not three. "I'm all right, we were arguing and I fell. See? I'm perfectly all right. Just surprised." Slowly and deliberately she got to her feet, to show how well she was. "But my poor gown! You had better send for the maid to undress me and then I think I'll go to bed." She tried to undo the velvet choker at her neck but her fingers were weak and she could not do it, and yet she had to keep trying so that they would believe she was well and not send for a doctor. She fumbled at the clasp. "Knocked myself over, so silly, I don't know what happened, the poor table! It's a wonder it didn't break." It was hard to fumble at the clasp and not to cry. "Mama, won't you help me with my necklace? I can't do it. It's pulling on my neck, I've gotten fatter again."

Mrs. Storace unfastened the clasp in one motion. The color had returned to her face. She glanced at Fisher coolly. "Forgive me, my dear," she said to her daughter. "I worry for you. In your condition."

"What condition?" asked Fisher.

Mrs. Storace pursed her lips. "Why, Mr. Fisher, I thought you had perceived. My daughter is carrying your child. It's the usual course of events. You should be more careful. There must be no more arguments of this nature or the baby will be put at risk."

"I didn't know," gasped Fisher. "My good woman, I swear I did not know."

"Three months, if I'm not mistaken," Mrs. Storace said, watching her daughter. "She did not wish to tell you until it was sure. Foolish girl. You must be more careful, Anna. You must not be so clumsy over dinner tables."

Anna sank into a chair, holding a hand to her head to make it stop hurting. So in the end it had not been up to her to say it. She had not had to lie. And here was John Fisher embracing her, pulling her onto his lap, kissing frantically at her cheeks and hair, and calling her his little dove, his sweet dove. Her back ached and so did her head and the baby was probably dying but she was tired, and had no strength of will, and so she melted against his body as if strength might come from him, as if he could give her his power, rather than leaching hers away. "My darling," he murmured, his lips and hands upon her. "My dove, my little fool, why didn't you tell me?"

But the baby did not die. It kicked and bothered her and made it impossible to sleep. She started walking in the early morning, in humble clothes, like a servant. When she walked, the baby quieted and she felt better. She crept out. Sometimes someone recognized her, and turned to stare. It wasn't proper for a lady to be out alone. In spite of this she felt less hunted, in the hectic streets of Vienna, with the snow and horses and pigs and running children. It was one of the largest cities in the world. She could disappear. If people looked at her curiously it was not with the probing, pitying concern that filled the eyes of her friends and made her feel as though she could not speak with them about anything, lest she be questioned and judged. Never could she be alone, unassailed. She felt her thoughts run riot and could not stop the panic. She built screens around her face. One could hardly see, through the slats, the roils of panic. Every attempt she made to free herself entangled her more.

She didn't know anymore which part she was playing, or for whom. She didn't know which face and character would please John Fisher and let her abide with him in peace. Sometimes when she was most short and angry with him he would swing her around the room and cover her with kisses and beg her not to frown anymore, and when he did that, she could almost not keep herself from liking him, from imagining what a fine father he would be and how the baby would make him happy and how happy they would be then. She actually laughed. Sometimes when she shrank into herself and cried like a little girl he would cradle her and say he was a brute, it was his Irish blood, his passion, and then she would stop crying and nearly forgive him. Sometimes when she was happy and laughing he was likewise. But for all these moments there were equally those when he would strike and slap her and push her down and yank her about. As an audience, a critic, he was unreliable. What pleased him once could not be guaranteed to please again. Everything had turned — it was impossible to say who she was and had been and would be, and what

185

any of it mattered.

Though her performances grew progressively more uneven they also provided the only times she felt secure in herself. She got to the theater earlier than she needed to. She told no one about her condition and concealed it well with her clothes. If they suspected they said nothing.

"Are you quite in health?" asked Michael one day. He had come to accompany her to a luncheon at the Mozarts'. Michael and Mozart liked to play billiards together. He peered at her as though reading a coded manuscript. "Not ill again, I hope?"

She kissed him. "Just a little peaky — slept poorly. There was too much in my head, too much music."

"I've got three tunes in my head at the moment," Michael said. "At the same time. Isn't your husband coming?"

She hesitated, then gave him a rueful look. "He's in a bad mood today. He said he doesn't like Mozart. I don't know what got into him."

"Doesn't like Mozart?" Michael raised his brows. "Well, then. Each to his own. I'm glad to have you to myself."

"Let's walk," Anna declared. "I want to be in the sunshine."

He drew back. "In this frost?"

She shook her head. "I need to breathe, Michael."

"If you say so," he said doubtfully. "Got your muff? I'll just send my carriage on its way, then. You're sure you're not going to freeze yourself into a faint?"

"Don't be so motherly," she said. "I never walk anymore — doesn't that seem unnatural? We used to walk everywhere in Italy."

"Only poor people walk. With no shoes on."

"I don't move," she exclaimed, flinging out her arms. "I want to breathe cold air and walk for hours."

His face darkened. He was going to say something about Fisher. If he came out with it directly she was not sure how she would answer. At last he asked, "Are you sure you're all right? You seem wan, Anna."

Her answer came without thinking, like her smile. It was the truth. "Mozart will cheer me. Come."

She finished fastening her boots and they went out. There was snow on the street and some sun shone weakly through the clouds. She strode along as if there was some marvelous treasure around the corner — she made herself imagine there was — with the air harsh in her throat and her eyes stinging from the vigorous chill. Michael Kelly, used to taking an easy pace in everything he did, found himself having to hurry to keep up with her. At the Mozarts' everyone was in high spirits, loud and raucous, a kind of madness in the air. Some of his instrumentalist friends were there, a flautist and a bassoonist, and they played something, and everyone sang bawdy songs, and there was dancing, and Mozart beat Michael at billiards. Then he recited some nonsense verse and Anna laughed so hard that tears came to her eyes. Then there was another game of billiards and she browsed the books in his library — Ovid, Molière.

"Do you like to read?" asked Constanze. "My husband carries a book in his pocket wherever he goes."

"I used to," said Anna. She touched a hand nervously to her face. She was sure Constanze could tell that she was pregnant. "I'm so busy now."

"So am I," Constanze said. She smiled.

Then there was shouting from the billiards room and they rejoined the rest of the gathering. Anna could almost imagine that this was all there was — that she lived here, too, in this jovial house, with these warm, boisterous friends.

She found other pockets of respite and

they kept her in sound mind, and reminded her that all was not lost, although sometimes it seemed so. On nights she wasn't singing, she watched the theater troupe perform Shakespeare in German, sometimes with Fisher but more often alone. She liked the comedies because they did not require anything of her. She could remain calm through even the most fraught of narratives, knowing it would end well. She understood, more and more, why people loved her opera buffa — why they found reassurance there, in that she always played the same stock role; in that the plots, the music, were all the same.

One needed sameness. One needed a feeling of order and reliability — of knowing that what was prophesied would come to pass, that those who were meant to love would love, that evil and good would be accounted for. There was reassurance in repetition, in familiar sounds and faces, as there had been from infancy. It was like walking slowly with her mother in the Stephansplatz, a large square in the center of the city, to the same rhythm of the same music in her head, past people and shops she had seen every day, knowing that the sky would not buckle, the earth not heave up its contents, the young soldier on his horse not give her a bruised knee or a bloody nose because she had moved in a way that seemed to him wanton.

ALL THE WORDS SHE COULD SPILL

As she was walking one morning — too early; she had hardly slept — Anna saw a tall, familiar figure stooping over some vegetables on display in an alley.

"Lidia," she said.

The other girl turned in surprise. "Oh, my dear one." She embraced Anna with all her strength.

They had not seen each other in some time. Anna had always been too engaged. "I thought I'd buy some bread," she explained now to Lidia.

Lidia looked her up and down. "Don't you have someone to do that for you? Why are you alone? In your condition?"

"Oh, yes, but sometimes they get the wrong kind, and I do like the fresh air. The walking is good for me."

Lidia observed that the air was not so fresh in town as in the country and it was not proper for her to be out alone. "You must have been up late singing last night," she added. "You should be in bed."

"I don't need as much sleep as I used to," Anna said. "Since my marriage. I'm entirely different now. It's extraordinary. You must try it, Lidia. You must marry."

"Only a widower with ten children would want me."

"Don't say that," Anna said. "I swear you are lovelier than when I met you." She pressed her arms together. "I'm only up early this morning because of some uneasiness in my humors."

"I never knew you to have uneasy humors," Lidia said.

"That I did not, because I had my dear Lidia with me."

Lidia looked at the ground, as though shrouding some pain. And there, in that flicker of pain, Anna saw the concern, the reproof, the solicitude that was every day in the eyes of her friends, and it came to her that Lidia knew. Someone had told her, or she had overheard some rumor. Madame Fisher's wicked husband was beating her.

"Tell me," Lidia said. "Would you like me to come back to you? To be your companion again?"

"Oh," Anna laughed, a laugh like a glaze, smoothing her entire aspect, "and face the wrath of my mother?"

"I don't think she would have anything to object to now that you're wed. I doubt she'd even notice me. I'd be quiet as a mouse."

Anna swayed on her feet. Last night after she'd sung, someone had given her a small silver watch. She wore the watch now around her neck. Beneath her cloak and scarf it was warm against her skin, where first it had been icy cold. She could feel the high tick of its heartbeat against her own, dividing the day into time, measuring out her breaths. It must be nearly eight. The sky, twilight-blue when she'd left the house, was bright and clear. How many sunrises she had missed. Last night while she'd slept the watch had ticked in its smooth purse on the table where a few weeks ago her husband had dropped her.

"I would have to ask John if you could come back," she said.

Lidia cocked her head. "Does he bother with your servants?"

Anna touched the base of her throat. "Please don't pity me. In truth I am fortunate. When I think of my life, of all I've done, all I've loved, it amazes me. Look, it makes me cry. I've always been so weak and softhearted."

"*Open*hearted, my dear one," Lidia exclaimed.

"And you mustn't — you must simply ignore John. Don't argue with him or he won't have you. He's very moody. He loves me in mountains and chasms. It's because of his genius — all geniuses are moody. And love isn't worth anything without storms and tempests, you know! But when he loves me best in the world it's the most wonderful thing I've ever known or felt and you mustn't get in the way of that, Lidia, only be as you are and just for me so that I might feel your calm, dear loving presence again when I'm lonely. I do get lonely, even now that I'm married and so fearfully busy. You were my only friend. My only true friend. Sometimes when I'm alone in the morning in bed and there's no Lidia to draw the curtains and wake me, the emptiness — the silence in my head, you see — I get so frightened! You can't believe what it's like!"

They walked on together, Anna leaning on the other girl's arm and talking as if all this could make up for their time apart, could disperse the isolation she felt, even here, with dear Lidia once again obediently listening and murmuring at her side, and all the words she could spill not doing anything to vanquish the silence, the reproach, the loneliness, of those horrifying mornings.

194

■ ■ ■ ■

Dear Anna,

Your last letter troubled me greatly. I wish I could see you. These are not the words of the girl I remember, the brave girl who was my best Cupid. What has happened? What can I do?

Ah, I am so far away.

There is no shame in sadness, my dear. Do remember how you are loved. You are the most remarkable young lady I know. You are quick-witted and strong. You uplift our souls. Isn't that good? Doesn't that bring comfort? I believe in you, and in your purpose. You must not give up. I don't know what is happening there but you must find courage and not give up. Do you still have my phoenix pin? Then you have me. You may carry me in your pocket or at your breast. And not only me but yourself, your courage, all our hours together. You mustn't forget, my Anna. Why do you think I gave it to you?

You say little of your husband. Let me tell you that there are times in life when everything seems darkness. When the

195

way becomes unclear. There is only a piling-on of blankets. Then the littlest things seem difficult. But there is a way out. There is always a way, if only in our minds. Remember who you are. You are Anna Storace and you have everything you need. If I was there I would show you. Well, I'm there in that pin. Write me and let me know you are better. You don't know how I worry. Of all young ladies, you must know joy — it's all I ever wished for you.

Ever yours,
Venanzio Rauzzini

It occurred to Anna early one morning, John sleeping beside her, that her husband might as well have been miles away, farther away than Stephen, dead like her father, or unborn like her child, for all that she was in any degree close to him. She sat up and looked at his square face and the thought came to her that this was no less true of anyone else she loved or knew; that it wasn't just because John was her husband or because he mistreated her. If he had not been her husband, if he had been kind, she would have been alone in the world all the same.

Rising from the bed she went to the

196

window and looked outside. The glass was thick and dirty. She could see nothing but a few shadowy figures who might have been ghosts. She felt as though she were regarding her own death.

"What are you doing?" John asked from the bed.

She turned. "I was thinking how alone I am."

His face in the dim light was unreadable. "You're not alone. I'm right here. I may be an old man but I'm certainly here. Come to bed. You have to sing later."

With a rustle of bedclothes he was asleep again. He spoke like that now and then — as if he cared for her. Anna looked at him for a few minutes. Then quietly she put on her dressing gown, the one with the peacocks and the French lace, and bound back her hair in a loose braid. She went to her writing desk and triggered the secret panel that contained her letters and treasures. In the gray light of morning she read Rauzzini's letter again. The part about how he believed in her, how she was remarkable. She took out the phoenix pin and turned it in her hands and pressed it to her cheek, as she had done a hundred times. John Fisher stirred and kept sleeping. The room brightened with morning. Anna took out some paper and her inkwell and wrote a letter to the emperor and had Lidia send it before her husband arose.

It was wonderful to have Lidia home. She was not afraid of Fisher and she gave Anna courage.

Sweet Bells Jangled

Joseph II received petitioners and meted out petty justice every morning at ten. Each appointment took between three and five minutes and was also attended by a number of secretaries and ministers. There was no music at these proceedings, although it might have made them pleasanter.

John Fisher entered the audience room in his finest clothes, with his violin tucked under his arm and the swaybacked bow dangling from his hand as if in lieu of a sword. It had snowed this morning and his boots were wet. There was something tender and melancholy about seeing him with the instrument under his arm, an instrument built so finely that it was as if the wood had been melted and suspended into shape.

The emperor cleared his throat, feeling put out. Why hadn't the men outside stopped him? "My dear sir. I did not ask you here for a concert."

Fisher looked around in embarrassment. The secretaries and ministers averted their eyes. "I beg your pardon, Your Excellency," he said in his egregiously accented German. "When I received your summons I couldn't imagine why — such an honor —"

"Mr. Fisher, you have injured one of my most valuable servants. A woman, indeed, who represents my interests. Therefore you have injured me. I believe you know of whom I speak."

"I do not, Your Excellency," Fisher said slowly. "I have never injured anyone."

"Then either you're lying," said the emperor, "or I wouldn't like to see your idea of real injury. For some time I have heard how you mistreat your young wife, Madame Storace-Fisher, the crown jewel of my opera company, for whom I pay a pretty penny. I have hesitated to intervene because the business between a man and his wife is not to be meddled with. When it affects her professional conduct, however — when she is unable to sing as she used to, and her physical well-being is threatened — when the woman herself writes me in the most piteous tones how she's driven mad by her oppressor — then can I only believe that I *must* act, as my conscience has urged these many months, before my people rebel,

200

before the nightingale herself is maimed or killed. Do you understand? You make no answer but I see from your eyes that you do. Very well. I could arrest and charge you but it would create a spectacle, and none of us would like that. Therefore I ask you to leave my city this evening and never return. These guards of mine will escort you. Your bags are being packed this moment. You may use my transport, for a fee, as far as Augsburg. John Abraham Fisher, I hereby banish you from Vienna."

Following this speech there was a long pause. The man, astonishingly, did not move. Joseph grimaced and retrieved a chocolate drop from his pocket. He rolled it in his hand but did not unwrap it. "Is there something you don't understand about banishment, Mr. Fisher? I could order the guards to take you out bodily."

Fisher shifted on his feet. He cleared his throat and seemed exceedingly uncomfortable. "Your Excellency. If you please. I have never played for you."

The emperor spread his hands, as if to say, *"Well?"* John Fisher shrugged his violin to his chin, with an air of apology, or sorrow, and began to play.

The guards moved forward but Joseph stopped them with a motion of his hand. It would not do to interrupt Bach. An oddly intellectual choice for this moment of John Fisher's public humiliation, although also, of course, being Bach, exquisitely old-fashioned and pleasant even in the most inopportune of moments. It was like one of those old Dutch paintings where the women are in peaked caps and the light and colors are so crisp and clear you think you could break them with a touch. One of the emperor's brothers was a duke in the Austrian Netherlands; Joseph had seen those poised paintings with his own eyes. So he let Fisher play. With the detachment of a fellow musician he admired the man for not rushing the tempo, not even in his distress, and for keeping the clear sweetness of tone he had cultivated over many years. One could almost understand, hearing this music, seeing the physical and emotional obtuseness turn to grace, how Anna Storace had been convinced to dash herself against his crags.

When the partita was finished, the emperor remarked, "You might have lived, sir, as you played."

Anna, surrounded by friends, waited for her husband. The emperor had said that he would send an escort but still she did not want to be caught alone. She had told Michael, and he had come to the house and had brought with him Benucci, Lidia, the Bussanis, and — of all couples — Aloysia Lange and her actor husband, Joseph. Mrs. Storace sat beside Anna with wet eyes, talking to Michael. Michael had said it would be better if there was a crowd when Fisher arrived, as he would be more apt to behave himself with so many watching. Anna was not convinced. Everyone had told her that she should be gone but she had told them that wouldn't do — it would be better for her own soul to say good-bye and see him gone.

Fisher, entering the drawing room, stopped short when he saw the assembly. They had heard him in the hall and gone quiet in anticipation. He had his violin case. His clothes fit him poorly, because he had been impatient with the tailor during their making. His face was red. The guards came behind him, looking sheepish.

As always he had eyes only for Anna. "A party?" he asked. "For you or for me?"

"John," she said. "I've had Robert pack all your clothes and things and I've given you some money."

"I wonder why you never surprised me on my name day, my dear, with such talents for secrecy."

"You hate surprises," Anna said.

"Ah, you know that? I suppose a good wife should know such things about her husband. One wonders why you are doing such a thing to me now as this."

"Look here," said Michael. "She's doing it because you're an ass, Fisher."

"And you, madam?" Fisher asked Mrs. Storace. "Will you renounce me, too?"

"It was a mistake," Mrs. Storace said. She gripped her daughter's hand. "Each of us has been deceived about the other. Won't you please go calmly and well?"

Fisher surveyed the room. The non-English speakers — Benucci, Lidia, the Langes, the Bussanis, the two imperial guards — watched with a kind of interested blankness; they were an audience whose comprehension was limited to tone of voice and quality of aspect; rather like a German audience at an Italian opera. Lidia knew the most English of all of them, and understood a word or two, while Joseph Lange, the famous actor and portraitist who had won Aloysia's heart from Mozart, could read their body language as if it had been written out for him in blocked letters. Benucci looked on edge. He leaned forward and asked in Italian if there was any trouble. Anna said there was not.

Fisher snorted. "What will I tell people?"

"What you like."

"Driven mad by your oppressor. Your oppressor! You were mad before you ever met me."

"Even so," said Anna. She felt as though there were fingers clawing around her collarbone.

Fisher rubbed his jaw. "And what about my child?" She looked at him with wide eyes and did not answer. He stood in front of them like someone to be judged. They had arranged themselves on Michael's suggestion to face him all in a row. Aloysia Lange whispered something inaudible in her husband's ear and Anna hated her for it. When she'd met the Langes at the door she hadn't wanted to let them in. They weren't friends of hers. If anything they were her rivals. But Michael had said that Fisher admired the Langes, Joseph especially, and would not want to create a scene in front of them.

"Is that Frau and Herr Lange?" Fisher asked, switching into his halting but forceful German. "Herr Lange here to watch me and see me break?" He rubbed his jaw again and continued in English. "Yes, I can see him taking notes about me now in his mind. Very good. How red my face is, how I clutch my violin case as if for my life. Well. I'll put it down."

"Good sir," said Michael Kelly, "why prolong this show? We're all of us quite ready to bid you Godspeed and farewell."

"Herr Lange is a great Hamlet," Fisher said. "As great as they can be in German. Do you remember, Anna, how we used to read those scenes together? It was one of the first things I loved about you, that you would read aloud the great tragedies with me and not think me grim. What a refuge this house seemed to me then, and you in it. Didn't you think we made a good pair of readers, madam?" he asked Mrs. Storace.

It frightened Anna that he was acting so politely. He should have been more angry. He should have tried to hurt her.

He crossed to one of the bookcases. "Come," he said. "Come over here and read with me. You know the scene I mean." He smiled with self-mockery and found the book on the shelf. "I'll read Ophelia. I wouldn't have you think I don't know who is banishing whom." No one offered a word of protest. Dorotea Bussani looked stricken. The room had a quality of helpless suspense and embarrassment. Outside, the day already seemed to be darkening, though it was not long past noon. Nobody had lunched and some of them — the singers and the actor — had been obliged to wake earlier than they were used to in order to be here for this scene. Fisher was like the worst kind of guest, one who made you feel at once bored and discomfited. Yet no one was ready to make the final push. They were all deferring to Anna. She seemed unwilling to end it. Instead it seemed she was setting down her crochet work and moving toward Fisher with all her gracefulness, her rounded belly, toward his mockery and his book; toward the performance he proposed.

"My lord," Fisher said to Anna, reciting fair Ophelia's lines from memory. *"I have re-membrances of yours that I have longed long to redeliver."* Casting down his eyes, he reached into his sleeve and retrieved a folded piece of paper. When had he put it there? What had he written on it? With a modest smile, he offered it to Anna. It was addressed, *To My Wife.*

She felt as if she were accepting a curse. She opened the letter and read: *Forgive me. I love you. John.*

Revulsion crossed her face. She slid the letter into the pages of the book. She read Hamlet's lines, his tirade against Ophelia, his orders to "get thee to a nunnery." Fisher tottered. Really he was a magnificent actor. It was as if her every word scorched him.

He wanted her to feel like a torturer. He wanted her to know how it had felt to push her down, to grasp her hips and pin her, to lift her up and let her drop. How powerful it felt and how cruel. But she would never know that.

He was on his knees now, facing front, his hands at his chest. Hamlet had made his exit and Ophelia was alone. He looked up. *"Oh, what a noble mind is here o'erthrown!"* His cheeks were wet with tears. The words, clad in his Irish accent, flirting with falsetto, were as beautiful and tender to hear as they would have been on any formal stage, and as wretched. *"The observed of all of observers, quite, quite down!"* Anna stood beside him, implacable. Benucci shifted nervously in place, as if waiting for a good moment to defend her honor. The rest stayed as they were, almost without breathing, a gravity on their faces of the kind usually reserved for the sickbed.

"I *say,* Fisher," said Kelly, "this is beyond batty. Have pity."

Fisher stretched a hand before him. *"And I,"* he whispered, *"of ladies most deject and wretched, that sucked the honey of his music vows, now see that noble and most sovereign reason, like sweet bells, jangled out of tune and harsh . . ."*

208

The rest of the speech seemed to wilt in the air. There was no applause. Fisher retrieved his violin and went outside to wait while the rest of his possessions were loaded into the carriage. Anna retired to her room with Lidia. The rest of the guests, sober and strained, helped themselves to the generous tea provided by Mrs. Storace, who thanked them for their company and remarked upon the weather.

STEPHEN'S RETURN

Stephen arrived from London one night in February while Anna was at a party. When she came home she felt the change instantly. The atmosphere was alive with it. Her body knew the fact of it before her mind did and she laughed and cried out before she knew why, before she heard English voices and strong, loud steps coming toward her from the parlor, before she saw the traveling trunk in the hall, the draped cloak, and all the wrapped parcels. There was Stephen, tall and bright-eyed and scruffy-bearded, taking her into his arms with great caution because he had never had occasion, until now, to embrace a woman who was with child.

Such a shock! They had been waiting for him for so long — so much had happened — and now here he was!

"Hasn't he grown?" asked Mrs. Storace. "Doesn't he look like your father? I thought

I'd seen a ghost."

"Look at *you,*" Stephen said to Anna, standing back to take in her belly.

She smiled shyly. "I'm sorry. I tried to stay smaller. We'll find a good costume."

"You're beautiful," he said.

They sat in the parlor, and all three were at a loss, unsure where they had left off or where to resume. Anna, after her first rush of joy, had come under the sway of more creeping emotions. Stephen asked for some wine.

"Did you get my last letter?" he asked at last.

"Yes," said Mrs. Storace, "but we didn't write back because you were just a few days hence."

"I half feel I should be writing a letter now," Anna said.

"What would you say?" he asked, turning to her with such encouraging imprecation that she knew she must seem lost and awkward indeed.

"Let's see," she said. She looked at the ceiling. "I would write that my dear brother has arrived safely and I am now the happiest girl in all of Vienna, because he is good and strong and embraces me even in my uncomfortable condition. I would implore him in my letter to keep warm and wear booties when traveling at night. I'd say we have no news."

"And here I am!" Stephen exclaimed, looking around him. "I have not seen much of it yet, but I love Vienna."

"Anna is admired here," said Mrs. Storace. "She can hardly take a step but someone is soliciting her or offering her his elbow."

"All the better for me and my opera," Stephen said with a smile.

"She's the only reason the emperor agreed to do your opera."

"Mama," Anna said.

Stephen shook his head. "It's all right — I'm not ashamed."

"Nor am I." She took his hand. "I need your music. Yours. Only yours. Everything else is so dull, I can't tell you how dull — it has no *relation* to me, my heart is elsewhere, there's nothing anymore to sing for —"

"Good gracious," Stephen exclaimed. "Who is this changeling? What have they done with my butterfly sister? Where has your joy gone?"

"So you see it was all for my own sake," she said, smiling helplessly. "And now I fear I've only made things worse — your prima buffa should not look like a ship at sea. I'll ruin everything."

"Nonsense," he said. The opera will be nothing without you. Nobody has heard of me."

"Yet," she said.

He laughed. "Yet! Soon the whole world will know, thanks to you. I always said we were going to be a team, didn't I?"

"John Fisher," Mrs. Storace said abruptly. She fixed her gaze on the ground. "It was John Fisher took the joy out of her, and I could do nothing to stop it. How many days and nights I wished you to come, Stephen, but she wouldn't write you."

"There was nothing to say!" Anna cried. "It's all over now and I'll have none of this about losing my joy, whatever in the world that means. How could I lose my joy when Stephen is here and it's almost springtime and I have a new Storace opera to present to everyone? I've never been happier. I don't know how I'll sleep tonight."

"Neither do I," Stephen said. "Oh, Anna. To have an opera of my own performed — on such a stage, with such singers, with you! To think I almost gave this up." He sprang to his feet and paced the room, glancing at himself in the mirror above the fireplace. "It's what I was born to do, just like Papa said. I've been denying God's will, denying my nature. Even the air is different here. It

213

hums. One can feel the music in it. But wait until you hear my opera. It will be like nothing anyone has ever heard. I can't help but think that this is the pinnacle — this, right here, this itself, or at least the beginning of the pinnacle, the pinnacle at the foot of some more majestic, higher pinnacle. Can't you help it, either? This moment is ours at last, just as Papa imagined us, ourselves united in the most beautiful, the most perfect art in the world, your voice and my music!"

"Stephen," Anna said, "you mustn't dream so hard. It makes me nervous."

"No matter! All you have to do is sing the thing before the emperor and all the great plush regatta of his court and concubines. That alone will be more than I have dared let myself dream even in my hours of greatest self-intoxication." And he looked at her kindly and patted her hand, as if he felt that all this would reassure her rather than make her feel more apprehensive.

Even with her husband gone she was still not herself. Her voice had lost its freshness. Rauzzini would have noticed the vocal strain that she battled in private but could not determine how to resolve.

Watching Swallows

Stephen found his sister more subdued than he remembered her. Her expression would sometimes sadden when she thought no one was looking, and she moved more slowly because of the baby. But her cheeks had a good color. Her eyes were as bright as ever. She had written to him after Christmas to say that her husband had been sent away because he hadn't been a good man. For a girl like his sister, who was all amiability and affection, to have married wrongly — married, perhaps, a scoundrel — was beyond bearing. There was no man on earth who deserved her love. But the evening of his arrival when he tried in his fumbling way to ask after her health, she smiled as if amused and passed on to easier subjects.

"This is my Lidia," she said. "She's my lady's maid and my true friend. You must get her to sing for you sometime, Stephen. She has a lovely voice."

"It would be my great pleasure," he said with interest, bowing to the girl. She was tall and brown, and had firm, honest features. He thought immediately that he would like to draw her.

"She's from Naples," Anna said. "She grew up in one of the girls' conservatories. But she's about to sink into the floor from embarrassment so we'll say no more. Come, let me show you your room."

His mother, too, seemed diminished. He felt he did not know her and had little to say.

Anna introduced Stephen to Mozart a few days later. She helped lay out the luncheon and was all aflutter that Stephen should meet her friend. She and her mother had a gracious dining area with a long table and rich paneling. Stephen could not believe how they lived here, in such luxury. He had taken John Fisher's old quarters, next door to Anna's, and it gave him satisfaction to paper over the impression and smell of the man. He spread his possessions all over. He rearranged the desk and bed and put up a few of his watercolor sketches, landscapes of England.

He told Anna she mustn't tire herself with this luncheon business, but she said with the brightest look that there was nothing wearisome about bringing together two of the best gentlemen she knew. Stephen hoped to take composition lessons from Mozart, and Mozart wanted English lessons, so that he could someday return to London. He had been there once as a little boy, before Anna and Stephen were born, and it would be just the thing for him, he said. But Anna did not have the patience to teach him English; she said she wouldn't know where to begin.

Mozart embraced Stephen like a brother and greeted Mrs. Storace cordially. He was a pale, slightly built man in his natural hair. His big eyes, Stephen thought, like agate stones, overset by soft reddish brows, seemed to seize and stare into one's very soul, such was the intensity of his attention and concentration. Yet he was also fidgety and shy. He had his neck wrapped in a checkered scarf because he had been ill. He ate with a ravenous appetite and avowed pleasure, two plates full; he had been up since six, composing, he said, and had taken no breakfast, only a single piece of cheese three hours in. He'd given up his opera. Nobody wanted an opera from him anyway. Now he was just composing piano concertos and symphonies, chamber music for sweet ladies, to pay the bills. How grand it was that Stephen had gotten an opera at the Burg — Mozart looked forward to hearing it. Stephen blushed and said he'd rather it was one of Mozart's operas and Mozart said that was nonsense. For Stephen to be only twenty-two and having his first opera premiered at the Burgtheater — that was something to be proud of.

Mozart wanted to know everything about London and the English way of being. There was a craze for all things English these days. They talked of politics and freedom and America. Mozart had just joined the Freemasons, though he couldn't tell them anything about it, only that it was marvelous and new. He had a friend there, a lodge brother, who was a black man, an actual African, working for his freedom from a nobleman. And by God he had nearly gotten it. He was a great fellow, married to a Viennese lady. Freemasonry, Mozart said, was about freedom and humanity, how to live, how to regulate one's mind to the highest capacity and discipline. It was a bastion of science, medicine, and all the arts.

"We used to see blacks in London," Mrs. Storace said. "Poor creatures. And of course one finds all kinds of Turks and Egyptians in this city. I never heard of one living so kingly as your man. I suppose he can't believe his luck."

Mozart looked at her. "Well, madam," he said at last. "I do not know if that is true. Perhaps someday you might ask him."

She blanched. "I do not go out often, Herr Mozart."

"She reminds me of my father," Mozart said to the Storace siblings later, when they retired to the music room.

"You, too?" said Stephen with a laugh. They had been talking of their childhoods, how all of them had been paraded for their musical skills — though Mozart's parade, of course, had covered all of Europe.

"Put her in trousers," Mozart said, "and I'd call her my own."

"She married very young," Anna said. "It was practically an elopement. But she was educated, you see. She really should have been a man."

"Our father was a bumbler," Stephen declared. "She's the one who taught us to read."

Stephen felt nervous and young beside Mozart. Mozart was an open, jovial fellow, but filled with such intensity — those fish-like eyes, that flushed pallor, behind which thrummed arteries of life and thought — that one almost wished to escape for air.

But composition lessons had already been

proposed, and Mozart suggested looking over some of Stephen's pieces now, why not this instant? Perhaps a selection from the new opera? Stephen could not refuse. Anna asked if she might sit and watch. Her brother, though he had not been expecting a lesson today and would rather have been taught in private, said that of course she might.

He and Mozart sat at the keyboard with one of Stephen's favorite arias from his opera and the orchestration to which he'd been setting it. Mozart proceeded to reduce it to rubble.

He was not harsh, but neither did he coddle, and for that, at least, Stephen was grateful. Mozart spoke in a low, mild voice, so that only they two could hear, and made small markings on the paper or played examples and ideas to explain his reasoning. When he praised, it seemed praise truly felt: he would stop to explore some surprise or beauty in Stephen's line or harmony, and wonder at how it worked, and speculate how it might be still improved, so it left one feeling oddly cheered, even in the wreckage of everything that was drab and hackneyed and ugly and wrong. Mozart's powers of concentration were all-consuming. The walls might have collapsed in flames around them and he would have kept murmuring and analyzing. He must do the same with his own work, one felt, only perhaps with still more strictness and rigor, and for this, too, one was wholly grateful even as one was stripped raw to the bone. Stephen hardly knew whether to laugh at himself or weep. It seemed impossible folly that his opera would go up in two months.

"We must do this again," he said to Mozart rather weakly after they'd gone through everything. "I'll pay you, of course. I'm going to have to think for days but I'd like to see you again — there are so many things I've got to learn."

"I like it very much," said Mozart, nodding at the page. He was silent a moment and then asked, "I wonder if you might indulge me in letting me play this aria with your sister? Would you mind singing, mademoiselle? It's been too long since I played with you. If we run through this aria I could show your brother what I mean about the accompaniment." His face as he said this had a dreamy quality; his eyes seemed the color of a briny sea. Flushed and smiling, Anna rose and went to the piano. Stephen with some reluctance took her place on the sofa. Her maid, Lidia, stood just inside the doorway. She'd come so quietly he hadn't noticed her. She had a chin, he thought, like an arrow's point.

Mozart smiled at Anna. There was a scarcely perceptible pause. Then he looked down and began to play.

Anna already knew the aria. She sang it easily and well. One forgot, watching her, that she was heavy with child. She seemed all girlish grace. Her color was high and her smile infectious. She got this look often when she sang, as though her life had become whole, as though she wished to do nothing ever but this. Now, however, the feeling seemed deepened. Had she not looked so happy one might have thought she was about to cry. Perhaps she was so affected because her brother had returned, or perhaps it was love and expectation for her child. Stephen had forgotten how beautiful her voice was and how unhampered by artifice. She sounded only like herself.

Mozart, however, was changing the entire accompaniment. Stephen, listening to his music in the hands of another — only altered, at times dramatically altered, by what this far more skilled composer suggested with harmony and texture and dynamic — felt riveted and strange. He was almost queasy. Was he so conservative as all that — so conventional? This particular aria had been his favorite. It had been, to him, one of the best things he'd ever done in his life. But it turned out to have been rubbish.

His sister was happy, singing with Mozart. He had come here expecting her to be troubled or wounded and it turned out she was happy and well. Watching them was like watching swallows in the air. He could not touch them. He was wholly barred. Though it was his music, the best parts of it were what they did with it, the phrasing, the tempo, the embellishments, such as would never have occurred to Stephen by himself. He could have gone on his knees.

"There," Mozart said. "You see? Of course it was only a little improvisation. You're a treasure, mademoiselle, to follow me."

Stephen groaned. "You're giving me headaches, Mozart."

"As my father always told me," Mozart said, putting on a long face, *"Learn or die! Learn or die, my son!"*

"I thought it was better before," Lidia said softly to Stephen as they were parting. "I liked yours better."

"Well," he said, with a wry smile. "You're the only one, then."

All the rest of the day Lidia's compliment bolstered him, and as the week went on, he began to think that his opera was not so bad at all, really, considering Mozart was nearly ten years older and had been composing since he was a tiny boy. And everyone always complained that Mozart's music was too complicated. Really, when one looked at it that way, *The Discontented Spouses* was an extraordinary opera and would be a smashing success — especially with Anna to sing it.

He looked forward to seeing Mozart again, though, and vowed to himself that the next time he would hold his own. "He's absolutely brilliant," he said to his sister. "I knew he would be — I daresay I've been his admirer long before he had many admirers — but I never would have guessed the *extent* of it. Why, if I had only the skill in his little finger! But I'm more practical than he is, I'm not afraid to bend to the wind of populism. Music should be agreeable above all else. Mozart knows this but *he gets in his own way.* My God, and I thought *my* orchestrations were complex! I wondered if *I* had gone too far! I would never dare go further than that, than what I myself have done, and yet look at Mozart going to the ends of the earth. If I didn't admire him so much, I'd have thought he had no care for his future or his family. And then you hear the bloody thing and can't help but be taken in, even as half of you is begging him to cut it down a little, for pity's sake, and let us enjoy the beauty underneath. Would that be so hard?"

THE DISCONTENTED SPOUSES

The Storace siblings were often remarking, as the premiere of Stephen's opera drew nearer, how amazed their father should have been at their change of circumstances. To have seen Anna sing in a royal house the music of her brother — to have known that Stephen had written it — well! At the time of the premiere Anna was almost nine months pregnant, although only her mother and Lidia knew that. Even her brother did not know. He had a vague impression that there were still one or two months remaining. Anna was calm, however. She knew the baby would wait.

In Stephen's face on the night of the premiere was a sort of patient excitement Anna had felt herself so often before — the feeling that everything that could be done had been done, that it was done extremely well, and could not help coming off like a perfect dream. The patience came from fullness of preparation and purpose, and the excitement, from the inconstancy of the theater, which was like the natural world in that events must occur that the actors could neither foresee nor control.

The Duke of York was in the audience, a guest of the emperor in the royal box. Laughter and applause greeted the first act. Stephen's music was charming, the libretto no worse than any other. Anna's costume disguised her condition tolerably well, although it was difficult for her to get a proper breath with the baby taking so much room. The other singers, because they loved Anna, were at their best. The orchestra did not indistinguish itself, and compensated, in its placid collective way, for Stephen's eager and somewhat impulsive behavior at the keyboard. So consumed was he by this moment, by the unbelievable felicity of his art made manifest — audience, stage, word, music — that he might have been forgiven for forgetting his own name.

What happened during Anna's bravura aria at the end of the first act could have been predicted by no one, least of all by herself. She felt no warning. All was as it had ever been. She was always at her best on stage — she felt it clearly — a better, more beloved Anna, an Anna of mystery and fortune and power.

What she would remember afterward was the time between ignorance and understanding, those few seconds or perhaps even minutes when none knew the extent of her misfortune but herself; when many indeed had not yet realized there had been any misfortune at all. There was a pain or spasm in her throat — a knife in her windpipe — then a blossoming of broken glass. She choked on the A-flat, on the word *dolce* — sweet. When she coughed and cleared her throat, and tried to continue, unknowing at first, there was no voice she recognized as hers, just rags and smarting air and pathetic wheezing. The orchestra kept playing. Stephen, almost deaf with excitement now that the moment of greatness was upon him, did not notice his sister stop singing, and was indeed one of the very last to look up. But Anna saw him. His forehead was knitted in happy concentration. It will break his heart, she thought.

The orchestra went on — oh, for many painful measures. Michael Kelly, on stage with her, leapt out of his part in an instant to be at her elbow.

"Is it the child?" he whispered.

Anna looked at him without a word.

"Is it the child, Anna?"

The hall had gone deathly quiet. The orchestra, divided between those who had noticed her distress and those who yet had not, limped to a halt. Stephen looked up and met his sister's eye, the enraptured smile fading on his lips. He would think she was joking, or that she hated him and was doing it on purpose. And in some selfish part of her heart she wished that were true, because this helplessness, this loss so sudden and unimaginable, was not anything she could remedy or bear. There was the emperor in his private box. There was the Duke of York with his medals and his disappointment. There was her mother with her hand over her mouth, and Mozart leaning forward in his chair as if he wanted to spring to the stage and finish the aria himself. Salieri, across the aisle, whispered something to his mistress. All of them were whispering now. The members of the orchestra looked up at her in alarm. Anna shook her head, once, *"No,"* for all their benefit, and someone had the sense to draw the curtain.

There was an uproar. They kept asking what had happened and if it was the baby and whether she could still finish the opera. She tried to sing, but it was no good. The voice had left her. She had done something terribly wrong, abused her heavenly gift, upset the balance. Now the work of years was reduced to nothing. Any girl might lose her voice, just as she might lose her hearing, her sight, or her life. But not so young — not, surely, at the flourishing of her powers.

She was made to recline on the floor; a physician was sent for. Stephen came running and was told everything.

"What will we do?" he asked wildly. "Who will sing it in her place?"

He had knelt beside her and seized her hand but looked away, all distraction and agitation. The desperation of his sister's case was not yet evident to him. She seemed distraught and mortified but otherwise in robust health, while his infant opera, his fragile, miraculous construction of thought and air, was in the throes of death. There were two more acts to be gotten through. Some other soprano could sing from the orchestra, while Anna put on a dumb show. He proposed this repeatedly to the crowd surrounding them. He helped Anna sit up in order to demonstrate that she was fit and well. He was urging her to stand — she was weeping and could hardly draw air from her panic — when the emperor's own physician came in and made her lie down again. Stephen hovered above them, muttering for a new singer and looking around frantically, but it would not do, this plan of his to save his opera from the brink. In the first place, there was no one else capable of singing Anna's part. In the second, the physician, who thrived on situations of public urgency, positively forbade Madame Storace from exerting herself in any way. She must be bled, she must drink bitter powders, she must have poultices applied to her throat and chest. In the third place, a new opera by an unknown English composer, without Anna Storace, was no opera that any Viennese wished to see. *The Discontented Spouses* died in Vienna that evening, at half past nine, and was ever after known only and infamously as the opera that muted a lark.

BLACK BILE

The doctor said she was not in danger of miscarrying; that had not caused Anna's distress. Rather the problem was black bile, in her chest and throat, which must find its way out. Black bile was the worst kind of bile, thick and noxious, seeping through all the vital organs. The black bile had filled her neck and burst out during the bravura aria, whereupon it had spilled into her bowels and lungs. If they did not release it, it would choke her heart. The doctor gave her ice baths. He made her drink bitter powders so that she would vomit, which only hurt her throat more. He bled her twice daily, until she was weak and delirious. Lidia became so distressed she threatened to take her own life. Finally Mrs. Storace, seeing her daughter white and parched as death, declared the doctor a murderer and sent him away.

Mrs. Storace found an old midwife, a

sturdy woman from the country, who swept in and gave Anna good food and cooling drink and bathed her and aired and cleansed everything. And though Anna still had no voice, at least there was no one talking anymore about the black bile and how she must vomit it out. The midwife did not believe in black bile. She said she'd never seen the stuff in her life. She gave Anna herbal drinks that were sweetened with honey and not bitter. She said Anna was a strong girl, and that there was nothing wrong with her. Anna was grateful for her kindness, and tried to believe her, but could not. Her throat hurt with every breath. She could barely speak. She was afraid for the baby and afraid, too, terribly afraid, that giving birth to it would kill her. She prayed it would not come out at all, so she would not have to feel any pain.

But she delivered the baby as well as the midwife had predicted. She was brave and strong. She hardly made a sound, to spare the rags of her voice. The midwife said she'd never known such a quiet young mother. But after the birth Anna became terribly ill.

The baby girl had Benucci's eyes. They sent it to a wet nurse. The wet nurse, though they did not know at the time, was sick, as well, and gave the illness to the baby, and it died a week old. They did not tell Anna for two weeks more that the infant had died, and when they did — for she had been begging to see her baby — her wails were like a banshee's, and after that she would not eat, nor speak, nor sign to anyone, and for a long time they feared she would not recover.

MESMER

The emperor came often to the Countess Thun's salons. He was as in love with her as everyone else. She treated him exactly as he most wished: as an ordinary man.

Her husband, the Count Thun, had lately become a devotee of Dr. Franz Mesmer and his miraculous magnetism, and their salons, in addition to the usual happy fare of some of the best music and conversation in all of Vienna, had attained a new and exciting air. The emperor, who loved everything modern, found himself tempted and intrigued by this new medicine, which worked on a patient with mere magnetic touch.

Dr. Mesmer had left Vienna in disgrace some years ago, after failing to cure a blind pianist, a young lady. There were some who saw Dr. Mesmer as a charlatan, and for years the emperor had counted himself among them. But there had been encouraging reports filtering in from Paris, Mesmer's new center of practice, and Joseph's own sister Marie Antoinette, the queen of France, spoke warmly of the speed and painlessness of the doctor's restorative cures. While the Count Thun had never had a session with Mesmer himself, he had invited the attentions of several young disciples, and seen some not insignificant improvements to his gouty foot. Tonight one of these disciples was installed in a side room, and into this sanctum the guests entered in twos and threes for treatments. The emperor declined to visit with the young mesmerist himself, but he watched the proceedings with curiosity. All things scientific interested him, and at a musical salon like this, one particular illness could not help but come to mind.

"I'm having a notion," he said to the countess. He sipped his wine and ate one of her bonbons. "I'm having a notion that it may be time to call Dr. Mesmer back to Vienna."

"Really, Your Excellency?" asked the countess. "How thrilling that would be for all of us — all who have these concerns, these weaknesses, about which the regular doctors are at a loss."

"Not *my* doctors," the emperor amended with a smile. The countess bowed her head and murmured something sorrowful. "But even they," the emperor continued, "have not the smallest notion how to make Mademoiselle Storace sing again. The poor girl has been bled nearly of her last drop, and doused in ice water, and seawater, and made to take all manner of powders, and been stood on her head and worked like a bellows, and all for what? Mesmer could be here in a few weeks. He might be just the thing for the Storace girl. He's good with nervous young ladies."

"Oh, yes," said the countess. "She has always seemed one to me who possesses more than the usual degree of the ether, as Dr. Mesmer calls it, which flows through all our breath and veins. I have felt a remarkable attraction to her on every occasion I've seen her — a pull almost physical in its strength. I grieve to know she's ill."

"Indeed," the emperor mused. "She does exert a certain pull, as you say."

"As do all great artists," said the countess with a smile. "They have that which I do not! How I envy them, Your Excellency. I do believe this is why I hold these salons, that I might see the great ones at close hand and absorb some of their radiance — their magnetism." She paused and let her gaze rest upon a guttering candelabra. "Yet it cannot be but that the force of the glow, the radiance — the white brilliance of that ether in them, so much thicker and hotter than our own — is also more subject to knots and blockages and clogging. Their risk is greater — they toy with all the passions and the profoundest beauties of the world, unbalance their humors, leave themselves raw to stoppages and despair. Do not you think so? And poor Madame Storace has had more to provoke her than even the calmest citizen could tolerate."

"Perhaps, madam. But it's just as well it died, before she could get sentimental. A single woman in my court is better off without such encumbrances. Far better off. She should be glad."

"Oh, but sir," interjected the countess with all her sweet modesty, "we women are weaker willed than you give us credit. All infants and children melt our hearts, and those — why, those we've carried *under* our hearts, of our own flesh — Your Excellency, the animal magnetism in such a case could not be felt more strongly. Oh, no, she felt the child's death. I am sure she felt it. I am sure she feels it now. It is little wonder she is ill-disposed for singing."

Chrysalis

The birds outside her windows reminded Anna of Tuscan songbirds. They had the same quality of rejoicing, of bathing in the April sky, recalling the gaiety of her former life. She would have liked to see more clearly what sorts of birds they were, but the windows were soldered shut and the glass obscured with dust.

One could not think of heavier matters than these. One must shut everything out. Still, the tears would squeeze from her eyes, songbirds being more dangerous than they first appeared — more dangerous even than music. Songbirds recalled love, and children, and cheer, and of all these was Anna bereft.

Broad afternoon and still she lay in bed. The new doctor had come in the morning and bled her and told her to eat more, go walking in the Prater. She did wish to go walking in the Prater — it took her breath away for wishing. She had been like this for a month. All her limbs and muscles cried out for use. But even to go outside, to bathe and dress and step into the harsh and foreign air, meant an impossible and terrifying exertion. Sometimes it seemed difficult even to lift her arm. She could lie on her left side for hours, wishing to turn to the right, but not doing so because it seemed too hard.

She leaked tears without warning or volition, as she'd once leaked milk. But mostly she was dry as bone, imprisoned inside herself. She felt her heart battering against the stony ribs. The first doctor had said there was black bile there, strangling her heart. When she remembered the girl she had once been, the girl who shimmered and danced like poplar leaves in the morning, whose only business had been to cheer others, and who now could barely speak or wish to move, how she pitied herself; how she became mired in this pity. There had never been anyone so sorrowful or weak or pitiable as she. "I did everything right," she whispered to herself. She could speak now. But the voice was not hers. She renounced it.

She had done everything right. She had been cheerful and good. Misfortune had

240

never upset her, never so completely as this. Even with John she had still been able to sing.

Stephen blamed himself for writing the aria that had torn her throat, an aria like a booby trap into which he'd poured all his hopes and somehow left buried Sleeping Beauty's spindle. They both remembered how Stephen had carried on that night, as if his opera were more important than she was, and he said he would never forgive himself.

For the first weeks she had communicated with a notebook and a pencil hung about her neck. She had not realized until then how much she had been used to talk. And since no one much cared to converse in that way, to a scribbling mute, and since she did not feel easy with others, she had simply stopped trying. And the more she stayed in bed the harder it was to conceive of leaving it. Lidia begged her to. She pleaded, ordered, and prayed. She took away the pencil and the paper, once it was clear that Anna could speak without harming herself. But still Anna said as little as possible, and only in the feeblest whisper. She still felt a pain. It was a distinct little pain. Just there. Her voice was a stained glass window and someone had thrown a stone through it. Rough air whistled around the shards.

If she could not sing she could not live. Like the poor baby had not lived. She had wished to hold it, after it had been born, but she had not been able to lift her arms, somehow, and then they had taken it away and Anna had turned her head and done nothing. And she could never tell Benucci now. The quail's egg had burst, poisoned her throat, filled her lungs with slime and broken shells.

Better not to think of all that. She needn't live if she couldn't sing. Without singing she was nothing, had nothing, no personhood, no purpose, no knowledge, no mastery, nothing with which to make anyone happy. She was without use. And the longer she was without use, the longer she did nothing, the more pitiable she became. One took these things for granted, voices, babies, then they burst and vanished. A knife at her throat and slime dripping from her ribs and the poor heart battering itself to death inside. The poor, poor baby. For two weeks they hadn't told her. For two weeks she had thought it living, imagined its smile, its black eyes and soft cheeks and waving hands. And all that time it had been already dead.

She was lying on her side, staring at the

wall, as was her custom, when she heard some music coming from downstairs. She turned her head and frowned. Stephen, playing the piano, trying to draw her out. Well, she wouldn't be drawn. Music was only painful to her now and he knew it. Of course he had to play for his composition and to keep his fingers limber, but somehow she knew on this day that he was doing it to draw her out. Every now and then he went through periods of trying to revive and cheer her, bringing little gifts or stories, coming in on tiptoe. Unspoken between them was the old truth that her life and art were more important than his own, that she provided income for all of them, that the entire population of Vienna awaited with impatience the news of her recovery or fall. She had become, in her distress, something of a legend. It was said she was in danger of killing herself. There were rumors she had murdered her baby.

She was indeed transformed. Stripped of all that had located her in the world, exposed to her essence, an essence which turned out to be very little at all, she had nothing left to hold on to.

Still frowning slightly, she turned onto her back and closed her eyes. But she could not help hearing the music that drifted so sweetly from downstairs. It was impossible to ignore. There were no other sounds and she had nothing to read or write or do. So she listened. If she smiled, it was only at her brother's folly, to think he could succeed in drawing her out. If she breathed more deeply, it was not from pleasure, however diverting the melody and countermelody — however long, it seemed, since she'd heard its like.

Then somehow she found she had climbed out of bed, by way of a footstool, and put on her peacock dressing gown and slippers. Her hair hung down her back. She saw the mirror and pinched her cheeks to brighten them. But no matter. She could look like this, or worse than this, forever, because she did not have to go on stage anymore, not for all her life. The music downstairs was blowing wide the curtains, letting in a smell of jasmine. One could not help but move toward it. Her legs were unsteady but somehow the knife in her heart had stopped its twisting — had gone quite still. If she moved with exquisite care, she could hardly feel it at all.

Grasping the railing like a drunken sailor she picked her way down the staircase. Apart from the piano, the house was wholly silent. Her mother must have been somewhere with her sewing or correspondence, and Lidia and the rest of the staff wrapped in their naps and domesticities. They had grown accustomed to keeping their own councils, during Anna's long illness.

As she emerged into the narrow hallway, the music became immediately louder and clearer and she knew then that it was not her brother. Stephen could not play like this. Not ever. Not for all the striving and study in the world.

Mozart, of course.

The door was open. It was the parlor and music room, filled with sun. She had never seen so much sun, never in Vienna. It came through the windows and sparked the dust on the ceramic shepherdesses on the mantelpiece. Even the big, heavy flowers in their vases seem to strain again for sun and belie their state of sustained dying. She caught herself at the doorway, remembering her thinness, her ashen skin, her mussed hair, the peacocks. She could not recall when last she had washed. The room billowed with music and sunlight. She could almost lean against it.

Mozart glanced at her with a calm smile, as if she were a rare nocturnal animal he had coaxed to the edge of a meadow. He seemed as if in a meditation, as one deeply

245

caught up, in this music which he did not write down, or read from, but tossed into the air like unstrung beads.

She stood in the doorway. It was as much as she could bear to stand there. But after five minutes, perhaps more, she was too tired to stand, and too enraptured to leave. She went to the chaise-longue and carefully laid herself upon it, while he continued to play without interruption.

When at last he paused, though with the appearance — his hands still on the keys — as if he would go on, Anna stirred and asked softly where was her brother.

Mozart said that he had come to give Stephen a composition lesson, but Stephen had been called away, and had invited Mozart, while he was gone, to try out the beautiful piano. Mozart was sorry to have disturbed her. He hadn't known anyone was at home.

This could not have been true. He must have known she was home, and practically bedridden. But she indicated, with a shake of her head, a hand on her heart, how profoundly undisturbed she had been.

In her absorption with her misery she had nearly forgotten him. His brightness, his inquisitiveness, his art. She pleaded with him softly to play something more. He gave a slight smile, shyly, and said there was

246

nothing he loved better than playing for her. And for another several minutes, she did not know how long, he obliged her.

She lay back with her eyes closed. If a few tears escaped from beneath her eyelids they were not the thick, remorseless tears of her imprisonment but soft, sweet tears. Tears bewildered by the peace, the gentleness, the clarity in which she now lay and which in her inconsolable suffering she had so perplexingly forgotten. Then he stopped. He said, hesitantly, that he missed her singing and could not rest or compose. He missed everything about her. He begged her to come back to them. But she shook her head and said she could not sing, she feared she was dying.

"Sing for me," he said, "and I'll kiss your hands a thousand times."

She gave him a dazed look. So this was why he was here. Not to play for her but to get her to sing. She felt again the slime, the heaviness. He wasn't a singer. He couldn't know. If his piano was out of tune, if a string on his violin snapped in two, he could call a craftsman, fix the damaged part himself, or commission a new instrument. Even if he were to lose the functioning of his hands, the ailment would be visible, the cause readily apprehended by a good physician.

Not so with the broken singer. As easy to diagnose in her a tumor that had been planted but not grown. She could not. She protested it feebly and firmly. Her will had left her with her song. It would be unbearable to have him hear her voice laboring and wobbling like a beggar's cart of rags and tins. She would not subject him to it — not humiliate herself before his ears.

He shook his head. "Do you think I'm such an ass as that? Do you think my ears are so inviolate they'll forget what you were?"

Were. What you were.

"One can't," he continued. "One mustn't succumb to the lure of the past. One must always keep moving forward, and never stop being terribly brave and good. To go the other way is incomprehensible. It doesn't suit you. You aren't a coward. You don't wallow and despair."

"Oh," she said in a forced whisper, with a false, haughty laugh. "Oh, signor, but I do. That is my métier. You've mistaken me for someone else. For one of my roles."

He straightened. The gesture had a youthful flair, as of a boy, neglected at school for his slightness, attempting to play the hero. "I've not mistaken you. I want you back."

She stared at him, her throat as taught

and painful as a bound whip. "Signor Mozart," she whispered. "I think you'd better find room in your heart for another soprano. You're wasting your time with this one. Better for you to be composing now, than asking a snapped string to knit itself together again. Not even God can ask a thing like that, of a poor little string."

This speech, the longest she had delivered to anyone in some time, was uttered in tones so low that Mozart had to lean closer to hear it. She smiled sadly and plucked at the long fringes of her robe.

"I think of you as many things," he said. "But not a poor little string."

"Well," she said, "that is your privilege."

He looked down at the piano with a frustrated expression and played a few bars of a slow movement. It had the yearning sweet-sad quality of a winter's dawn, rising in a series of suspensions as if to break the long-held dark.

"This piano is very fine," he said. "Mine is also fine, but in a different way. How lucky I am to be able to move between my instruments."

"Yes," she said. She smiled at his acknowledgment; she would never have another voice, just as she would never have another life. His eyes were kind, the brows pale in the light. His skin had the luminous pallor of the inner coil of a seashell. His neck was straight and so was his spine. He had taken off his overcoat and sat in his plain waistcoat and loose shirtsleeves, and though his shoulders were narrowly built they were strong, and strong, too, his arms and wrists, from the many hours mastering his instruments.

She had noticed, often, a certain smile of his, an inward-looking smile, that barely touched his lips, a smile of confidence and calm that was probably unconscious, unbidden, a reflection of some secret feeling. This smile was there now as he looked at her so kindly and sadly. "Would you like me to go?" he asked.

She shook her head.

He rose, glancing at her, and paced the room. He examined the ceramic shepherdesses, the flowers. He shook his arms and wrists to relieve them of the exertion of playing. His feet were narrow and turned slightly inward. The sleeves of his shirt touched his knuckles. He worked his fingers, stretched wide his arms. "To live like this! How can you stand it? How can you do this to yourself when you're so young and pretty and there's so much to be lived and done and sung? I should've gone to you when you married that pig. I was an ass not to do it."

"You tried," she said. "You were the only one who tried."

He shook his head as if in great agitation and said quickly, "I don't believe you can't sing. Not for one minute. If you can speak, you can sing."

She shouldn't have come down. She shouldn't have let him draw her.

"I know what it is," he said, "to lose an infant. I know what a woman goes through to bear a child." He knelt at her side. His eyes were clear. "Sing for me, Anna," he murmured, "and I will kiss your hands a *hundred thousand times.*"

She shook her head and whispered, "No." Mozart took up her hand and kissed her palm.

She gasped. The room was bright with sun. He leaned at the edge of the chaise, brushing her side. He reached across her lap and took her other hand and kissed that, too. Then he drew down her face and kissed her lips. Her unbound hair fell around them.

"See," he said quietly, studying her with wide, anxious eyes. "That's three already. Now you must do it, mademoiselle. I've given you a head start."

But she refused. She could not. She could

251

not even speak. After a moment he got to his feet, and she thought he would leave, and prepared herself to be alone again. But instead he went to the piano and played without pause for half an hour longer, until Stephen came home. He played as though she had given him all he desired. As well as she had ever heard — so well it was impossible to think of anything else. His fingers bestowed the kisses on the keys. Her hands lay in her lap, where he'd restored them, as though they had perished there.

ETHER

Mesmer set up treatment for Anna in the music room. She was a private patient. The emperor had paid for everything. Mesmer brought with him a small replica of his *baquet,* a magnetized oaken tub with which he treated groups. The small one was about the size of a side table, circular, covered with a warmly finished lid and inlaid with Masonic symbols. The lid was rimmed with a number of hook-shaped cast-iron rods, like the legs of a spider. Mesmer explained to Anna that these rods were held in place, inside the tub, by glass bottles that stood upon a bed of crushed glass, sulfur, and iron filings. The tub was filled to the brim with magnetized water. It took two men to carry it. To one side of the *baquet* stood the doctor's glass harmonica, a musical instrument made from circular glass tubes. These tubes, when turned upon a spit with a crank by his assistant and touched with dampened fingers or cloth, produced high, hollow, spinning tones. To this music Franz Mesmer conducted his cures.

He had requested that Anna wear a loose cotton smock and nothing beneath it, to ensure the efficient transference of magnetic energy. He arranged a series of Turkish screens in such a way that she might feel secure in her near-nakedness while he was treating her. Lidia and Anna's mother sat outside the circle of screens.

Mesmer retired to put on his robes, and Anna stood barefoot in her airy smock waiting for the doctor to reappear. She was almost sure he was a fraud, and would not have agreed to see him but for the fact that Mozart knew Mesmer. Mesmer had put on Mozart's first opera, *Bastien and Bastienne,* in his private theater, and he was friends with Mozart's father, and a Freemason. Mozart had written to Anna to assure her that the doctor could work miracles. It was a week since he had played for her. Every night when she went to sleep she held the memory in her heart. But everything else, it seemed, remained the same.

Mesmer emerged wearing yellow slippers and a long purple robe. His wide-set eyes had deep frown lines between them, as though he had spent much energy imagining the pains and travails of others. It was a face wholly compassionate and open; a face to inspire faith, confession, and trust. He reminded Lidia and Mrs. Storace that they must be silent and respectful, lest they risk disturbing the transference of energy. If Anna needed assistance she was to ring a bell.

"Begin the music," he said, and his assistant spun the glass tubes on the crank, drawing forth the clear, ethereal sound of the glass harmonica, a sound like a choir of miniature castrati singing in an overlapping cascade.

"Now," Mesmer said gravely. He rested his hands on Anna's shoulders. They felt like tender weights — so heavy and so filled with understanding, and she gasped in shock and nearly collapsed. He looked into her eyes. "I see," he said. "My poor girl, what a state you are in." And to her surprise — to her relief — he folded her in his arms. His thumbs rubbed into her back. Her face was in his shoulder, and he smelled of incense. "There," he murmured, embracing her ever more tightly. "Do you feel that? That is our magnetic energy, mine and yours. That is the force that runs through everything, every animal and human. Yours is weak and thick, it does not flow, but mine is a torrent, I give it to you freely. Don't you feel it?"

"I don't know," whispered Anna. One of her knees buckled. She would have stumbled to the floor had the doctor not held her fast.

"There," he said softly, hoisting her up. "That's one of your blockages gone. We must dislodge them all. You must help me channel the astral tides and release your ether in a clear beautiful stream." He drew back and took her hands, rubbing the tops of them rhythmically with his thumbs. "You've gotten yourself all dammed shut. The pools of your life force are stagnant. How can one sing when inside one is a festering pool? One cannot! One grows weak and mute with putrid inner sores!"

The keening waterfall of the glass harmonica spread around them. "Where is your anguish?" Mesmer whispered.

Anna closed her eyes. She had not expected to be moved by this. At worst she had thought the treatment would leave her the same, and at best, that it would give her an hour's diversion. But this doctor made her legs shake and her head feel light and empty, as though her mind were spreading thin as beaten gold. With an unsteady hand she touched her throat.

Mesmer nodded. His eyes half lidded in concentration, he felt along the sides of Anna's neck with his open palms, and again the sensation was of a great and tender weight, hot and tingling, as the magnetic energy roused and churned between them.

"I feel the heat," said Mesmer. "I feel the deadness — the void — yes, there, there." His fingers massaged firmly and gently along her neck, turning her head with the movement as though sculpting clay. Then his hands fell down her collarbones to her arms and he guided her to a kneeling position in front of the *baquet,* crouching behind her with his robe flung around them. He said, in a fervent voice, "When I tell you, you will grasp a rod in either hand. You will feel a shock. But you must not let go. You must keep holding the rods. The shock will travel through your body and make you convulse. It is the only way you will be healed. Do not be afraid."

She felt dizzy with his voice and the smell of incense. "I don't want to," she said in a faint voice.

His hands went under her arms, under her breasts. "You must," he said.

As if in a dream she saw her hands reach toward the black iron, saw them grip the rods and convulse. In the next instant she was rocked by a surge of magnetic force that came through her neck and blossomed at the top of her head and shot down her spine to her belly, and even to the soles of her feet, and she cried out and shook from the feeling and sank back against Mesmer, who grasped her to him.

"Is she all right?" called Lidia anxiously.

"Perfectly, madam!" shouted Mesmer in a voice hoarse with effort and emotion. He held Anna close, warming her with his body, speaking softly into her ears, clearing away all the blockages and deadnesses and voids, massaging her, while she sobbed and shuddered. They put her to bed and she slept like death.

THE RED SASH

Softly, as she did every morning, Lidia went into Anna's room to draw the curtains and see if she needed anything. Lidia no longer stayed with Anna at night. Her mistress was not anymore that fluttering, needful sweetheart who had burned for Francesco Benucci's secret kisses. Her cheek had grown hollow, her gaze turned thoughtful and inward. She had a waxen complexion, she who had been always flushing pinker and pinker. The doctors, Lidia feared, had bled her of every drop. She was grown so thin, she who had been so strong and plump. Lidia admonished her that there would be no more riding or dancing if she was not nourished, but Anna only sighed in her languid way and said it did not matter. She refused to see her mother.

Lidia had watched Anna go in to Mozart that afternoon; she had heard the music and the murmuring through the walls and seen

Anna creep up to her room again afterward. That had all gone according to plan — a scheme of Stephen's to draw his sister out. But Mozart, who had seemed shaken from the experience, said he did not know if it had done any good. He had not come again. And yesterday had been the famous cure of Dr. Mesmer, but no one knew whether or not that had done any good, either. Everyone was always urging Lidia to use her influence, to get Anna to move and eat and laugh, but Lidia was at her wit's end. Mrs. Storace, for her part, since her daughter would not see her and she had no wish, she said, to force herself upon her, had taken to spending long hours in study and prayer, like a nun or a penitent. She was not as harsh, Lidia noted, as she had been. But Lidia thought a little harshness might have been helpful now. If they could only douse Anna in ice water — if they could only force her to eat. That was what she needed, Lidia thought. Anything but the closed bedroom and the black ruminations with which she lay there, day after day.

As Lidia eased open the door on this morning she was surprised to find the room already light. The curtains had been drawn. The bed was empty and the coverlet feebly dragged across it, one end still trailing to the ground.

In the window seat sat Anna, quite upright, dressed in a white morning gown — the laces at the back undone — with a red satin sash about her waist. Her hands were clasped in her lap; her pretty feet were bare, resting on a velvet stool. The gaze she turned to Lidia was transparent and calm. "I've grown so thin," she remarked quietly. "My dress doesn't fit properly. I wonder if you could bring me some hot porridge with honey and dried currants and butter and cream? And a little pot of coffee with chocolate? Would you be so good, dear Lidia?"

And though she looked at Lidia with a clear, level expression, behind it lay a flicker of pride, as if she had pulled off a great trick. Lidia stood for half a moment with her mouth agape and then turned and bolted downstairs.

Anna had been up since daybreak. She had woken and felt a sudden desire to open the curtains before Lidia got there. So she had done it, one two three four five six, and had only got a bit out of breath. To anyone else this action would be as nothing. She watched the sky brighten and the people on the street begin their work and play. Then it had seemed necessary that she dress herself, although she was not used to dressing herself. She pried open the wardrobe and selected a likely looking gown, one of the loose modern ones that had light skirts and nothing rigid or heavy in the bodice. With painstaking care she changed into a clean chemise and pulled the dress over it. Since she could not do the laces she tied up the waist with a sash. Stockings were beyond her — she was afraid of ripping them. She kept laughing at her own weakness, how fumbling and timid she'd become. Even this act of dressing seemed so bold it made her afraid someone would find and scold her before she was ready. She combed out her hair and pinned it in a sort of bun and washed her face in the basin and was seated in the window, panting with exertion, by the time Lidia came to wake her. And the look on Lidia's face was worth all the effort in the world.

Yesterday she had seen Mesmer. Everyone would think he had cured her. When she had woken this morning and decided to open the curtains she had been dreaming of music — a delicious, calming dream, the details of which had instantly escaped her, though for a moment, a remembered melody had brushed her thoughts and lingered there like a trail of smoke. She'd had a feeling of wonderment, unstained, without remorse, to think that her life could contain this music. And in that moment of remembering her dream she'd realized, as if seeing herself from afar, that what she was doing was not what she wanted.

It seemed she had never been so hungry. When Lidia came in with the porridge and the coffee she almost could have wept but she did not want Lidia to think she was sad. She set the bowl in her lap and the warmth spread through her legs and the porridgy steam wafted up into her face. The bowl was a white ceramic. Her hand quavered as she took the first spoonful, the porridge and the cream and the black currants and the thick golden strands of honey that had been made from sun and bees and flowers. And when she put it to her mouth it seemed there was nothing so beautiful and good as this, so sweet, so filling, and she felt her mind which had been clouded revive and thrill, and her throat glisten, and her stomach, in one motion, unknot and welcome. And the coffee — the coffee was the nectar of the gods, bitter and warm, and rang awake all the hunger for life that had been sleeping in her core.

"Could you help me with my dress?" she

asked Lidia. "Is my brother home? Would he like to go driving with me in the country? I'd like some air. Perhaps we might be able to walk a bit if he would lend me his arm."

And Lidia, who could hardly speak, lest she break the spell, said that all this would be done; and she went outside to report the news to everyone who was waiting in the hall.

The sky was a hazy blue, as though draped with gauze, and the tall magnificent trees backed with sunlight, their leaves bright and some of them in flower. She had not been outside in a long time. She kept turning her head to some flickering of light, or new smell, some breath of mossy air, some animal's movement or call. Stephen beside her was at his very best, in his thoughtful, painterly aspect, pretending that all this was normal.

She'd suggested he bring his sketch paper and his watercolors. When they found a likely spot on the bank, they spread themselves out and he sketched the Danube, and then, against her protestations, Anna, leaning on one thin arm in her red sash, the spring light about her, her gaze on the great river, with its boats large and small, its people, its diving birds and nibbling fish,

264

her straw hat thrown onto the ground beside her. She had not gotten Lidia to fix her hair. The bun listed to the side and threatened to unfurl; one or two curls fell down her neck.

"Stephen," she asked him. She was still not used to speaking. Her voice was hesitant but it was still hers. "If I don't sing again, will you hate me?"

He put down his brush to consider. "Yes," he said. "I believe I shall. I'll cast you off. You'll be no sister of mine."

She leaned toward him smiling. "Don't!" she cried. "You must tell me. You must swear truthfully."

He touched her arm. "Sweet Anna. I love you no matter what you do or don't do."

"Even though I ruined your opera?"

"You did not ruin my opera."

"Say I did."

He shook his head. "Never. You did nothing wrong."

"Ah!" she exclaimed, a light, high sound that was itself almost singing, and lay back on the ground, to keep herself from weeping. "I don't believe you. Look at the sky. Look at the leaves tossing."

"You can't lie down," he said. "I'm not finished."

"But I'm tired. And the sky, look at it,"

she said, pointing. "That's vastness. Nothing was ever so vast."

"Sit up," he laughed. "Look at the river again. I'm not finished."

"Ah," she said, propping herself up again. She wiped her cheeks and her hair fell down. "The river is also vast. And look how it runs and runs."

A little later she asked, "Can I see?" and he showed her the picture. She studied it, tucking back her hair. "There I am," she whispered. She drew a finger down the page. "How good you are. Just think, there might have been a baby with me." When he did not reply she looked up with a sad smile. "I wish you could paint the baby in. Then I could keep it with me to remember her by. Did you ever see her? Before she died? I sometimes wonder if I imagined her. I never believed she was real, anyway. Perhaps she wasn't. But then I don't know why I'm so sad."

"Don't be sad anymore," he said impulsively. "The baby is in Heaven. The baby wouldn't want you to be sad."

She smiled again, looking before her. "No," she said. "I will be sad. I did everything wrong. Everything until now and even now I'm still sad, and afraid I'll do wrong again. I never thought of her, Stephen. I tried very hard to believe she was not there and would never exist. And now I will think of her for as long as I live. How old she would have been, how she would have looked, whether she'd have liked me to teach her singing." She paused for a long moment and then added, "I think she would have been a fine singer."

"Yes," he said.

She smiled and looked down. "I don't think Mama wanted her to live. I don't think I did, either. In my heart. Deep in my secret heart. But then I should be happy now, and not sad." She turned to him again, with her wan, thinned face, her cloud of dark hair. "Do you think we killed her? With wishing?"

"Never," he said again. "I don't believe you wished anything of the sort."

She looked at the painting. "But of course you say that. You couldn't very well say the other thing."

"She's in Heaven," he said again, helplessly.

Anna shook her head. "A little baby all alone in Heaven? But who would take care of her?" She handed the picture back to him. "You don't believe in Heaven any more than I do."

"I suppose not," he admitted, flustered.

She lay down again. "Nor in Hell."

"No, I don't suppose I do."

"There's a comfort." She laughed. "I haven't talked so much in months. Let me lie here quietly awhile and then we'll go home."

THE KEY OF F

She told herself that it did not matter if she sang. The important thing was to live, as well as she could. But when she started to feel strong enough, she thought she might try. She had to play all sorts of tricks on her mind so that she would not get too anxious, or hope too much. It was best not to hope for anything at all.

She stood alone and imagined Rauzzini beside her. His gait, his voice, his flashing rings. She murmured to herself his familiar phrases and admonishments. She watched herself in the mirror with his eye, watched her head and torso and the intake of her breath. She remembered his breathing exercises as she remembered her name and yet it was as though she were performing them for the first time. For days she did nothing but breathe. Then she decided it was time to sing.

She chose an F, not too high and not too

low. When she struck it on the keyboard — though she knew what an F was, felt it in her body, just as she knew C and A and G — it seemed that everyone in the house, everyone in the city, must have heard it. She had to wait a moment for the panic to subside. Then she took a good breath and struck the F again and hummed it. Her lips rested together and her throat was open and the breath caught and spun. The sound of F rang inside her. Then she took another good breath, before she could have time to think, and sang *"Ah,"* as Rauzzini had taught her, with a small *messa di voce,* from soft to loud to soft, and the voice was clear, and it was strong, and it had not left her, and she burst into tears and collapsed to the ground as if a weight of iron had been lifted from her lungs.

At first she sang only for ten minutes at a time, then twenty, then thirty. She sang with Rauzzini's method, a regimented sequence of scales, arpeggios, staccati, and vowel exercises. She was firm with herself and strict. She pretended there was no one listening, though they were all listening. Let them.

She remembered Mozart's kiss like a child might take out a delicate toy, which must not be played with too much, or too roughly, lest the paint chip or the fur get matted. If she did not think of it too much, it would not grow old, it would not tarnish. She would not indulge in fevered dreams, as she had done with Benucci, until everything was distorted and confused. She would not allow her thoughts to drift to a hopeful or anxious future. All she could do was take the memory out and look at it, when she was safe and alone, and then quickly put it aside. How he had played for her and kissed her when she had been so pitiable, kissed her as though he couldn't help it, drawing her face down with both his hands. When she thought of the kiss, it seemed in her memory that both of them had been surprised and neither of them had wanted it to end, and that she had felt all this in his body, the surprise and the pleasure and the longing. It had not been so on the night in the terrace garden. That in comparison to this had been children playing. This other was shocking and strange. She really had wished for it not to end. She had felt almost dissolved of her own person.

But she could not remember the kiss too long or she would not be able to act normally when next she saw him. She must tidy her dreams away.

271

For the Recovery of Ophelia

"My dear," said Salieri to Anna. "My heart reposes to see you so well. We cannot tell you how great has been the scope of our anguish." The corners of his mouth lifted in a kindly smile and then dropped down again.

"Madame," murmured Lorenzo Da Ponte, squeezing Anna's hands.

"Abbate," said Anna warmly. "Thank you for your poetry."

"There's no effort in writing," he said, leaning his head cozily against hers, "when it's for darling you. How we've missed you, my dear. You gave everyone such a fright."

Da Ponte, the court poet, a Venetian, had been born a Jew under a different name, and had converted in childhood for the sake of patronage. Then he had gone on, somewhat improbably, to become an ordained priest. Thus was he known as the Abbate, but laughingly so, for he was a priest who liked rude verses better than scripture, who gambled and kept mistresses, who engaged in love affairs with the wives of his patrons, and who was in short more suited to the theater than anyone in the world. He had a large chin and large, limpid eyes. When he spoke it was softly and disjointedly, with a lisp and a broad Venetian accent, a gentleness in his tone that implied sympathy and sensuality and disguised a pointed wit.

Da Ponte had written the libretto to a new solo cantata for Anna, *For the Recovery of Ophelia,* which she would sing to mark her return to health and the start of the new season at the Burgtheater. Salieri, Mozart, and Stephen had jointly composed the music. Da Ponte named the cantata not to reference *Hamlet,* but after her character in Salieri's new comic opera *The Grotto of Trofonio,* which would be played at the Burgtheater in October. But the name of Ophelia could not help but also recall the tragedy, and there, even before she read the poem, Anna found in Da Ponte a kind of genius. For it did feel sometimes as though she had gone mad and drowned, and been brought back to life.

"Where's Mozart?" Salieri demanded. "Is he coming? That man is always late. One thinks one has ahold of him and then he squirms away."

"I told him to come," Stephen said. "Perhaps he got the day wrong."

"He'll come," said Anna. "It's not struck two."

She had not sung for anyone since she'd lost her voice. Stephen had heard her through the walls but the others would not know what to expect. She imagined herself failing. She imagined them all falling away like a crust. And she felt inside herself the steel of Rauzzini. She trusted her technique. She had done the exercises. The voice was there and it did her bidding. A voice did not depend on sorcery and miracles. As long as there was no permanent injury, the skill and the beauty came from training, just as for any dancer or rider. But she was afraid of standing on that stage again, where it had happened. She would have to see Benucci.

"Where is he?" Salieri demanded. "He knows I can't stay past three. You'll have to sing it without him. This is just a formality anyway. We all know it will be marvelous."

But of course he did not know that, and wouldn't until he'd heard her. A strange thing, this notion she'd once had, that if she could not sing, she could not live. That *this* was all she was: this formality, this standing at the piano before a few smiling gentlemen hoping to make them like her. But patently she could live. When she'd been an infant she had lived. When she'd woken last spring, and heaved back the drapery and watched through the thick windows the breaking day, and had put on her dress, and put up her hair, she had lived. She had looked at her strange face in the mirror and whispered, "You don't have to," and had felt an interesting affection for that dark-eyed girl, no longer a soprano, now a kind of nothing, who was somehow still alive.

Now it was autumn. "Have we decided who's going to play the piano at the concert?" Salieri asked. "It can't be me, I don't play anymore. I'm all thumbs."

"Of course Mozart must play," said Stephen, at the same time that Anna said, "I thought Stephen would do it."

"Well. It can't be me," said Salieri, "and Mozart isn't here, so that leaves you, Storace. Unless you want to hire someone, but it's a little late for that."

"My sister prefers to sing with Mozart," said Stephen, looking at her.

"Nonsense," she said. "I prefer to sing with you." She felt, as she spoke, a hot blush come to her face. The clock read twenty past. Da Ponte yawned and picked up a book.

Stephen laughed. "I can't play Mozart's music with Mozart in the audience. It would be like painting over a masterpiece."

"It's your music, too," she said.

"And mine," pointed out Salieri. "Aren't you worried about playing *my* music with *me* in the audience, Storace?"

"Certainly, sir. But you said yourself you don't like to play, and Mozart's the best pianist around."

"*You* play," said Salieri. "You're perfectly adequate. I know Mozart. He'll add all sorts of notes and harmonies when no one can tell him otherwise, and by the time he's had his way with it I won't know my own work. Moment he gets his paws on it he'll change everything, just you watch. He's got no self-regulation. I don't like him smirking at me. Give that man an edge and he rides all over town."

"Your statement has no sense," Da Ponte observed sweetly.

"It's half two," Salieri retorted. "It's been half an hour."

"I concede," said Stephen, and went to the piano.

"Oh, good," exclaimed Anna, to hide her disappointment.

They started the cantata. Immediately Anna saw Salieri and Da Ponte brighten and relax. A few notes were all they required to be reassured she was well.

The first aria in the cantata was Stephen's: light, charming, English. The last was Salieri's, and quoted cleverly from *The Grotto of Trofonio.* The second stood alone. It was both happy and sad. The sadness contained joy and the happiness was veiled in suspense and unease. The text related a moment of darkness, yet it was mixed with light. The vocal line, through-composed and wrenchingly dissonant, languished and rallied and languished again, while the piano rolled and fretted beneath it, until finally the voice gave four soft cries — *"Ah! — Ah! — Ah! — Ah! —"* and stopped midway through the bar. Perhaps it was morbid, enacting the moment when Anna's voice had failed her, but after all this was what drama was for: to render control by turning the chaos of living into an orderly story, something that had a beginning and an ending and that happened to someone else.

Anna tried to feel cheerful but she was irritable, full of a sudden ennui. It was all so tedious and small. None of these men were listening to her, not truly. She had expected something joyful in this moment. This was entirely too dull.

He hadn't come. He would not hear her.

277

She had taken out the memory too often.

So preoccupied was she with these dismal frustrations that when the door slipped open at the beginning of the second aria, Mozart's aria, she assumed it was Lidia or her mother or some other servant. She was distracted by Stephen, who kept playing the wrong accidentals. He dragged the tempo. She was angry that it was Stephen playing and not Mozart, and that Stephen would play in the concert. But still it was painfully beautiful music. She supposed this was a mark of a good composition, that it could remain beautiful even when performed inadequately, and in foul moods.

The intruder eased his head through the door — Mozart, of course — and engaged Anna with an expression of such tiptoeing repentant agony that she almost laughed aloud. The floorboard creaked and he ducked out of sight again, leaving the door ajar. But neither Da Ponte nor Salieri seemed to have noticed him. Da Ponte was smiling dreamily and winding his long fingers around his cane. Salieri was fixated on the clock. And Stephen did not know the music well enough to take his eyes from the score.

As she began the next phrase she saw one white hand, wreathed with lace, appear with

278

a flourish from behind the tall dark door. For a moment it hesitated in the air, like a bird in flight. Then it gave a sort of sigh and began, pompously, to conduct her. But Stephen did not see the hand and kept getting out of time with it, which infuriated the hand and made it writhe and shake.

Somehow she managed to continue singing. But it was hard going — she almost split apart with laughter. A large, capable, expressive hand it was, rather thickly made, as though padded with unusual degrees of muscle and fat. She tried not to look at it but she could not look away. So expressive it was, so bright and dancing, it compelled her, indeed, to follow.

The second aria ended. The hand retired behind the door. But Salieri was impatient and there was no time for delay, so they ran immediately into the recitative that preceded the third aria.

For the whole of the first two sections of this last aria, which was a rondo, with verses and refrain, there was not a stirring. She thought perhaps he had gone away. She began letting down her guard. The last was a light aria anyway — it didn't matter if her eyes sparkled, if her voice took on a joyful quality. She thought she was safe; she truly thought she was in the clear. But then, perfectly in time with the last four bars, there appeared in sequence from behind the door four largely written and elegantly lettered cream-colored cards, which read:

ICH-

BIN-

EIN-

ARSCH-

It meant: *I am an ass. Forgive me. I am a fool.* She burst out laughing and immediately converted it to a violent cough. The *arsch* card vanished in a fright.

"Are you all right?" Salieri shouted, rising.

But there was no Mozart in the hall. Nor anywhere in the house. Stephen asked what Anna was looking for, what was so funny, and she said she'd thought she'd heard something and was just giddy to be singing again, and then she twirled him around the room in a dance.

THERE WAS NO WOUND

For Francesco Benucci, seeing Anna for the first time after the months of her indisposition was a shock of the greatest kind. She was lovely. He had never seen her so lovely. She was not the little girl, round of cheek and light of step, who had danced with him and pushed his hand down her bodice in the dark. She was not, either, the girl he had watched marry John Fisher, a girl in a kind of trance. She had always been someone who slipped away, as if covered in scales, vanished in weeds and glassy water. But now when she looked at him she stayed where she was. She did not fidget. The angles of her face had grown sharper. There was almost a hardness, now, in a certain look she had. Her pretty, full lips had firmed like her mother's. The slight sharpness of her cheek, the slight thinness, made her eyes appear larger, darker, and when she set them upon him somehow she did not slip away. It was almost an uneasy feeling; it gave him an ache almost of apprehension. Though she laughed and was merry, and acted like her old self, this strange, penetrating gaze she would sometimes turn on him, this sudden almost hardness, changed her into something she had not been.

But her voice was Milan. She sounded sixteen again. Sweet incomparable Anna. They had all worried. John Fisher had roughened her, shaken her breathing, flattened her tone. Perhaps the public had not noticed, because Anna Storace could act her way out of anything, but for trained singers like Benucci and the rest there had been a marked difference after her marriage. They'd felt it in their own throats. They'd cast each other secret looks of dismay. The night she'd damaged her voice had rocked them as if the damage was their own, their own the grief and shock. They all feared that the instrument might never repair. This sweet girl whom none of them had helped. It was as though they'd watched her put out her eyes.

But she sounded sixteen now. There was no wound. The voice was responsive and fresh, holding all her old sweetness, all the truth and warmth and openness that made it hers and no one else's. Hot tears sprang to his eyes when he heard it. He was in Milan again, marveling at her honesty and ease. The true, warm sound, a voice he would have known anywhere, a voice to match his own.

But then she turned those eyes on him, the hardness, the sharp hollow, and he did not know her anymore.

Anna tried very hard to deceive herself. It was just another concert. A hall like every other. But when she stepped out with Stephen onto the stage and saw the familiar boards, the rows of chairs, the tall windows, everything elegant, white, spare, Viennese to the core; when she smelled that smell like nowhere else, a smell of wood chips and roses, and stood in the place where she had been in love, once, where she had triumphed, where she had been frightened and humiliated, she wished she had someone to take away the responsibility. After they bowed, Stephen sat at the piano and she turned to him and whispered, "I don't think I can do it."

Stephen looked handsome tonight and relaxed. He had walked in the market with Lidia. He had remarked earlier that he had decided not to try so hard; he did not like to remember how he had behaved over the failure of his opera. He had an easy quality now, as if he were going around feeling slightly amused at himself. He raised an eyebrow at his sister and whispered, "We'll find out." Then he began the introduction.

She tried to think of nothing but the words. It was as though she were on a tightrope and if she looked down she would fall. She must set herself inside each word, believe in it wholly, think of nothing but the word. She was not herself now. She was some girl singing *"Felice," "Tradito," "Piange."* When she pretended to lose her voice at the end of the second aria she felt the horrible feelings, and yet they were feelings felt by another, and inside her remained the impassive coolness of Rauzzini.

"It doesn't matter," she told herself. "Nothing can be worse than what has already happened." But that was no comfort. There was always something worse. When she'd married Fisher, that had seemed the worst, and then worse events had followed. But she supposed the point of it was that she had prevailed. It had marked her, surely, it had left her something different than she had been before. But she still had her spirit. She had. She could laugh and play and sit in the sunshine and have that be true, not acting, but just as she was.

284

And the joys were finer, then. She noted them more, felt them more deeply, and yet also more gingerly, knowing they might pass at a moment's warning, or with no warning at all. In her essence she rested unchanged. She hoped she would never forget how it felt now to sing, how precious. That this should be her life's work — that she should have been given another chance —

As always, she could not judge accurately for herself whether she sounded well. The only way she could tell that she had sung sweetly was by the quality of the applause, like a thunder crack, sudden and loud, and the triumph on Stephen's face. They took their bows and beckoned the other singers back on stage, her colleagues who had sung earlier in the concert, and she was so happy, and so relieved, but then a gentleman in the upper balcony stood and shouted for everyone to hear, "She killed her baby! She killed her baby! Murderess!" until he was drowned out by boos and hurried from the building.

SAY NOTHING

There was a reception after the concert, but Anna had disappeared. Benucci went down and knocked on the door of her dressing room.

She said, "Come," and turned toward him with wet eyes and a hopeful smile, and he realized that she had been expecting someone else.

He shut the door. "Are you all right?"

She put a hand to her mouth. "I had to leave. I'm sorry. I couldn't face them. They were being so good. We were all pretending so hard."

"No one cares about a madman."

She rose, clasping her fan loosely in her hands. "It's horrible," she said in a low voice. "I know what they think about me." Her voice broke, slightly. There had been cruel speculation in pamphlets that Anna Storace had killed her baby, and lurid cartoons depicting her in sexual consort

286

with the emperor and with women.

"I hate them, too," she said. "If they knew what I feel — they are the torturers, they the murderers!" She hugged herself, staring before her. It was almost impossible to believe that half an hour before she had been glittering on a stage, a girl of sixteen, incomparably charming, commanding, poised. Anna Storace could light a hall with the way she held her hands. But of course it had been a mask. Benucci knew that better than anyone.

"Anna," he said. "Is it true?"

She looked at him blindly. "Oh, no," she said. "Oh, Francesco."

"I'm sorry," he said, but there was a challenge in his voice. His voice was too loud for some rooms; it carried a challenge, sometimes, where none was meant.

She looked as if she did not know where to go. "No," she whispered. "It's not true, Francesco."

He put his hand on the door. There was a long silence. She did not move, nor look away. She was a remarkable picture of stillness. He might have been leveling an arrow at her heart. "It was mine," he said, "wasn't it?"

She faltered and closed her eyes. The arrow struck, quivering, at the base of her throat. Her voice was not loud but perfectly placed, melodious, clear: "Yes," she said.

He grasped the door and saw her marrying the Irishman, in her silk frock, saw her mother like a queen refusing to speak to him. He heard himself say, "And we're still friends. That's the main thing," and saw her again and again turning her head and saying, "Yes." He saw her more than a year ago in this same room, a plumper, sweeter, ardent young girl who clung to him and kissed him and wept from her love and he saw himself taking her in a vindictive passion, hurting her and not caring, caring only to silence and give her what she thought she'd wanted, caring only, too, for his pleasure, hating himself yet feeling the pleasure still. He saw her in her frock marrying the Irishman, again and again saw her turn from him and say, "Yes." Saw her singing with him all year long, smiling, slipping away, collapsed with her big belly behind the stage with her idiot brother squawking above her. He saw the Irishman hurting her, the rest of them pretending he was not.

"Oh, God," he breathed. "How could you do it? How could you look me in the eye?" She went white and said nothing. He cast his eyes around the room desperately. "What kind of man do you think I am?"

"You didn't love me," she said. She swallowed. "You loved Aloysia."

He stared at her. Then he said in a sharp voice, "Aloysia? Aloysia Lange? When did I give a fig for Aloysia Lange?"

"She said you did. She said you wrote her love letters."

"When have I ever sent any woman love letters? When would Francesco Benucci have time for love letters?"

She listed forward as if he had struck her. "Oh," she whispered. "Of course you didn't."

"Would you have let me dandle the child on my knee?" he said. "Would you have lied and lied? All that time, Anna, and you said nothing —"

"Don't I know that?" she cried out wildly. "Haven't I known it every minute?" She put her hands to her cheeks as if she was afraid she would break apart. "Oh, God! It was horrible! Oh, God!"

He stared at her and took a few steps back. "I never knew you," he said. "I don't know you now. We're worse than strangers. You never told me. You never did. You married him and never told me."

She let down her hands and stared vacantly before her, tears hesitating on her cheeks, as though waiting patiently for him to strike her down.

He gave a helpless groan and passed a hand over his forehead. "I've done you wrong," he said suddenly. "Forgive me . . . please forgive me." Then he turned and left the room.

Upstairs, in a mirrored hall with a checkered floor, the reception was still going on. "My gentle friends!" called someone in heavily accented English. It was Mozart, red-faced, wigged, on the arm of his wife. "A most good evening to you."

"Hello, Mozart," said Stephen. "Practicing your English, are you?"

"If I do not practice," said Mozart, delicately articulating each syllable, "I shall not advance."

"Very good," said Stephen, laughing. "And if you don't advance you'll never come to London. Good evening," he said to Constanze in German.

She nodded to them both and said to Anna, "I'm so happy to see you well."

"Thank you," Anna answered, and felt a kind of panic rise inside her. Not the panic of stage fright — decidedly not that. She had returned to the party ten minutes after Benucci had gone. No one there mentioned her absence, nor her reddened eyes. They were all kindness. They avoided speaking of the madman, and the rumors.

Stephen had had a few drinks and was relaxed and amused. He had played well tonight. "I say, Mozart," he continued, still in German, "awfully good of you to join us. Awfully bold. We missed you at our rehearsal for Anna's cantata."

"I was sick that day," Mozart protested. "Feverish indigestion. Wasn't I, my dear? I wrote Mademoiselle Storace and she absolved me."

Saying this he pulled Anna toward him and whispered quickly in her ear, as if a caricature in a play, "I am an ass. Say nothing. You sang beautifully, beautifully —" but his grip on her arm was firm and his lips grazed her earlobe.

"Stop it, my love," laughed Constanze, pulling him back. "You'll muss her hair." She looked around them composedly. "My husband has had too much wine."

"I have not," cried Mozart.

"He really was sick that day," Constanze continued. "He hasn't been that sick in ages. But he wouldn't let me write you because he insisted he'd be well enough. He kept saying, 'I must be there, I must hear her,' until I thought he'd have a fit, so finally he went, but by then it was too late and he came right home again. I thought it was a lot of fuss for nothing when he was so unwell."

"It's not true," Mozart said. "I was not sick, I was fatigued. My wife is trying to defend me. Wasn't sick at all."

"You *were* sick," said Constanze, frowning. "I was most anxious. I didn't want you to go out. But you insisted."

"You didn't come all the way to our house, did you?" said Stephen. "Why the devil didn't you say hello?"

Mozart looked at Anna and shrugged a little. "I was too late. I hadn't realized, in my state, how late it was."

"Well," said Stephen. "I'm rather glad you weren't there; I played your stuff abominably that day. I fared much better tonight."

"You were so charming," said Constanze. She smiled and patted Anna's arm. "Both of you were so charming. Everyone is so happy."

Mozart Riding

Mozart rode out on his horse lightly and easily, humming to himself, occasionally talking to the animal or patting its neck. There was a special grace in being a small man upon a fine horse. One could observe the world from height. One guided the animal and was carried by it. The ears swiveled, the hooves clopped, there was a bellows of breathing and low, conversational snorts. The balance was elegant and lively, always at the edge of thought, like when one hit a special place of concentration where the notes seemed to run of their own accord and one was afraid to eat or sleep or take a piss lest one topple down again into the slog of tedious labor and confusion like the poor fellows who walked.

It was good to have a horse. He hoped he wouldn't have to sell it. Sell the horse and move to the outer city beyond the Prater, where the cheap rents were. With a horse one could see everything and get places quickly and independently, and look a certain way, tall, refined, powerful. He was not really any of those things, without his pretty horse, without his piano or some other instrument. On his own he was small and bashful. Always saying some nonsense. He could never say quite what he meant. His own face made him laugh in the mirror, the jutting nose, the pitted skin, the eyes like a frog. When Aloysia Lange had broken his heart he had stared at his face for a long time. He did not do so anymore, he only laughed. His father, though, was stringently handsome. But Wolfgang resembled his mother. She had died with him in Paris, the worst days of his life. His father had blamed him. He would never go back to Paris. Not for all the horses in the world.

He would stop at his best friend Gottfried's house for lunch, teach a lesson, meet with Da Ponte, pick up his new coat, the one with the white and gold, drop off a few easy piano pieces for a princess, and have an English lesson with Georg Kronauer, his brother Mason. Stephen Storace was rubbish for English lessons, and Anna — well, he couldn't speak English with Anna, she made him tongue-tied in English — she pattered on in her lilting way and he gaped and stuttered and made a fool of his own foolishness until they were both constricted with laughter.

There was never enough money and never enough time. He thought of his death every day, not from morbidity or fear but to remind himself that it would come. He wasted so much time. Just this morning he had overslept and then had had to write a couple of letters and suddenly he was late for lunch at Gottfried's and had not a line of music to show for himself. If he died today he would leave his family poor and his best work — he felt it there, dormant in his heart — unwritten. So it would be better not to die today, please God. Since becoming a Freemason he thought he had made his peace with death, which had used to frighten and anger him so much, but yet there were all these things waiting urgently in his heart to be written, waiting for money and time and peace and concentration. He could have written them today if he had not overslept. These piano pieces he was selling for the princess were drivel, rubbish, worse than any mincing, timid, derivative opus of his peers. But they had to be mincing or she could never play them and he would never get his fee and would never pay the rent. Not that the fee would cover the rent.

But he had to have the white-and-gold coat for performing in. He had to look richer than he was. A fine set of garments was as important as a fine horse — more so. When he wore a coat like that, then he was handsome. Striking, if not handsome. When everything fit just so and the fabric was heavy and rich and the buttons were like pearls and the collar was high and everything sharp and straight and fine and smooth. He was a peacock but he did love it. Then he could be easy with himself, then stand tall and play beautifully and banter with the duchesses and not be so nervous and shy. Most of the time one would not know he was nervous and shy. He had learned early and well to disguise his feelings with revelry.

Lovely, graceful, funny Anna. He felt he had always known her; he'd felt that from the first. And yet he'd never met anyone like her. This little English Italian soprano. Her waist fit neatly in his hands. Her hair was dark and soft; softer still were her lips and her cheek. How many hours he'd spent dreaming of her cheek, of it resting against his naked chest while he stroked her downy temple.

He loved his wife. She made him laugh. She took care of him. When he was stuck in his work he would go out and chat with her or play with their son and that would revive him. He loved her breasts and her rump, loved taking her to bed. When she looked at other men or behaved with immodesty he became jealous and enraged. But she was so ordinary and uncomplicated. She was like a lamb. Lower-class, simply taught. He was sometimes afraid she would say something ill-bred and then he was ashamed of himself. That was his father in him, his father who could be proud and stubborn. And Constanze — it could be that he had been rushed into marrying her. He had been boarding in her home, still in love with her sister. All he'd wanted was some nice companion, someone to kiss and squeeze and do all manner of delicious things with. After all, he'd been just a boy. It was true that after he and Constanze were engaged, her mother had made him sign a contract, with witnesses, stating that if he did not marry Constanze he would pay her mother as settlement a large annual stipend for the rest of her life. He hadn't minded; he'd been sure he would marry Constanze. He would have signed anything. And when she had found out about the contract, Constanze in a fine fury had made them rip it up. But still. It had been there. He had perhaps been rushed. And he had not known, then, how much he would change.

That night he'd stolen Anna's slippers he'd been angry with the world and restless. He had worked himself nearly to death that week. He'd longed for playfulness and release. And when he saw the new Italian company perform Salieri's opera it was as if his soul caught fire. A hundred ideas crowded into his brain at once. And at the center was the pretty soprano who knew everything to do and yet made her every word and action seem spontaneous and new. Her voice captivated him. The sound held simplicity and beauty and a quality of being direct, crystalline, unadorned. She could create all manner of colors and moods, as if she were one of those acrobats whose strong and flexible bodies defied the rest of human experience, yet the voice at its core was clear, truthful, only hers. She achieved such acoustic resonance and subtlety of tone, and had access to such ranges of dynamic and emotion, that Mozart felt it almost physically. She was perfectly in tune. Her voice in all its clarity and honesty, in its precise, direct skill, cut him to the quick. Listening to her he remembered everything he aspired for in his music. The human voice at its best had no companion nor rival. All other arts fell abject before it. A baby's cry, a lover's vows, a sob of grief, touched the heart more readily than any crafted instrument. While Anna was singing he could not move, nor think of anything else. He almost shouted out, like an animal. He had wanted to possess her. He, with his wife beside him, wanted to do such things!

But that, too, his insensible lust, testified to Anna's voice and ability, and he laughed at himself as if he had been a character in a bawdy story. He vowed to write for this remarkable soprano. To fit his music to her voice so perfectly that when she sang it, she became her best self.

What he had felt that night when he'd first heard her had been the product of a fevered imagination. He'd known nothing about her. If anything the desire and frustration had arisen from the fact that this new company was here and Salieri got to write for them, and any other man got to write for them as long as he was Italian, as long as he was not Mozart — the German, the small fellow, the one whom everyone still thought of as a seven-year-old boy. Mozart could not write for them. Mozart must sit stewing in the audience, lusting after the exquisite, incomparable new soprano . . . but he loved his wife . . .

At the reception he'd had to talk to that windbag Herr Gosta and a hundred other windbags who knew nothing of what he did, who had no life in them and no souls, who cared only for what mattered least. He'd escaped to the courtyard, where there was nothing and no one, no fear, no lust, no wife, only himself and his frustration and the trees and the darkness. Then he'd turned and seen her, on the bench, the very girl he'd been longing for all evening. She'd followed him out. She had not seen him. He'd watched her take off the slippers. He'd said to himself that if he lost this chance he did not deserve to live.

He had not expected her to accept his kiss. It was as if they were in a romance, exchanging the requisite motions and words. She could not speak German then but her Italian had been beautiful, and her speaking voice more melodious than he had even imagined. She had hesitated in his arms and then leaned against him.

After they'd gone inside that night and he'd seen his honest wife — he loved his wife — he had wanted to feel ashamed for what he had done but he had not. It had felt nothing but a game then, a game he had won. Salieri would never have done anything so bold. Salieri was too stodgy. He had not the necessary recklessness.

Mozart should have been a Kapellmeister by now, rich as Gluck. All of them knew it. He was almost thirty and had nothing. He should have had more time for composing if he hadn't had to do everything else. What? Did they think he'd stay forever? He'd go to London and they'd never see him again, no matter how they begged and implored.

Anna's voice came to him in dreams. Sometimes he imagined another life, in which they lived together in London and he could hear her in the next room, and anytime he wished he could talk with her, tell her something that had happened or interested him, laugh with her, press his face into her shoulder. When he was with her he was happy and lively, and the time sped along without his noticing, as it did when he was in the middle of a good composition.

Until that day when he'd played for Anna in her illness, he'd thought he was safe. He had cared for her, had worried for her, but had not allowed himself to love.

That day, he sat at Anna's fine instrument and imagined her upstairs, in the bed he had never seen. He could almost pretend he was alone with her in the house, as he'd imagined them being alone in London. He did not like to think of her upstairs lying

301

there as if waiting to die. The piano was perpendicular to the door. Along the wall were the chaise-longue and various side tables and chairs. Books lay about and flowers drooped in vases on the mantel. The sun flooded in and made everything hot. Mozart had to remove his jacket.

Exploring a fine piano with no aim or ending point was one of his greatest pleasures. Every worry abandoned him. His concentration was so steady, and yet so abstracted, that he could have no thought of the past or the future. He became loose and calm. He had a sensation of watching himself from afar, of admiring his hands and fingers and wondering how they managed it, and what might come next. Musical convention made some turns more likely, even required, but even so there was always an element of randomness and play. He would watch himself running toward a certain corner and at the last minute turn the opposite direction. Or he would send himself deliberately somewhere hazardous and strange just to see if he could get out.

He could always get out. This was a point of pride, even when there was no one there to hear him. He never felt so full of power as when he was at the piano. So potent, so calm, expert and whole. If he had only time in a day to practice, to compose, then he was happy, then he found his life's meaning and equilibrium. So he was almost always happy, and his life almost always had meaning. He thought of this now when he played for Anna, because her meaning had left her.

After a while she appeared at the door, in the corner of his vision, and it was all he could do not to go to her. He had not seen her in ages. But he must not startle her nor imply that there was anything strange. So he smiled a little and pretended to be slightly bored. She wore a shimmering robe, blue and green and gold. Her hair was down. Sweat dampened his brow. She stood in the doorway and he played as if she were not there and yet every nerve was tuned to hers.

At last she closed the door and came in. Her gown like water around her, her face thin and pale, unadorned, her eyes dark pools of yearning and regret. Until that day he had been safe.

ORANGERY

"The winner is Salieri," the judge declared, and the hall broke into polite applause. They were in the orangery of the emperor's pleasure palace at Schönbrunn, transformed for the occasion into a double theater and banquet hall. It was bleakest February, almost a year after Anna's crisis, and the emperor's brother was visiting from the Netherlands. The emperor had decided to welcome him with summer. The humid air smelled heavily of hothouse flowers; the guests had left their hats and furs piled in the hall. They were seated at a long table overflowing with a royal feast. The vaulted glass ceiling seemed to touch the stars. The orange trees rose about them and made them feel in a fairy grove. Here could be no thought of snow.

On each end of the hall was set a miniature stage, ringed with lights, and on each of these stages this night had been fought a mock battle between German singspiel and Italian opera buffa; between Mozart and Salieri. Each had written a one-act opera satirizing his respective genre. And Salieri had won.

"It isn't fair!" cried Aloysia Lange. She had sung in Mozart's contribution, *The Impresario,* along with the rest of the new German company from the Kärtnertortheater. The Italian company, from the Burgtheater, with Anna and Benucci and the rest, had put on Salieri's *First the Music, Then the Words.* Both offerings were comedies about the backstage politics of the opera theater. Mozart's music was superior, anyone could tell, but Salieri outranked him, Salieri was Italian, and Salieri had better singers.

"Well," Mozart said in a low voice, smiling quickly at Aloysia and applauding with the rest, "we couldn't expect otherwise."

Aloysia watched the Italian company rejoice. They didn't even have the courtesy to act surprised. She had sung well. She was not as good an actress as Anna Storace, but she had sung well and been unafraid of making fun of herself. But she was not Anna. Anna with her perfect breasts and beguiling eyes and velvety low notes. Anna with her unshakeable legato, her naturalness, her charm.

"Pig," said Mozart genially to Salieri. "What's the prize, another watch?"

"Mozart, my boy!" laughed Salieri, striking him roundly on the back. "My child! You actually had me worried for a moment."

Mozart winced and rubbed his shoulder. "A dainty opera," he said. "It reminded me of all your others."

"And yours," chortled Salieri, "had so many notes it reminded me of none." He patted Mozart's cheek. "And the words! God bless you, my boy, for thinking anyone can sing German without foaming at the mouth."

Mozart smiled tightly. He had long been a proponent of German opera for German-speaking people, and his greatest success on the stage to date had been another singspiel, *The Abduction from the Seraglio.* But Italian opera still had its hold. The aristocracy, perhaps, did not wish to hear its own language.

He went to Anna. He could not help himself. But there was no harm in going to her, surely. He had every reason.

Months had passed since the Ophelia concert to mark her return to the Burgtheater. They had seen each other since then on many occasions, dinners and salons and such, and each time it seemed to Mozart he was more nervous, could speak to her even less, yet also that he was more filled with joy. He was composing an opera for her with Da Ponte, based on the second Beaumarchais play, *The Marriage of Figaro,* even though it was banned for being politically subversive. But Da Ponte would take out the politics and leave the comedy, and then there could be no objection. Mozart and Da Ponte wished for the new soprano, Luisa Laschi, to play the Countess Rosina. Luisa had more stateliness. But Anna was famous for her Rosina in *The Barber of Seville* — she might be displeased, think that Susanna was the second to Rosina. But the opera was Susanna's. They would make her see that. It should have been called *The Marriage of Susanna.*

Every morning when he sat at his desk to compose, it was as if he were engaged in a private dance with Anna. But whenever he saw her in the flesh, she was not as he had remembered her, at once plainer and more beautiful, because she was real.

Impulsively she gave him a hug, and touching his shoulder exclaimed, "Oh, I wish you'd won! It isn't fair."

"That's what my sister-in-law said," he replied, smiling into her eyes. "I am happy you won. You sang beautifully."

She shook her head. "I meant to sing awfully, so that you'd win. But then I couldn't do it."

"I'm glad you didn't. It was rigged from the start."

She looked back at him. In her eyes there was still a shadow of that sorrow that had made him love her, veiled in that bright good humor that had made him love her more. Then she kissed his cheek and moved on to talk to some patrons. He laughed and watched her go.

"What were you talking of with Frau Storace?" Aloysia asked Mozart, coming to his elbow. "I fear we'll lose you to our enemies."

He smiled, still looking after Anna. "Oh, this and that."

"I was just having a tête-à-tête with Benucci," said Aloysia in a disinterested tone. "He's madly in love with her."

There was a short pause. Mozart cleared his throat and said, "Is he really?"

"Oh, yes, quite desperately. And she loves him. They do make a beautiful pair, don't they? They're both so handsome, are they not? I daresay Benucci is the tallest gentleman in the room. He was asking me what he should do, poor man. He really wants to marry her, but of course she's already wed.

And she, poor lady, begs him to disregard her honor and live with her in sin. She says she's had too much unhappiness. All she wants is peace and love. She cares nothing for honor."

Anna and Benucci were talking to the emperor now, laughing and bantering. Mozart watched them. A high color was in his face. "What did you tell him?" he asked Aloysia.

She gave a sad, compassionate sigh. "I said to do it. I said she was free in the eyes of everyone but the law — even in the eyes of God. I said that a great love must be cherished — that this life of ours goes all too fast."

He turned to face her. It was curious to think he'd once been in love with Aloysia Lange. She could not act to save her life. "I don't believe a word of it," he said. He looked back at Anna. "Mademoiselle Storace has too much dignity."

"I assure you it's true," Aloysia exclaimed.

He shook his head. "Benucci might love her," he said, "but she, my beloved sister, does not love Benucci."

As they were departing the orangery, Anna and Aloysia arrived at the exit at the same time. Their skirts bobbed together and they held their fans on opposite sides in the air.

309

Mozart and Salieri were coming up just behind them.

"After you, my dear," said Aloysia, smiling and bowing formally.

"Oh no," Anna said, with her own sweet curtsy. "After you."

"You are the victor," quoted Aloysia through her teeth, and graciously inclined her head.

Anna laughed and gestured kindly to the door with her fan. "But you are my senior."

Aloysia's mouth fell open. "Ah!" she exclaimed. She gathered her skirts. "There, my dear, you have trumped me." With a fixed look of lightness she glided through the doorway. Anna followed behind.

"I'm using that," said Mozart into Salieri's ear, roughly linking arms with him. "You are not allowed to use that, you bastard."

Salieri laughed, delighted. "Oh, please," he declared, "be my guest. I wouldn't touch those girls for all the money in the world. I leave the difficult ones to you, Mozart. I like my women like I like my music, obedient and mild."

Mozart shoved him away. "That's not what I meant. The *scene*. Their tone — their smiles."

"I know what you meant," said Salieri, smiling easily. "You can have it, my man,

310

with pleasure. I wouldn't know what to do with it anyway."

Mozart gave him a blank stare and then laughed. "That's right. You wouldn't. Forgive me, Salieri. Sometimes I forget you're not as clever as I am."

"Do you really?" asked Salieri dryly. "That's the most flattering thing I've heard all day, Mozart, my boy. I'm sure I never forget it for a moment."

THE EXECUTION OF FRANZ ZAHLHEIM

Their first day back in rehearsal, two months after her concert, Anna and Benucci could at first say nothing serious, not with everyone there, but they smiled, tentatively at first, and there was relief in those smiles. He had had time, perhaps, to recover from his shock. At last she found a chance to take him aside and say how sorry she was, and he grasped her shoulders and said, "No, no, it's my fault, it's I who ask pardon of you," and he hugged her tightly, and the humanity of that embrace washed over them both. Though nothing could be as before, yet they could go on. For the first time in weeks she had no nightmares.

But John Fisher sent her letters. She balked to read them, felt the old shadows slamming around her. He was in France. He said she was still his wife. And she was. He claimed he had no wish to see her again. He only wanted money. Even the penmanship made her ill. She gave the letters to Lidia to file away. Then she decided she must witness the execution of Franz Zahlheim.

Franz Zahlheim had murdered his young wife with such brutality that he had been sentenced to the kind of torturous public death not seen in Vienna in forty years. His wife had been so beautiful and the murder so gruesome, so entirely without cause, that the public clamored for suffering. His execution was scheduled for March 10, 1786, Lorenzo Da Ponte's thirty-seventh birthday.

Da Ponte, disgusted, declined to celebrate.

Michael Kelly did not want to go, but Anna insisted. She had loaned Michael money for a gambling debt; he was in no position to deny her anything, however perilous to his ease of heart and stomach. Michael was a gentle, pleasure-loving fellow; he had no affinity for blood sport and screaming, for being squeezed and pummeled by the rapt and heaving crowd. But Anna said that she had an interest in men who murdered their wives.

"Have you ever seen a man executed?" Michael asked, exasperated. "Stuck with hot coals and broken on the wheel?"

Anna gave him a soft look. "Now and then

I thought that John was going to kill me. I'd set him off, somehow, and I'd be absolutely certain it was going to happen. Wouldn't that have been a scandal? If he'd killed me?"

"Not a scandal," Michael said. He rubbed his forehead. "A goddamned tragedy."

"Of course I didn't *want* to die. Lidia will tell you, I still have nightmares. It was as though I was only made of fear — I couldn't think — I was suffocating in it. But, you see, sometimes I wanted him to do it. I did, Michael. I wanted it so that he could never take it back. I wanted him tormented. I wanted it to be in the newspapers. Everyone would have been so shocked and sad. . . . But then he didn't kill me, and no one knew a thing, and it wasn't in any newspapers, and we all went along."

"Some of us knew."

"Not really," she said.

Michael said, feelingly, "You should resist pain, Anna. You shouldn't invite it in. You know that story already."

"I want to see if he looks like John."

"Of course he won't."

"In the eyes."

"You won't be able to see his eyes!"

"If we get close enough I will."

"We will not get close enough. I won't have you swooning on me with blood spattered upon us. I'd lose my breakfast."

"I deserve it," Anna said, feeling a kind of stillness fall across her.

"What? His pain?" She shrugged and would not answer. Michael took her by the shoulders, his eyes wide, his face red with emotion. "You *don't* deserve that. You *don't.*"

"It's not my pain, Michael — it's my pleasure."

"Do you hear yourself?" he cried, looking around him as if to seek more sympathetic ears.

"Are you sure you don't want to go back to Ireland and become a seminarian?"

"Don't mock me," he said.

"Please," she said. "As my friend — my dearest friend."

He gave an indignant snort. "Fine. But only because I owe you money. And we're not getting close."

"Close enough to see his eyes," she said, and kissed him.

She wore her black veil, in the hopes that no one would recognize her, and leaned on Michael's elbow. He was wordless, thin-lipped.

Lidia and a big manservant pushed a way through the rolling crowd. The smell was bad. One could not help bumping against men — most of them were men — of every rank. On the streets and lanes, from shop fronts and carriages, all eyes turned toward the square, where stood the scaffolding and all its flags and barbaric accoutrements, soldiers ranging before it. Anna was surprised at the number of children. Sometime later the soldiers brought out Franz Zahlheim — a thin man in soiled clothing, with a shaved head — and bound him to the wheel while he wept and struggled hoarsely and feebly. He was twenty or thirty yards away. The noise of the crowd seemed to blot out all thought, all freshness, all peace. But there was a great hush when the bludgeon was raised to break Zahlheim's first flailing foot. The hammer swept through the sky and there was a crack and thump and then the rending scream, and the cheers and shouts of the crowd. Anna, in all her career, had never heard a crowd like this, so huge, so rapt. In spite of her veil she was flayed by her senses.

She had wanted to place John Fisher's face over Zahlheim's. To see him hurt — to see him, in agony, die — this would release her, she had thought; would bring a feeling of vengeance, an end. But there was no end. She did not wish to see this man suffer. She did not wish to see him tortured and killed.

She had been tortured herself once. The wife of Zahlheim remained murdered. And these crowds were wild with excitement, they were laughing, vivid, exultant, to see the murderer wracked and killed. She suffocated among them. It was they, as much as the spectacle, that stunned her, and made her wonder who she was. It was as if they had never known pain themselves, even though this, what they were doing, was nothing else. She plugged her ears but the sound only seemed greater. Stumbling against Michael, who pressed a handkerchief over his mouth and against his tearing eyes, she begged him to take her home, but their progress was so slow, and the executioner's so swift, that Zahlheim's body had been broken and branded long before they could struggle free.

Her mother was at home doing some needlework. The dogs lay sleeping around her.

"How was the execution?" Mrs. Storace asked. Anna put her face down to Bonbon and didn't answer. "I saw a few hangings when I was a girl. Thieves and such. Poor creatures."

They were quiet for a while. Then Anna asked, "Mama? Were you afraid of my

317

husband? Of John?" Her throat was dry. She petted the soft, dreaming dog.

Mrs. Storace continued stitching so steadily that for a moment it seemed that she had not heard. But at length she sniffed and said, "I curse myself every day for letting that man into my house."

Then Anna, her heart full of sadness which was also a terrible warmth, rested her cheek on the arm of her mother's chair and watched the needle pinch and thread as if for all eternity. While she watched she did not have to think of the broken man and the wrongs. She had only to think of the needle, pinching and threading forever in her mother's elegant hands.

IN HEAVEN'S NAME

Mozart was home, waiting for Anna. She'd said she would sing Susanna only if her last aria, *"Deh, vieni, non tardar,"* was a showpiece rondo. He was good at writing rondos. He liked to put them in his piano concertos. They were long and vivacious, in the form of verse and refrain, and demanded a skilled technique. Anna's aria would have decorations and roulades, low notes and high, show off everything she could do. It would stall the action, but leave no doubt which soprano was the prima buffa of the Burgtheater.

She was coming over now to try it out. His rondo. He had cleared his afternoon appointments. What time Anna did not need he would reserve for *Figaro*. *Figaro* must be everything now, as nearly everything as he could make it.

At lunch Constanze had remarked that he was fidgeting. That was what he did when he was nervous. He had not been alone with Anna since that time when she was ill.

He tried to play but it was shit, his hands were shaking all over. She was late. Perhaps she would not come. Perhaps that would be better.

Then there she was, cheerful and smiling, with her bright, dark eyes, and it seemed that both of them were nervous, remembering the last time they had been together alone. So long ago that was now. He had tired himself out, finishing his opera. It consumed his thoughts. He wanted little to eat and little sleep — only to finish it, to see it whole and perfect as he had it in his head. He forgot to wash, forgot household matters and social engagements and his appearance. Nothing like that could hold in his mind. Only *Figaro* — only Susanna.

His wife was out for the afternoon with Karl, visiting her mother. They went every Wednesday. Mozart disliked his mother-in-law. She was always wanting money and smacking her lips. She was superstitious. But she was good to Karl and devoted to her daughter.

It was now late March. Soon it would be full spring. Since last he'd seen Anna, Mozart had come to believe that Aloysia must have been right about Anna and Benucci. After all, their characters in his opera possessed an ideal love. And it was better that way. Benucci was tall and free. Mozart was small, and bound to Constanze. He had no time for infatuation. It would be much better if Anna loved Benucci. He would encourage it. He desired nothing but her happiness and she could not find happiness with him.

Carefully she removed her hat. She seemed both lively and relaxed. She talked of a fair she had been to this morning, a trinket she had bought.

"It's wonderful to be here," she said to him, smiling. "I feel so comfortable with you."

This pleased him enormously. He fussed with his papers. *Benucci,* he told himself. *She loves Benucci.* But he didn't believe it. "Here it is," he said, not able, really, to meet her eyes. "A *grandissimo* rondo. You'll be disguised as the countess, and Benucci is hiding in the bushes thinking you're waiting for a tryst with Almaviva. But really you love Benucci, and you *know* he's hiding, so you play a trick on him and pretend to sing a love song to Almaviva, whom you detest, in order to mock and serenade the man you really love, Benucci, who's listening. This is that love song."

"Figaro," she murmured, studying the score.

"What?" he asked.

"You mean I love Figaro. Susanna loves Figaro."

"Yes, right, Figaro. So you see it's really very clever. It's double-edged. She's driving him mad with jealousy but in her heart she knows she's singing for him alone. For Figaro. So it's two things at once, you see?"

"Yes," she said. "It's wonderful."

"I'm sorry. You know all this already. I'm an idiot."

"It's all right."

There was a brief silence. "Well," said Mozart, turning to his keyboard. "Shall we?" She nodded her assent and they played through it.

Of course it was a wretched aria. Completely wrong. She was a breathtaking singer but she had been wrong in this. He'd known it would be wrong to do a big rondo. So he had composed it in the wrong key. Ha! It was very clever. He'd written it in E-flat. E-flat was entirely the wrong mood. And Benucci's aria was also in E-flat. One couldn't have two E-flats in a row. *"Deh, vieni"* must be in F. But it couldn't be in F, and be a big showpiece rondo. That would be ridiculous and impossible. So he'd written an alternate aria in F, which was waiting at the top of the piano, a sweet little thing, almost a folk song it was so simple, the kind of song a girl like Susanna would sing to her lover on a hot summer evening, to bring him to his knees.

Anna would not like this one in E-flat. He knew her too well. So he had the other one waiting, the one in F.

It would have been easier to play if she hadn't been standing so close to him. The aria was wretched but her singing was exquisite. He could see her breast expanding and declining with every breath.

"Well," he said grimly when it was finished. He almost spat on the score. "There's your rondo."

"You don't like it," she said.

"What?" he asked. "Why would I write anything I didn't like?"

She hesitated and wet her lips. God help him, her eyes . . . "To teach me a lesson," she ventured. "To stop me from being so vain."

He broke from her gaze, flustered, and looked at the keyboard. *I married Constanze,* he told himself. *I love Constanze.* "Look," he said rapidly and almost with irritation. "It's the middle of the night. She's waiting for her lover. Longing for him. The place is

323

crowded with enemies but in spite of the danger she means to sing for his ears only. In a minute the climax will come, the dénouement, a great hubbub, but for now she's alone with him. In this grove. In Spain. In summer dark." He took a long breath. "Do you think she wants to show off her *fioratura*? Her high notes? She already has him. In heaven's name they are already married. The aria should be a caress, a breath, an ache in the heart. Anything else is showmanship."

She was silent for a long moment. He couldn't see her face. He didn't know what she was thinking. He could only hear her breathing, the breath that touched her lips and nose and throat, that moved her perfect breast. Then she said, softly, "Did you have something else in mind?"

He swallowed back the lump in his throat. He remembered kissing her in the courtyard, how she had sighed against him, her sweat and her perfume, the silkiness of her dress, how she'd let him pull up her stockings and almost go higher. He reached for the other manuscript. "Yes." He was surprised at himself, how natural he sounded. "I do have something, as it happens. I have it here. Would you like to try it?"

"Of course," she said.

"I think it might be just the thing. There's this part here, you see, where I'll have the winds cooing, a very special effect, very lilting. I think it will be just the thing to drive Benucci mad."

"Figaro," she murmured, correcting him.

"Figaro," he said. He could not look at her. He could speak quite naturally, but he could not look at her. His own breath was coming quickly, a steady, nervous rhythm — nervous, he told himself, for fear she wouldn't like the aria, because really he was rather fond of the aria, rather proud. It *must* be this one, the one in F, with the cooing winds.

They began with the recitative, the dialogue-like speak-singing that led into the aria proper. *"At last,"* she sang in Italian, *"the moment has come when I can enjoy myself without care in the arms of my beloved."* And as she sang this he felt her hand come to rest on the top of his left shoulder.

Her left hand it was. He shut his eyes. She sang, *"Timid fears, depart from my breast! Do not come, to disturb my delight,"* and stroked his shoulder in three soft circles.

He played the rushing interlude of piano notes, her hand on his shoulder, all his life in his shoulder, and when he got to the last chord of the sequence he turned his cheek

325

to rub against her hand on his shoulder and kissed the top of her first finger. The finger lifted to stroke across his lips and he wheeled around in an agony of desire and buried his face in her breasts.

"Oh, no," she gasped, urgently, over his kisses — her neck, he wanted to devour it — "Someone will notice, I have to keep singing or someone will notice," so he pulled her forward and sat her in his lap and played the next chords with his lips nuzzling her nape, her hair, the sweet downy slope of her shoulder. Laughing, breathing against him, she somehow continued the recitative, about the beautiful Spanish grove, the earth, the sky, the night, welcoming and responding to her desires, and then she turned around and kissed him like someone dying of thirst.

She rested her forehead against his and stared deeply and laughingly into his eyes. "The aria," she whispered. "Now the aria."

Thank God he had it memorized.

He played the introduction as slowly as he could — slower than it ever should go, and with ridiculous errors — while she kissed and caressed him and fumbled with his trousers. She missed her entrance.

"I'm sorry," she exclaimed, a little thickly, but clearly enough for anyone outside to

326

hear. "Frog in my throat. Could you start again, maestro?" And as she was saying this she found an opening in the trousers and he gave a scarcely audible groan. He began the introduction again. She turned, resting on his knee, an arm about his neck, the other in his pants, and sang the first phrase. Then she stopped and fell against him and he held her as tightly as he'd held any girl in his life and both of them were laughing breathlessly and silently. He pushed up her skirts, felt again the sweet soft thigh, touched for the first time her strong, perfect rump.

"Such long phrases!" she gasped. She pressed her face into his neck and turned around again so that her back was to him. He caressed her waist, her breasts, inhaled blissfully her sharp, exquisite scent. "We'll have to try it again. I'm afraid," she said, sounding remarkably sober, "I haven't quite the breath to do it justice today."

"You're doing very well," he declared. Lightly he nibbled her ear. "It's an experiment. It's so new."

"Yes," she sighed, a sigh as if of ecstatic respite, leaning against him in his chair. "And so abominably exposed."

"You have the best legato," he said, running his hand up the inside of her thigh, all

327

the way to the top, "I ever heard." She gasped and thanked him kindly, and wriggled like a fish.

The door was not locked. The house was full of people. Anyone might come in, without a knock.

"Are you sure?" he whispered.

"Oh, yes," she said, adjusting herself. "Let's start again from the beginning. Let's see — I mean — ah, yes — I mean, let's see if I have the breath." She turned the page back to the beginning, to the recitative, and then he was inside her.

It was absurd, sacrilegious, that he could keep playing, and she singing, in such circumstances, with such feelings and motions. Yet somehow they managed. They stopped and started, laughed, made great shows of chagrin and apology. Her tone was perhaps not as strong as it might have been. One or the other of his hands were sometimes occupied with other things. Sometimes she got the tune wrong, because she wasn't looking carefully enough, and he had to sing it to her, in his soft tenor, moving in time with it, conducting it upon her body. Twice he bit her shoulder — once she broke off singing entirely. It was perfect in F. There had never been anything so right or so whole or so good.

SPRING IN VIENNA

If music were an intoxication, Anna never wished to be sober. Her mind thrummed with melody. At night, in bed, as she had done since childhood, she sifted through all the musical themes running through her head and chose one to fall asleep to that was most like a lullaby.

She and Mozart saw each other every Wednesday, even if it was only for a few minutes. She lived and died for Wednesdays. Sometimes she kept him company while he composed. Now and then he'd ask her opinion — whether she liked this better, or that; whether it sounded best with this tempo, this articulation, or another. Always he was delighted with her answer, even if he did not agree.

When she was with him, her contentment was absolute. But as soon as they parted she was restless and upset. She became envious of his wife, envious even of his little boy. When she was lonely or tired, she could call up some memory of Mozart and that would restore her, but the feeling would not last.

They did not talk of the future. Rehearsals for *Figaro* had started and they were both extremely busy. Mozart would conduct the first few performances of the opera. He was still finishing the last acts.

"You seem strung rather thin, Anna," Stephen remarked. "Aren't you getting enough sleep?"

"It's my Susanna," she said. "She consumes me."

"Your part's too long," Stephen declared. "Da Ponte's got you on stage every moment."

"But what would we cut? There's nothing. It all runs together."

"Trust Mozart not to leave any seams," Stephen said with a laugh. He was writing a new opera, based on *A Comedy of Errors,* which he hoped to premiere in the fall. The emperor had said he might have a second chance, and Mozart — in part to be nearer to Anna — had been giving Stephen composition lessons.

Mozart and Da Ponte had wanted to have *Figaro* ready by winter, but it had been delayed and postponed and now would not be performed until the beginning of May, the very end of the season. Even with the delay Mozart could not write quickly enough. Anna would go to his house, or the house of one of his patrons, to read her part with the others, and Mozart would greet them like a ghost, cracking his distracted jokes and handing them new pages. His fingers were blackened with ink and appeared to grow blacker every time she saw him. When one hand got tired of writing he would switch to the other. In addition to composing *Figaro,* he was still performing concerts and giving lessons to his students.

The company had divided into factions over the new Mozart opera. On one side, resenting it, were Stefano Mandini, his wife, Maria, and Luisa Laschi. The Bussanis swayed with the winds but were usually found over by the Mandini-Laschi border, leaving only Anna and Michael Kelly solidly championing the opera. Benucci refused to ally himself one way or the other.

The root of the problem came down to matters of laziness and pride, and a reluctance to do anything unfamiliar. Mozart, try as he might to compose in an Italian style, was Austrian, and this bothered some of them. His opera was exceptional in its length and difficulty. They were used to

331

singing dry recitative, as easy and natural to them as speech, easy duets and trios, and simple arias. But Mozart put everything together so that one musical number ran into the next without rest. He did not only require them to sing duets or quartets: he required *sextets.* Performing one of these elaborate ensembles was like baking a new dish for a king, on pain of death, when none of the proper ingredients were at hand and everyone had only fragments of the recipe. Everything must be memorized and perfectly timed.

"Why must he," asked Mandini, "make everything so thorny? He's a splendid pianist and I enjoy his concertos. But an opera is not a concerto. Mozart has his genius. Let him stick with it. How can he be expected to set an Italian text? How can he have any instinct for it? The music is too rich. It sinks with its own weight. And we'll be the ones who pay for it."

"Come now," said Michael. "Anna has the most to sing of all of us, and do you see her complaining?"

"She never would. She's got Wolfgang Mozart in her pocket."

"I do *not,*" she exclaimed. "Signor Mandini, I'm shocked. You know I haven't any pockets."

Mandini laughed. "Then you're keeping him somewhere else."

"Don't you dare," she cried teasingly, flying at him. He shouted and ducked. It was all in jest — at least it seemed so. Surely Mandini didn't know. Surely none of them knew. There was always this kind of talk and teasing among musicians. But her heart was racing.

"Come," said Michael. "Enough. They're waiting for us."

Mozart and the stage manager were in the saloon of the Burgtheater, a pleasant open hall with the chairs pushed back. The whole company had assembled. They were to rehearse, for the first time together, the extensive second act finale.

Mozart rose, seeming anxious, and said to them, "I've been looking forward to hearing this — all of you together. It's tremendous. I've been dreaming of it."

The action of *The Marriage of Figaro* took place over the course of a single day. The Count Almaviva wished to claim his *droit du seigneur* and take his wife's chambermaid, Susanna, to bed on the night of her wedding with Figaro. Carrying through it all was a subplot involving the page Cherubino, played by Dorotea, who loved the countess. In the section of the opera they were rehearsing now, the jealous count had discovered that Cherubino was locked in his wife's closet, in a state of undress. After that, various characters rushed in and out until they were all singing together in a frenzy. The finale went on for half an hour without break, and if any element collapsed in its structure the rest would soon follow.

"Well," Mozart said, after their first attempt. It had gone terribly. He looked at Anna and smiled. In spite of how messy it had been she felt cheerful and pleasantly tired with the feeling that could only come from singing for a half an hour the music of the man she loved. "It could be worse."

"It's so fast," said Bussani. "There's no time to breathe."

"Don't be glum!" said Michael Kelly. "You sound like Zeus himself; you make my bones rattle. If anything it was too slow for you."

"It must be at *least* that fast," said Mozart.

"Otherwise we'll not be home before daybreak," said Mandini.

"If I may," said Bussani, "the short duet between my wife and Signora Storace is most delightful."

"Isn't it a hoot?" asked Dorotea. She put her hands to her head. "If only I can get my tongue to obey my brain."

"Maestro," said Mandini with soft gravity to Mozart. He stood and took some space among them. "We will spend all afternoon on this one finale alone. It's not even the finale to the *opera* — just the second act. We've not begun to master it. I guess the length of your opera will be five hours at the very least — I shouldn't be surprised if it stretched to five and a half. How are we to be expected to know it by the first of May?"

The room had grown still. "Four and a half hours, I should think," Mozart said at last. "At most."

"You're not accounting for encores."

Mozart passed his gaze over them, pausing when he reached Anna. "I'm aware of that," he said. He turned back to Mandini. "My opera is so long because it can't be any shorter. It's exactly the length it needs to be. I would offer to cut the count's aria, but you sing it so magnificently —"

"It's impossibly difficult," Mandini interjected.

"And you told me that you like it and it suited you."

"It *does,* too, by God," said Michael.

"Can't deny that," said Benucci, smiling.

"I'm not suggesting you cut my aria," said Mandini.

335

"Perhaps your fair wife's?" Mozart said. "Yours is perhaps the least important to the plot, madam," he said to Maria Mandini, "but I would not wish you to leave the opera without an aria of your own."

"That, too, must remain," said Mandini. He coughed. "It's not a question of the arias."

"Then what?"

Mandini opened his mouth, hesitated, and shut it again. "The whole thing."

"The whole thing?"

"Some of us" — he hesitated again — "are wondering if perhaps you've overreached yourself."

"Ah," said Mozart, smiling and leaning back. "Maybe I have. I suppose we'll find all that out on the first of May."

Mandini sighed and bowed his head. "I suppose we will."

"You can't deny it's a magnificent finale," Michael said to Mandini as they were leaving. "I mean, as long as we can pull it off."

"But we *can't*. There isn't time. I see no good in it and very probably harm."

"Harm? It's opera, Mandini. We are not going to war."

"Your part is nothing. If we fail, it's I who'll get egg on my face, I and Benucci and the prima donnas."

"The opera is superb," Benucci declared. He touched Anna on the back and she looked at him with surprise and gratitude. "Best thing I've ever sung. I won't soon forget it. Wait until you hear my aria in the second act, Mandini. The man makes me sound like a god."

"You always sound like a god," said Michael happily.

Mandini snorted. "Where's your loyalty, Benucci?"

"With the music, ass. I don't mind anything if the music's good."

"Barnacle," drawled Mandini. He gave Benucci a push. "It won't be any good if we can't sing it."

"We can sing it."

May 1, the day of the premiere, came too soon. As they assembled in the familiar round of the Burgtheater there was within the cast of *The Marriage of Figaro* a degree of nervous tension not usual for them. There were obstacles of vocalization and memorization. The instrumentalists were out of their depth. Mozart had used his opera orchestra as he used it in his symphonies and concertos, but the orchestra of the Burgtheater had never played such symphonies. He'd meant for the instruments to be in dialogue with the singers, nearly their equal, commenting on their action, but too many of them had not sufficiently learned their parts. They were not yet moving in the same breath, with the same mind. Everyone felt uneasy and unmoored.

Anna stood backstage holding hands with Benucci in the dark. She had taken his hand because she was frightened, and he'd accepted her touch without a word. Of them all he was the most composed. But Anna perceived him taking measured breaths to calm himself. It was always like this with a premiere. One didn't know it well enough. One could not anticipate how it would go over.

After a moment she transferred her hand to the crook of his arm and let him take a portion of her weight. On her head was Susanna's wedding cap. Her shoes were pink. They could hear the chatter of the audience and the fiddling of the orchestra. It was not yet dark outside — there must be an hour or two left of daylight.

"Why do we do this to ourselves?" she asked Benucci in a low voice. "I'm ready to faint, if you weren't here holding me up."

"We do it," he murmured, "because we haven't found anything we like better."

She seemed to have lost the use of her

right ear. Her vision was blurring at the peripheries. But it was too late. The overture had begun. She and Benucci went to their places in the darkness behind the curtain, he to measure out the space for their marriage bed, and she to admire her pretty cap. Then the curtain was drawn and warm light poured on her and she saw from the corner of her eye the shifting audience and the heads of the players and Mozart in the center, at his piano, as tranquil and focused as he had been in rehearsals, and she loved him, and could be frightened no more, for it was of utmost importance that Figaro be drawn from his work to admire the little cap she had made for their wedding day.

Running through the evening she had the sensation of balancing a ball on her nose like a bear at a circus. When it stayed balanced, even with all her dips and dodges, it seemed a miracle. Every now and then she would have the sensation of watching herself. But if she observed too long, everything would threaten to come crashing down and she'd have to scramble. She was ever having to loosen her awareness — and become, in that way, *more* aware — in order to steady her brain, which wanted to comment upon her actions rather than sinking into them as deeply and resolutely as it must. This evening she failed, she feared, more than she succeeded. The audience was restless and vocal. A knot of rowdies in the balcony — hired, no doubt, by Mozart's detractors — had set themselves to booing, and this distressed and distracted her. Da Ponte had done the best he could in adapting the libretto from the French play, but the plot could not be jarred, or it lost its sense; yet jarring, it seemed, was all they did. The singers missed their cues and confused the audience. When Anna played her guitar to accompany Cherubino's second aria — a song within the opera, which Cherubino had written for the countess — it seemed the first time in the evening that the restlessness stilled. The impartial members of the audience gave many bravos but it seemed not enough. The finale at the end of the second act nearly fell apart. Everyone came off stage in a black humor. They had not rehearsed enough. Mozart had overestimated their abilities.

"Cheer up, my ducks!" shouted Dorotea Bussani, breathless from jumping out the window to escape the wrath of Count Almaviva. She mopped her brow and blew out her lips and stretched her mouth like a lion. She enjoyed strutting around in her tall boots and snugly fitting trousers. She had told Anna the garments made her want to gallop on a horse. Her husband sliced an apple for her. "The worst is over now. Nobody remembers the middle of things. They can read the libretto during the interval. Only two acts to go, my chickens! The easiest acts yet!"

"The orchestra is out of time and out of tune," said her husband.

"Well, I thought our duet went splendidly," said Dorotea to Anna. The duet between Susanna and Cherubino, with the two young servants singing over each other in panicked whispers, was a comic masterpiece, over in the blink of an eye.

"Yes," Anna said absently. She had hoped Mozart would come backstage during the interval, but there was no sign of him. Somehow it seemed that if the opera failed tonight it would be her fault.

"Mandini's aria will set us right," said Benucci, clapping the other basso on the head. "Nobody does it better. Elegance, farce, it's all there."

"Ah," said Mandini. He adjusted his wig. "We'll see." But he added, "I'm rather fond of the third act."

Luisa Laschi, who played the countess, gave Anna a hug. She was a sweet girl about Anna's height and they had become friends.

341

In the third act they sang a duet in which the countess dictated a letter, while Susanna repeated the lines back to her. Although the text was ironical, Anna and Luisa's voices mixed and slipped across each other like silk in a breeze. It was one of the most exquisite moments in the opera and showed, Benucci had remarked, Wolfgang Mozart's profound and uncanny understanding of womenfolk. Mozart had laughed and said it was because he had a sister.

"You sounded beautiful," Anna said to Luisa. "I listened to your aria."

Luisa shook her head. "I was sure I'd run out of air." She gave Anna a kind look. "I'm sorry I doubted the opera, Anna. You were right. It is a marvel. But I'm afraid we're not showing it to its best."

"We will," said Anna.

"Of course," said Luisa. She bowed her head and moved away, murmuring her lines. She'd had some memory slips in the first half.

"How are you holding up?" asked Michael. He was in his judge's costume. He took Anna's arm.

She leaned on him with theatrical weakness. "I'm so tired," she exclaimed. "I've sung enough for one evening, thank you. I think I'd better go home."

"You can do it," Michael said. "Don't be afraid."

"How like a judge you are," she said, admiring his costume. Then Benucci swung her away from Michael and lifted her into the air, and she let herself become excited again, because the opera was still wonderful, and for all her fears there was still nowhere she would rather be, just as it had been when she was thirteen, than inside an opera house.

The third act was the best they'd ever done it. When it was over and time to commence the last, although she had already sung more than she was used to, she somehow felt she had new energy, as if nearing the end of a long fast.

The fourth act was the act of mistaken identities, of lovers' assignations in summer evenings. The stage was in semidarkness. The little girl playing Barbarina went out alone to look for the lost pin and sang a melody as melancholy as anyone had ever heard. The child reminded Anna of herself, when she had been young. Then came Maria Mandini's aria, then Benucci's, and finally it was time for *"Deh, vieni,"* Susanna's last aria, the one in F.

She went out, disguised as the countess, more alone than she had been all evening.

Figaro hid behind a tree. Anna lifted her veil, to breathe the sweet evening air, and saw Mozart in the orchestra, dressed in white and gold with a gold insignia at his breast. And she understood then that she had not failed. She saw it in his face. He did not care if it was imperfect.

She flitted about the stage for the recitative and then settled, kneeling, on an imagined bed of moss, among fragrant nighttime flowers, for the aria.

She could never sing it without blushing.

Here, this evening, for the first time in nearly four hours of stage play, she paused in her disguise to reveal her heart. The aria was gentle and lulling, delicately exposed, achingly sensual. The range was as narrow as any popular song. More low notes than high. A serenade. Yet amateur young ladies after dinner could not have sung it as Anna did now. As with much of Mozart's music, its greatest difficulty lay in its seeming ease. An amateur would not have had the breath for it, would have wobbled and staggered, run sharp or flat. To make it sound as it must — simple, guileless, a breath of desire — Anna had to draw on all her reserves, that the line not fail, the silver ball not waver in its balance. And this time she did not falter.

Now came the ending, the part that transcended nature, the part where she begged her beloved to come to her, to this dark copse of trees, where the flowers were all smiling — to come, come, *"Vieni, vieni,"* that she might crown his brow with roses. Mozart watched her from the piano, remembering their sacrilege. She sang it to him.

The Dearest Friend

They gave three more performances of *Figaro* in May, and as the listeners and singers became familiar with the work, its worth began to show. The little duet between Susanna and Cherubino was encored countless times. The emperor ordered a special performance of *Figaro* that summer, at his pleasure palace in Laxenburg, and Mozart was confident there would be many more performances come autumn. The press, after some initial hesitation, had declared his opera a masterpiece.

And all through the summer Anna and Mozart were lovers. As nearly as they could be. Once his opera opened, and then after it had closed, they had little excuse to be alone, with her so busy at the Burgtheater and Mozart putting on concerts and composing everything he could. He was always tired. He felt guilty and was afraid his wife suspected. He felt he could not give Anna everything she needed. He talked of moving to the outskirts of the city, where the rents were cheaper. If he moved there, Anna would see him even less.

The only times she ever felt at peace now were at his concerts. Then she could sit quietly, watching him, and sate her heart. In his music was where he lived and revived, and where she'd first loved him. And she knew, always, always when she was there, that he played for her. That he had always been playing for her. He had told her so. But she would have known it, even if he had not told her.

The touch of his hands was like nothing she had ever felt from a man. It was wholly gentle. His fingers did not demand. They did not coarsen or insist. She could have devoted her life to the memory of a single caress. When she saw him play, she wanted to laugh, for he touched her in the same way that he touched the keys.

It was as though the world was a dream and they the only real ones in it. Sometimes she would meet his eyes across the room, and only they would know, and no one else, and it would seem unutterably awful that she could not go to him, and tell everyone her love, her joy that was like an open wound. For it could not last. Even this, this watching and being watched by him, in crowded rooms, while the nonsense of dream-world conversation rang about them — this stealing of kisses and caresses whenever they safely might, which was hardly ever, which was almost never — could not last. She feared it would wreak him. He was always getting sick and never had enough money. He borrowed from others but refused to accept anything from Anna, no matter how she begged him. His face was tired. Sometimes when he looked at her, behind the cheer, behind the jokes and teasing, there was distress in his eyes. And what right did she have to do this to him, to take him from his work? What was the good, if they could never be alone? What, must they wait for the next opera? Must they scheme and suffer that long? He already had a wife. They had been happy, he and his wife — they might be happy still. Anna was nothing but a lonely girl whose baby had died, whose husband had beaten her. She had no right. She tried to express this to him, and at first he brushed it away. He said he loved her and that was that. He said he would be happy just to see her, kiss her cheek, hear her sing.

He would not leave his wife. Nor could Anna ask him to. At times she found herself almost wishing for some harm to come to Constanze, and this frightened her more than anything. This secrecy, this fear, this selfish need, were what she had become.

One could not live forever in a dream. Dreams never reached their promised end.

They performed *The Marriage of Figaro* at Schönbrunn Palace near the end of August. The singers stayed a week there, in resplendent luxury. Mozart came to conduct the last two nights, and the evening before the performance he and Anna arranged to meet on the grounds. They had not been alone in nearly two weeks.

There was a gazebo at the edge of a long lawn. She was late. As she hurried across the lawn she saw his slight figure leaning against one of the posts, regarding her. The day had been hot but it had rained briefly tonight, and the air smelled wet and green and there was a soothing breeze. It was after midnight. A few of the emperor's guests still gathered outside the palace, drinking and dancing in the open air — this was why Anna was late — but they would not come as far as the gazebo.

"There you are," he said, and she fell into his arms with a sigh. She always forgot how dear he was. But as soon as she remembered

349

she became so afraid of losing him that it seemed better to forget.

They rested awhile, hidden in the dark, facing the wood. The tops of the trees swayed and rustled in the gentle breeze.

"Anna," he said. He grasped her hand. She tried to think of something else, of the trees and the sky. The trees were alive but unthinking, they knew nothing and everything. The stars were clear. But she knew by the way he said her name what would come next. Francesco Benucci had sounded just the same, the day he'd said he didn't love her.

Mozart told her that his wife was going to have another child in the autumn. The deception and anxiety were killing him. He was not himself. He could not work and could hardly sleep. He was afraid that if they went on like this, everything would fall apart, and he would hate Anna. It could not go on, not in Vienna, not now.

His voice was high and strained. He clasped and reclasped her hand. She wiped her tears on her sleeve. Then she said, "I know, I know, Wolfgang," and he turned and held her and they stayed like that for a long time while the noise of the party filtered to them from a distance and the tops of the trees swayed like great sails.

When they drew apart she said quietly, "Stephen wants us to go back to London when my contract is up next spring. He thinks his operas would do well and I could sing at the King's Theatre or Drury Lane." She took a deep breath. "He says once we're there, we could get you a commission. It's almost a sure thing."

"Next spring," he said. He looked at the woods.

"Maybe it would be best. You wouldn't — I wouldn't trouble you so, if I were away."

"But for how long?" he asked, like a child.

She smiled, tearily. "Oh! A year. Just a year. Then we'll come back. Or you'll come to London. And we'll have gotten used to being apart by then. We'll have forgotten each other. You'll have your pretty babies. We'll just be friends, the best of friends, in London."

He embraced her again without answering. She pressed her face into his shoulder, trying to hold and remember every part of him. He had not answered yes, but neither had he asked her to stay.

A Rare Thing

Late in October Anna held a party for her twenty-first birthday. She rented a hall and there was dinner and dancing. Benucci and Bussani put Anna on their shoulders and marched her around the room while she shrieked and nearly collided with a chandelier. The guests were made to wear paper hats. A cherubic child was led around on a miniature pony distributing party favors to the guests.

"Who are you supposed to be?" asked the Countess Thun as she bent down — steadying her paper hat — to accept a charm bracelet the child offered her.

"I'm Cupid," the little girl recited in a high voice. "I come from heaven to pierce your heart and then you fall in love."

"Oh?" said the countess. "Then I should be frightened of you. But you are too pretty. Will you kiss my cheek?"

The child nodded and raised her face to

oblige, and with a rustle of silks the good lady momentarily enveloped her. When she rose, her face sparkled with the gold powder with which the child had been dusted. The pony jingled its bells and the procession moved to the next guests.

Mozart was there without his wife, who was nearing her confinement. Anna had brought in a billiards table, at great expense, for him to enjoy, and he did so with relish, beating Mandini out of several florins. But he and Anna had hardly spoken to each other all evening.

She made her way to the table to stand beside him. He missed the shot and Mandini took his turn.

"I hear you're leaving soon," he said.

"I thought you knew." She shook her head and played nervously with a rose that Michael had tucked into her bodice.

He nodded. His expression was neutral. "When? If there's any chance of reviving *Figaro* I must be sure I have a Susanna."

"After Lent, when my contract is up. The end of February."

"Ah," he said.

It was his turn to play. Fidgeting with the flower, Anna smiled at her well-wishers. Mozart was steadier now, regained his concentration, and won the match. Mandini

353

declined to play another.

"Will you play?" Mozart asked Anna. He was just the same. It was all she could do not to cry.

"I don't know how."

"Why do you have a table, then?"

"I had it brought for you."

He tilted his head. "For me? You should do better things with your money."

"It's my birthday. I can do anything I like."

He looked at her and shook his head. She sighed, took his arm, and leaned against him. She felt him relax. "You," he murmured, "can always do what you like."

"Not always. Not now."

"We must teach you billiards."

"Billiards is not a game for ladies. I couldn't hold the stick properly. My bodice is too tight. I couldn't raise my arms. And when I bent over everyone would be scandalized."

"Then we should play when we're all alone and you're able to move in comfort."

"If you'd show me how."

"I think you'd be a fine student."

"We'll see each other soon," she said. "It won't be long — a year, no more. Stephen and I will bring you to London. Once I'm there it will be so simple to gain influence and find someone to invite you. They have so much thirst and they've never heard anyone like you. They're not so stodgy as the Viennese. Everything will work out for the best. We'll revive *Figaro* before I leave. Or you'll find another soprano."

"Another soprano will make me change the last aria."

She smiled. "That's good. I don't want anyone else singing it."

He shook his head, wincing. "I'll miss you. I hadn't realized how much."

The little girl playing Cupid came up to them on her pony, led by Lidia. The pony had a wreath of hothouse flowers around its neck. The little girl listed complacently from side to side, clutching the pommel of the saddle. Goose-feather wings were fastened to her dress and a gold ribbon bound back her curls. A bow and arrow bumped gently at her side.

"Would you like a party favor?" she asked Mozart in a loud voice. He smiled and said he'd like one very much.

"My first role," Anna explained, "was Cupid."

"Were you as young as this little one? She's not much older than my Karl."

"I was thirteen — a good deal older. I felt already grown."

Lidia helped the child pick out the favor

that had been chosen for Mozart, a ceramic whistle in the shape of a bird. "Listen to that," he exclaimed, delighted, after he opened the box and blew upon the toy. "Wolfgang Mozart whistles at last!" It was a long-standing joke between him and Anna that he could not whistle. He bent down to the little girl and thanked her warmly.

"You're welcome, sir," said the girl, who had been well trained. She proceeded along to the next guests.

"Were you on a pony, too?" Mozart asked Anna.

"Oh no, but the child insisted. We should never have convinced her, otherwise. I want to take her with me. She could order everyone about."

"When I was ten I was in Paris," he said, watching the child. "I went back later with my mother and she died, so I can't think of it without sadness. But I've never seen a more beautiful city. You must stop there on your way home. You belong in such a place."

"A sad one?"

"No, a beautiful one."

Da Ponte came up to them. "My dear Mozart," he said, "did our muse tell you she's leaving us? I mean to follow her. Without Mademoiselle Storace, I don't know how I'm supposed to live."

"She did tell me," Mozart said. He spread his hands. "I'm completely distraught."

"I'll see you again," Anna cried. "You act as if I'm joining a convent."

"I can't imagine you in a convent," said Da Ponte. "I have a very particular idea of nuns and you are nothing like them. And I am an ordained priest."

"An impious one."

"Nevertheless."

"What are they like, then, your nuns?"

"Oh — rude, stiff, shy."

"I'm rude!" Anna exclaimed. She appealed to Mozart, "Am I not rude?"

"Extremely," he said.

"But why aren't you dancing?" asked Da Ponte.

She looked at Mozart. "No one has asked me."

"May I?" Da Ponte said, and offered his arm. "I'm almost as good a dancer as I am a poet." He looked down at her fondly. "And I shan't have many more chances to dance with you."

She did not wish to leave the billiards table, but she could not refuse him, and perhaps it would be better not to be seen too much in Mozart's company. She and Da Ponte danced. Vincente Martín y Soler, the new Spanish composer, was dancing the same set, and Anna took a turn in his arms. "Ah, my Lilla," he said, "so fresh you are. I feel I'm breathing new air."

"Rake," Anna called to him as she turned herself round. Martín y Soler had arrived in the city last spring. He beguiled everyone he met. Already he was known in Vienna as a god of melody. Lilla was Anna's role in his new opera, *A Rare Thing,* which was to premiere this month. Da Ponte had written a libretto for Martín with a plot quite like *Figaro*'s, but simpler and shorter, to suit the ear-catching, guileless melodies, derived from Spanish folk music, at which Martín so excelled.

As she danced she was aware of Mozart watching her from the billiards table. All she had desired this day was to feel happy and at ease, and to make her friends feel the same. To that end she had brought these people here; to that end gone to such extravagant expense. But she had failed — failed utterly.

A *Rare Thing* was the most successful opera in living memory. If Anna had not been lauded before, she was now. Women blushed in her presence, and diligently emulated Lilla's dress, coiffure, and manner of moving. Men stopped her on the street to declare their adoration. Every night four hundred hopeful listeners were shut out on the street, disappointed for tickets. And those were the ones who could afford tickets. It became difficult to enter or leave the theater for the throngs gathered around it. The music from the opera spread to every rank. On every corner, in houses rich and poor, at gatherings crass and fashionable, the air was filled with the Spaniard's tuneful melodies.

There was nothing difficult, no uncertainty or fear. A feeling of rightness had been on the cast almost from the beginning. The labor was hidden, the gears basted in silk, and no effort was required, even of the most easily distracted listeners, to apprehend the opera's beauty. When Anna sang Martín's melodies, the heart swelled and reposed. Da Ponte's libretto amused the spirit but did not attempt to challenge it. The course of the action was predictable even in its surprises, and therefore it, too, was right and good. The audience left the theater reassured in the goodness and virtue of the heroine, Lilla, and in her ultimate triumph. Melodies from the opera came into their heads unbidden, at odd moments, and made them feel again that same reassurance and pleasure. *A Rare Thing* became a point of commonality. One talked of it over dinner, read references to it in papers, looked forward to the chance to hear it again, as many times as was possible, in order to relive and ingrain the same sweet first impressions: the feeling of witnessing, here, with all these collected contemporaries, a great event.

There could be no more talk now of reviving Mozart's *Figaro* before Lent. Anna did not see Mozart after the opening, though she had known he was there. The baby boy born to him and Constanze in October had died two days ago, on November 15; he was disinclined to mingle socially. Anna imagined him sitting perfectly still, watching this great setback unfold before him at the hands of his friends. He sent a note later to say that he had enjoyed her performance and that some of the melodies had been very pretty.

THE EMPEROR'S CHOCOLATE

Joseph II received Anna in the study where he breakfasted, looking drawn and irritable. "What's this?" he asked, brandishing her letter. "You're resigning at the moment of your greatest success? In the middle of the most celebrated run anyone has ever known?"

Tossing his head he looked at Anna, it seemed to her, with bitter contempt. "Now I know," he said, "how your husband felt."

Anna fixed her eyes on the pattern of his desk, red and fawn and black, inlaid to resemble a starburst. "My brother has arranged a contract for us both in London. I've been too long from my home."

"Your home!" exclaimed the emperor. "You come here spouting this nationalist claptrap to me? Do you think I've nothing better to do than listen to my star soprano express her ego? What, do you want me to increase your pay, is that what it is?"

"My brother needs me with him in London," Anna said. "I can make his career."

"If you leave," the emperor said, "you'll never work in any of my cities again — not in my entire empire. You'll be shunned in France, Burgundy, Italy, anywhere I have influence. Do you have any idea how many *children* my mother had? My brothers and sisters rule the world. I don't take these things lightly. Neither will they."

He had gone red in the cheeks; the rest of his complexion was white as lilies.

"I'll work in England," Anna said.

"Never to return? Never to leave? What madness is this? All for your brother? What's he done for you that an emperor cannot?"

Anna looked away. No longer was she the unstrung girl who had sipped the emperor's chocolate. She did not care what he thought. She would not live anymore in Vienna. "Loved me — cared for me."

"I dispute that," cried Joseph, as if he had just witnessed foul play in a game of whist. He grasped her wrists and pulled her toward him. "What of your debts to me?"

"Debts, Your Excellency?"

"Your husband banished, your brother given an opera to botch. *Two* operas! He's putting on another one! In *my* theater!"

362

"It wasn't my brother — that was all my fault."

Joseph bent his face to hers. She leaned away. "I see," he said abruptly, releasing her. "So you owe a debt to both of us now, to your brother and me, and blood holds more sway than the imminent disfavor of one of the noblest and most important men in the world, the most liberal and generous of patrons to you and your profession as you're ever likely to find. I see."

Anna's smile was small. "There are times," she said carefully, "when love holds more power than reason."

"Rubbish," Joseph said. He fished in his pocket and came up with nothing. "Love is but lust."

She looked at him steadily and then dropped a slight curtsy. "Forgive me, Your Excellency. Nothing you can say will make me change my mind."

"Stuff and nonsense!" the emperor exclaimed, banging open a drawer. "You're the same as everyone. You're just waiting for me to give in."

"Give in, sir?"

"Proposition you. Entreat, beg you to stay. Tell you I'll pay you more, that I'll expect nothing in return, not a gesture, not a look — not a foot, a toe, extended in a pink slipper for me to hold in my hands and kiss."

As he spoke he banged through all the drawers in his desk, opening them with an agitation Anna had rarely seen him display, going over their contents with eyes and hand and slamming them shut again.

Anna took a small step back. "I'm waiting for nothing, Your Excellency." Her slippers today were yellow and cream. They had almost never been pink, not since *Figaro.*

"That's what you'd like me to think," said the emperor, glancing at her. He rang the bell on his desk and a servant entered. "Gregor," he said tersely, "why do I find myself left without chocolate? Has there been some crisis of state? A revolution? Has the sky fallen in? Have we gone bankrupt?"

Gregor blanched and muttered something about killing himself and hurried outside.

"Louse!" Joseph called after him. He leveled his gaze at Anna. "Well. I can't pay you any more. You're already costing me too much. I could hire forty soldiers for two years on your salary. Frankly I'd have been just as happy to get rid of you, during your absence, but that I'd thought it would smack of cruelty and make me look bad to the people. And then I found myself, oddly" — his voice lowered a little — "missing you. I was as glad as any of my dimmest subjects to have you back. And now this — betrayal! Too much!"

This last was almost shouted. During the long pause that followed, Gregor returned with a tray piled with chocolates and left again. The emperor stuffed a few into his mouth. "Well?" he demanded.

Only John Fisher shouted at her like that. "I am in love," Anna said in a choked, angry voice, "with someone who can't have me. If I don't leave your city I'll kill myself."

The emperor stared at her, incredulous. "My dear girl. Life is not an opera. Wait a few months and it'll all be over."

"I've already waited."

"If you go now I'll never have you back. You think I shall but I shan't. I never forget a betrayal."

"I know," she said. "I don't care."

He snorted and waved a hand. "Fine. Good riddance. Whoever this fellow is — damn his eyes."

VIENNA NOCTURNE

In December, a cold, bright day, with two and a half months remaining before Anna's departure from Vienna, Mozart called on her, on her afternoon off. He had ridden his horse and his nose and cheeks were bright with chill.

Anna had been reading in her room. Stephen was out with Da Ponte and her mother was at Mass.

They embraced, just for a moment, though they'd promised each other not to, and then drew apart. He was weary and preoccupied. He'd come to tell her that the Czechs wanted to put on his opera in Prague, in January, and that he would go there to direct it and to concertize. The Czechs adored him.

"Our *Figaro*?" she asked.

"I could hardly have wished for better luck. To get away for a bit." He paced in and out of a low band of winter light. The room was warm with the fire. "Everywhere I go I hear *A Rare Thing*. My own wife hums it in her sleep."

"How long will you be gone?"

"I'll be back for Lent and Carnival — to send you off. Constanze goes with me."

"Oh," she said with a slight gasp. She felt an ache in her chest, deep and low, as though there were a hot coal resting lightly and inexorably against her naked heart. "Then we've no more time."

He placed his fingers on the ledge of the window, where it was cooler. His reflection looked back at him, broken by hoarfrost and strips of lead.

"It wasn't when I first saw you that I lost myself to you," he said. "It wasn't when I kissed you in the garden." He swallowed. "It was when you were so ill and came down to me. I could've whispered you away on the air. It was all I could do to just sit there — if I'd been any kind of man I'd have cradled you."

She smiled gently, remembering. "So you played."

"Yes." He cleared his throat and gave a quick shrug. "You know I don't think I've ever played with more intent. Only concentrating on you, on the cradling. The way you listened."

"I couldn't help it." She added, wryly, "I did try."

With a restless movement he went to sit at the card table. The clock chimed. "When I was a little boy in Holland," he said in a low voice, "my sister and I were very sick. I was delirious — had such strange fantasies that even when I think of them now, they make me shiver. I knew I was dying. Knew from the way they talked around me. I was angry with myself. I thought I'd failed. There we were, in the middle of our tour, and it was so important I be well, or all the concerts would be canceled, all the visits, all the money." He rubbed his eyes. "I remember looking at my arms and hands all covered in spots and wondering if I'd lose the use of them. Then I'd make no more music, unless I played with my nose or something. And it was my fault."

He opened the backgammon board and fiddled with the pieces, red and black, which clacked and sifted like stones, placing them in rows of alternating colors, stacking them in threes and fours, rolling them from hand to hand. "Then I lived. My sister lived, as well. We had some scars — here, on the cheeks, and hands — to remind us. Sometimes I look at these on my hands and forget why they're there. They've faded since I was such a little boy. I was only a few years older than my Karl. Six, seven? But I felt like a man." He smiled, stacking the pieces higher. She sat beside him and put her cheek on his shoulder, breathing the sweet, warm scent of his body. He had been smoking his pipe. She loved to watch his hands. They were always in motion, always fiddling with something or other. The scars were faint. "I suppose that's what makes me stubborn. Your Italian friends call me arrogant. My father told everyone I had a gift from God. There was always that expectation. Even on the commode. I had to produce these God-given shits."

Anna laughed. He took up one of her hands, his thumbs meeting at the joint of her wrist, his fingers pressing gently against the curve of her palm. "Do you know," he remarked, smiling, "when you come into a room, I always feel you bring the sunshine. Even when you weren't well, I felt that. It's like that when you're on the stage. I think we watch you for that. We bare our breasts to you and you lay on us your warmth and light."

She stirred. "I couldn't do anything without your music."

He squeezed her hand. "My starling died," he said. "Did I tell you? I was unaccountably broken up about it. I wrote him a funerary poem. I'll send it to you. Such a winter this is — our poor baby, you know." He looked toward the window, unblinking, and then shook his head. "I'm glad to be going to Prague. The air's no warmer in Prague, but I think the people are."

"And then you'll come to London," she said. She was crying again.

He sat up and made a show of kissing the tears away. "I had an idea," he said, "that I could write an aria for your farewell concert. I have just the text. A rondo I set for my *Idomeneo* last year."

She had not been to that concert, a private revival of his Munich opera. "A proper rondo?" she asked. She took his cue and tried to perk up, tried not to think how long he would be gone; how long it would be, after he came back, before she saw him again.

"Yes, exactly," he said. He squeezed her hand. "A proper rondo. The rondo I didn't give you in *Figaro.* In E-flat. I mean to write a piano part for myself, just like in one of my concertos. Only you'll be singing along with me, and I with you, the pair of us, with the orchestra. It will be a duet. The grandest kind of parting anyone has heard."

"What's the text?"

"Don't fear, my love, for you my heart will always be faithful." He gave her a rueful look and pulled her to him. "That sort of thing. It's by Varesco. He's no Da Ponte, but it will suit perfectly. You'll be telling the people of Vienna you're not abandoning us; that you'll always hold us first in your heart; that you'll come back, etcetera."

She looked at him cheerfully, so he would feel better. "And you'll play with the orchestra?"

"Yes," he said, caressing her knee. "It will be for myself and you."

Then they had to break apart, because Lidia came in to light the room. She rattled at the door before she entered, to give them time.

"Kind lady," said Mozart to Lidia, "you come at just the right moment. We were about to play a game of backgammon and can hardly see the dice."

"Indeed," Lidia observed, "the sun has nearly set."

"So it has." Quickly he arranged the backgammon pieces, a familiar expression of gaiety and interest on his face, as though the black-and-red disks were the most engrossing collection of objects he had seen in his life. "Do you know it's been years since I played? But I remember all the rules.

I used to love hearing the thunk and clack of the men as you run them around the board."

"Oh, Lidia," Anna asked her, as if in passing, as the girl was leaving. "Will you see we're not disturbed? We shan't need anything else. No wine."

"Yes, Anna."

They finished the game and she beat him handily. "Ah," he said. "You're beautiful triumphant. Look at those black eyes trying to contain themselves — those hot cheeks. You're like that when you've been singing something marvelous. On my lap. In your underclothes."

"I hate to lose. You made silly mistakes."

"I left too many blots. Next time I'll do better. For now I rejoice in my losing, if it gives Mademoiselle Storace such eyes."

"I'm sorry," she said, laughing. "I should be more gracious."

They were silent a while. Then he said, "It's late," and rose. And there it was: their parting. "Constanze will think I've been taken by highwaymen."

"Oh, stay," Anna whispered, rising, too. "Please don't go yet. Stay a little longer."

"A little longer," he murmured. He rested his chin on her shoulder, as if willing his body to dissolve there.

"She knows you're here. She'll think we're practicing our music."

"We've no music to practice. She knows that very well."

Anna pulled back, frowning and crying. Mozart watched her without speaking. She slipped off her shoes. She took off her stockings and put them down her bodice. Then she stood there trembling.

"Give me back my boots," she whispered, in German. "Please. Please, Wolfgang."

He lifted his hand and traced the line of her cheek with such tenderness she thought it would kill her. "Never," he said. "Never in all my life. You'll never have them."

"Give them back," she whispered, weeping. She let her head turn with the motion of his fingers. He kissed her neck where it met the jaw.

"Never, Anna."

"And your debt to me," she sobbed, rubbing her nose into his shirt, holding his slender, breathing, dearest back. "The kisses —"

"What debt?" he whispered. "What kisses?"

She tried to laugh, to pretend that none of it mattered, but all that came out were unrelenting tears. "Sing for me, Anna, and I will kiss your hands a hundred thousand times."

"Oh," he murmured. He bent his head and kissed her collarbone, kissed the space between her breasts. "Forgive me," he whispered. "I'd forgotten. There's two already. There's three. And I love you. I love you."

THE YOUNG LORD

"My German's wretched," said Stephen. He helped Anna up the stairs. It was January and they were going to a party at the Thuns'. The Mozarts were in Prague. "It's embarrassing. You'll have to tell me if I make a faux-pas."

Stephen was smiling and at ease. His new opera in Vienna had been a success, redeemed him completely, and he was looking forward to going back to London. He planned to write English operettas and pastiches, in the mode of Italian opera buffa.

Inside, the countess with all her graciousness was wearing the bracelet she had received as a favor from Anna's birthday party last year. "I have someone here who especially wants to meet you, my dear," she said to Anna.

The gentleman pushed himself forward. "Oh," Anna exclaimed. "Lord Barnard."

"Miss Storace remembers my name," the

young man said in a voice of low rapture, closing his eyes.

"Now, Lord Barnard," Anna said lightly, glancing at their hostess. "You mustn't speak English like that in mixed company. If you insist on being so rude, you and Stephen may retire to a corner and talk between yourselves."

The young man shook his head and said in rather broken German that he would speak any language to stay by Miss Storace's side.

"Oh, dear," Anna said into the countess's ear. "Either he doesn't know what he's saying or he's a fool."

The countess smiled genially at the young gentleman. "Yes," she said in a low voice, "but there is a place for puppies, if they have wealth."

Barnard was an English lord of twenty-three on his first European tour. His hair was russet gold, his eyes wide and watery. He had a booming voice and would not have made a bad singer, if he'd had more art and less fortune. He was handsome in the rich, well-fed way of his class. Lord Barnard got what he wanted. His youth merely added to his confidence. And he was besotted with Anna.

The spell had been cast last May. He had

come to the opening of *Figaro,* had heard Anna sing, with such exquisite sensuality, *"Deh, vieni."* Although Barnard possessed little Italian, he had a romantic soul, and he had fallen deeply in love with Anna that night. She had been singing to him, he felt. The sense of recognition was no trick of drunkenness or fancy. She was his to worship in whatever capacity she would let him. He was young, clever, and rich. He did not doubt that these charms would prevail.

Anna that night had not been in any mood to receive him, so he had attended every subsequent performance until she had. Then he had left Vienna to continue on his European tour. He had returned yesterday evening.

"I meant to spend more days in Rome," he said, "but something pulled me back to Vienna." He gazed at her and began again speaking in English: so frail was his German. "You, mademoiselle, if I may be so bold, called me to this place, this city exquisite in my memory, not for its spires and vistas but for something — someone — who shall, when she leaves it, render the poor city drab and dark. For a pair of eyes, mademoiselle, as rich and promising as velvet. For lips, cheeks, as soft and pink as new roses. For a voice that has made me wish to renounce my place in heaven."

"Dear Lord Barnard," she said laughingly in German, "you have many words and nothing to put them in. That must be very hard." She took Stephen's arm and left him.

But after that meeting he called on her nearly every day. Sometimes she was not at home. On those occasions he left behind some token of his presence, a flower, a fine piece of ribbon, a lace fan, a jar of perfumed ointment. Now and then there might be a curiosity from the Orient, a hair ornament of wrought ivory, exotic earrings, silk.

"He thinks I can be bought," Anna observed to Lidia.

"Then he's a fool," Lidia said. Anna tossed the earrings into a drawer.

A Proper Rondo

A package arrived from Prague with the aria Mozart had written for her farewell concert. There was a letter, as well. She read it in the dining room over her breakfast. Morning frost sparked at the windows. It was now the end of January. Mozart had been gone a month. He would mark his thirty-first birthday in Prague. He apologized for his handwriting and his spelling. They were having a tremendous success. He could not describe his satisfaction. He was certain she would like the aria and he longed to hear her voice again. The Prague Susanna was nothing compared to Anna. She need not be envious. The Prague Susanna was as stiff as a board. He kept saying to everyone, if only they could hear Mademoiselle Storace sing it, *then* he'd be content, *then* he'd know his opera was being shown to its best.

The aria he'd sent her was in his own hand, a clean copy that yet gave an impression of haste. He had a strong, careless script. Across the top he'd written, *für Mlle Storace und mich* — "for Mademoiselle Storace and myself."

"The famous rondo?" Stephen asked. He snapped the package from Anna's hands and went into the music room and sat at the piano. She scrambled after him but it was too late; he was already playing it.

"What does he say?" he asked.

"Hm?"

He glanced at her. "In that long letter you read so quickly and blushingly."

The music distracted her. Stephen, sight-reading, still half asleep, played feebly and inaccurately and yet it was beautiful, it was perfect.

"I didn't blush," she said. "I was warm from my coffee."

Stephen laughed. "You were not. He was teasing you about something, the devil." He leaned his chin in his hand, searching the manuscript. "This is a good piece. I don't do it justice. One can tell he wrote the piano part with himself in mind."

Anna moved to lie on the carpet, on her stomach, her cheek on her arm and her legs crossed at the ankles. Stephen cast her a dubious look and started to play again. "Are you quite all right?" he asked. She didn't answer. He continued to play. She heard the click of the instrument's mechanism and felt the light tap of his foot against the floorboards. There were dog hairs on the carpet, brown and white. The air down here was cooler. She felt her chest pressing against the floor, her heart beating into it. When she closed her eyes she could hear one of the maids in the next room singing a tune from *A Rare Thing.* Stephen fumbled and hummed along with Mozart's aria. Whenever he came to a particularly interesting or difficult passage he played it over slowly, breaking it into segments, talking to himself. Anna, listening, breathed against the floor. One of the dogs ventured to join her and she scratched its belly. When Stephen finally paused, she got up and went to the sideboard in the dining room to get more coffee.

"A proper rondo," she called back, forcing herself to be light, to smile.

"Just as he promised," said Stephen.

Lidia came in to announce Lord Barnard and Michael Kelly.

"So early?" Anna asked. She drew her morning gown around her. "Doesn't Lord B realize I'm never at home before noon?"

Lidia glanced at Stephen and smiled. "It's past noon."

Anna looked at the clock in surprise. "So it is. Well, they're friends. Show them in, then, Lidia."

Barnard's hair was dressed in a kind of puff and wave that ill became him but gave the impression that great care and expense had gone into its formation. As he entered the room he held a silver snuffbox to his nose and discreetly sniffed. Michael Kelly came behind him, jolly and red-faced, in his customary finery, and kissed Anna thrice on the cheeks. "Still in morning clothes?"

"And yet here you are," said Anna. Lord Barnard brushed her knuckles with his soft lips.

"You *should* be dressed," Michael said. "It's nearly one."

Mrs. Storace entered the room and greeted the visitors. "Not dressed?"

"I was finishing my breakfast."

"Look, Mama," said Stephen. "We've gotten a package from Mozart — the aria for Anna's farewell concert."

"Have you? How pleasant," Mrs. Storace said. She smoothed her apron. "And then we return to London."

"Let's hear this aria, then," said Michael. "Let's hear the good-bye."

"It's not a good-bye," said Anna. "It's a farewell."

382

Barnard lit up. "Dear Miss Storace, do sing for us. There's nothing I like half so well as your singing, and you know how much I admire the music of Wolfgang Mozart."

She felt herself grow dizzy. "I can't," she said. "I've not sung yet today."

"Just a few bars," Barnard pleaded. His hair bobbed and he spread his arms. "Just to give us the gist of the thing, as your friends."

"I shan't," Anna said, "give you the gist of anything." She sat by her mother. "I've had quite enough of all of you. Coming so early and treating me like someone to do tricks for you."

"I'll sing it, Barnard," Michael said.

"You won't," cried Anna.

Michael looked at her in delicate puzzlement. "Come, dear, there's no harm done, is there? You can spare your voice, and Barnard here can hear the tune. We're all friends."

"I must say, Kelly, yours is not the voice of my dreams," said Barnard.

"Sir, I take no offense. You know only how to speak your mind. I may submit, however, that you've only heard me sing in comic melody, when I was distorting my voice for effect." Michael went to Stephen, who was leafing through the manuscript. "My friend, shall we make a run of it?"

"We can try," said Stephen doubtfully, "but I'm afraid I'll have to leave out a few notes here and there. He wrote it for himself, you know."

"Michael," Anna said softly. "Please."

"We would all be grateful to hear you," said Mrs. Storace to Michael. "You always had such a lovely Irish tenor voice."

"I thank you, madam."

Stephen could barely play the solo lines, unpracticed as he was, but Michael read well and did himself credit. They jerked and careened, joked with themselves, remarked in passing about the plangency of this and the felicity of that. But Anna was quiet. She did not entertain Lord Barnard's flirtations, nor smile at Michael's jests. The aria was beautiful. It was beautiful and yet it was not sad. Rather it was a kind of rejoicing. *Do not fear, my love: I will never leave you, I will always be yours.*

Für Mlle Storace und mich.

ZOROASTRO

At last Mozart returned to the city. She had counted the days. She was nervous to see him again and yet he blanketed all her idle thoughts with soft contentment. Nothing was so right and good as to hold him in her mind and heart like a jewel. There he sat, all her waking and sleeping. She would wake before dawn and lie with her eyes closed in the warm dark, listening to the clock chime, holding the memory of him in her heart until it almost hurt. When she could no longer pretend to be asleep she would push back the bed-clothes and watch the dawn spill across the city, violet and gray, whispering, *I love you, I love you, I love you.*

She saw him first at the Countess Thun's Carnival party. All of Vienna was there. There was a press of people in all of the rooms, everyone masked, dancing, shouting, and singing. Anna recognized Mozart's back, its straightness, the slightness of his shoulders. He was dressed as Zoroastro, and passed out amusing philosophical riddles. Her own mask was from her days in Venice, golden, with a star the corner of the eye. Her gown was new, black and red.

She touched his shoulder. "Excuse me, sir," she said in English. "I've no one to dance with."

Beneath his feathered turban his eyes brightened. He bowed, the feathers bobbing and waving, and led her to the hall with the dancing. His thumb pressed into the top of her hand, circled there; pressed and circled again. For the whole dance there were only their hands, touching and releasing, first playfully and then with enough strength to cause a little ache, a brief stab; and saying, thus, with the only touch and pressure allowed them, and for which none there could fault them, how greatly, how ardently, they esteemed and admired each other.

THE TOPIARIES

How beautiful and terrible it was to be in the Mozart home again, to greet the lady of the house and the sturdy little boy who had grown so big and tall. Whatever Anna looked at, she would be leaving. This place, where she had been so happy, in such secrecy, which was hers and not hers, she would never see again. It became necessary to breathe more deeply, that she might remember everything as clearly as possible. She had left too many places carelessly.

The Mozarts' rooms were warmer than Anna's — tidier, brighter; aromatic of baking, wood smoke, and herbs; fuller of noises and of people. A home to be lived in and loved, a home too much for their means but theirs in every way save that. Anna and Constanze sat in the large main room where Mozart sometimes gave his chamber concerts. The chairs were jumbled and there were papers everywhere. A basket of darning rested by the fireplace and Karl's toys were scattered across the floor. The coffee Constanze Mozart brought Anna was spiced with cinnamon. She apologized for the disorder of the rooms, a consequence of their late arrival from Prague, she said, and herself and her servants being such flibbertigibbets. She kissed Anna on the cheeks. The little boy resembled her. He kept trotting over to Anna and handing her objects to admire: a spoon, a button, a piece of red ribbon.

"Thank you," Anna said to him, over and over. She didn't know how to behave with children. Constanze Mozart scooped him into her arms and hung him upside-down and he whooped in delight. When she put him down he fetched a rattle from the floor to give to Anna. She shook it for him and he took it back, smiling, as if she'd done a great trick.

Mozart was out, giving a lesson, but expected back soon. He had suggested they meet at his house to rehearse the farewell aria, because his own piano was there, and it had independent pedals, built for him specially by Anton Walter, the great piano maker.

Constanze Mozart had square hands, which she was always folding together as though she wished in that way to make them look more elegant. "My husband will miss you when you're gone," she said. "It's so difficult to find good singers. Do you know what I mean? He is so particular. That is, he will write for anyone, as required, but he would prefer to write for someone like you. You are so musical. It is good of you to include him in your concert."

The conversation dwindled. Anna smiled at the little boy and Constanze got up to straighten the chairs. Anna asked if she could help. Constanze politely declined. There seemed nothing to say.

Mozart was convinced that Constanze did not know.

At last they heard him in the foyer.

"Is Mademoiselle Storace there?" he called. "I've just run into my sister-in-law, she'd like to hear our aria. She says you invited her to tea, Constanze."

"Don't shout from the other room, my love," said Constanze, going to the door.

"Is she here?" he bellowed.

"Yes, sitting patiently and listening to all my prating."

Mozart bounded in, a high color in his face, and kissed his wife and child. His hair stood out and his shoes were damp around the toes. Anna's heart constricted. "Didn't

389

you find your slippers in the hall?" Constanze asked, frowning, and went to fetch them and bring little Karl to his nurse.

Anna rose. Mozart stopped short before her. "You're here," he said. He hesitated and studied her. "I've been looking forward to this all morning."

"As have I," said Aloysia Lange, rustling forward to greet Anna. "How good it is to see you. How do you do. We're all so broken up about your leaving us. It is really too bad. Do you much mind me listening? I was coming to visit my sister and I would so much love to hear you. You're so gracious, my dear. What a lovely frock this is! Just like a rose. How I wish I had your youth. My family is quite well, I thank you, the children in good health, by God's grace. How pretty you are. Isn't she pretty, brother? It must be months since I've seen you. Constanze, isn't Fräulein Storace looking well? How we shall miss her."

"We hope she'll not be parted from us for long," said Constanze, coming back into the room. She helped her husband with his slippers.

Anna stood smiling. He was here. Her friend. She must remind herself to breathe. The jewel in her heart had dropped to her belly and become grotesque and leaden. To smile, to speak a nicety, meant dragging the weight through a current of water, neck-deep. There was only the press of water and numbing cold. She had trouble attending to what was said and yet every instant was like a drop of dew on her skin, finely delineated. She was conscious of herself in the room, and of Mozart's every gesture. Here he was, in plain daylight, with his wife and his wife's sister. She recognized him — what he was, how dear and how right — with a certainty so serene and assured it would not be undermined. But she could not go to him. She was forbidden. She felt the heaviness, the water coming over her chin, the cold winter light reminding her that everything was comical, petty, implacable.

They all crowded into Mozart's music room. The two sisters, one prettier, the other happier, sat side by side at the far end, their skirts overlapping and their hands entwined.

But Anna could not mind the sisters watching over them. She would have undergone many more discomforts for the exhilaration of singing with him again. The aria brought her joy, just as he had intended. There could be no greater gift. She could not help, once they'd gone through it, swinging to him with such open delight that it turned to laughter.

"You like it?" he said, pleased.

She draped herself across his instrument, her head on her arm, as if swooning there. "I adore it."

He smiled. "Don't break anything."

"I'm very gentle," she murmured.

"Is she all right?" Constanze asked. She and Aloysia were about eight feet away.

"I think my brother has made his favorite soprano faint," Aloysia said. "She'll recover in a moment if she's not too far gone."

"Why, you've made all three of us giddy, my love," said Constanze. "You don't know your powers."

Anna drew herself up. "You do," she said to Mozart. "You know very well."

He shrugged, proud. "It's a proper rondo."

"As promised."

"Anything for you," he said in Italian. She gave him a sharp look.

"I think they're talking about us," observed Aloysia to Constanze.

"They're talking about the music."

"I wish he'd write music like that for me."

"He did — don't you remember?"

"Not like that, sister," said Aloysia.

"Well, you're not having a farewell concert."

"Perhaps I should."

"But where would you go away to?" asked Constanze blankly.

Aloysia snorted and dabbed at her nose with a handkerchief. "Why, nowhere. But that's the point. My brother doesn't want Mademoiselle Storace going away, so he writes her this. He knows I will never go anywhere, so he writes me nothing."

"Hush. We'll disturb them."

Anna turned to the ladies and bowed graciously. "I'm so sorry. Herr Mozart's playing overpowers me."

"As it does us all," Aloysia said. "As it has done ever."

"It's beautiful, Wolfgang," Constanze said.

"And the text," added Aloysia, "is so affecting. I understood almost every word. Eternal faith, and so on. Even though they are parting she will always be loyal to him. The *amato bene.* The 'beloved,' Constanze. You understand? And of course she means that *we* are her beloved ones, all we of Vienna. There will not be a dry eye in the house, as they say."

"Surely not mine," said Anna. "I'll be happy if I can only make it through to the end without weeping."

"Oh, you shall manage," Aloysia said tartly. "You always do."

Anna dropped her eyes.

Mozart laughed, uneasy. "Three of my favorite ladies all in the same room, and all of them flattering me. I'll get a big head."

"Too late for that," said Aloysia.

"If only my sister were here," Mozart said. "Then there'd be four of you."

"What would she say?" asked Anna.

"She might want to play it herself."

"Why, then I don't want her here."

He gave her a warm look. "You would, if you heard her. She's a better player than I am."

"I can't imagine any better than you," she said.

"So naive," exclaimed Aloysia. "La, madame! You cannot find your way to my brother's heart by praising his playing. He's been praised for his playing since he was no older than Karl."

"How may I do it, then?" asked Anna lightly.

"By stealth and cunning," Aloysia said. "Like my sister did."

"Aloysia," Constanze exclaimed. "You'll hurt my feelings."

"Oh, my dear, you know I was only teasing. It wasn't stealth but your sweet, gentle nature, your simplicity; your grace. Let that be a lesson to you, Mademoiselle Storace."

"Oh, yes," said Anna with a smiling glance

at both sisters. "Whenever I see Madame Mozart I wish I could be more like her."

"But we can only be ourselves," said Aloysia. "That is our great tragedy." She looked at her sister and dabbed her nose.

The two women observed the rest of the rehearsal as though sitting judgment on it. The next time Anna and Mozart rehearsed this, it would be with the orchestra.

They would not let her be alone with him. She would never again be alone with him.

Still the ladies in their observance insisted that Anna and Mozart rehearse just as they would have done without anyone watching. The ladies in their observance would be but flies on the wall, making not a peep or motion, simply absorbing the charming union of the famous soprano and her chosen composer. After the first flurry of compliments they remained silent and impenetrable as seated topiary trees, unmoving except for a slight listing of their bodies, a shivering in the still air of their lace and bows.

But Anna and Mozart were yet able to enclose themselves in a private dialogue — a few soft words, here and there, in Italian, a language neither sister knew well, while discussing their music. They said nothing of any great matter, but it was a nothing for themselves alone.

"A little slower here, I think."

"Here I imagined you as a soldier, a revolutionary."

"Man or woman?"

"Man. But only for these bars and you mustn't tell the emperor."

"Welcoming my death."

"Yes — a hero."

"And this, here, must be a great change."

"That is love."

Their eyes touched and touched again, while the topiaries watched and shivered.

"You see? Here we faint and there we faint doubly."

"Exquisite — exquisite . . ."

"We can do more with this climax, mademoiselle."

"How do you find such strength in your left hand?"

"Practice."

"Again, again."

"And you see this will go over the orchestra."

"I love this part," she said. "Where we faint."

He laughed. "You're blushing to say it."

"That's how you may tell it's truth."

"Could I ever write you less?"

"Hush, my dear one."

"The world may hear. Could I write less for you, Anna?"

"Not my Christian name. The world may not hear you say that."

"And yet you call me dear."

"No, that was the music." She shook her head. "Let me sing that part again. The part where I faint and you carry me up."

"It should be more beautiful. I'll improvise around you."

"Inside me, rather."

"How may I do that?" he murmured.

She laughed, remembering his touch, which she could have no more. He said, "Sing now — sing and I'll find you."

As Anna was leaving, Constanze grasped her hands and said, "You are so dear, mademoiselle, and good to us. I tried to be as quiet as a mouse. The concert will bring you and my husband much glory."

Caught in Constanze Mozart's regard, held so firmly in her strong, square hands, Anna was nearly deprived of speech. Here, again, was the ordinariness, the truth, the lead in her belly.

"We'll see each other again," Constanze said. "Don't be sad. There's no need to be sad."

■ ■ ■ ■

Lord Barnard opened the door in his dressing gown, his fine wheat-colored hair hanging around his shoulders. It was four o'clock in the afternoon. "My dear Miss Storace," he exclaimed, "you catch me in *dishabillé.*"

"Did I wake you?" Anna asked. She couldn't smile. She had been almost home from the Mozarts' when she had directed the driver to come here instead. She gathered her skirts and entered his small parlor, which was sparsely furnished and rather chilly, testifying to his transience and carelessness. Through the door she could see his rumpled bed. The street on which he lived received poor light and the room faced north. It was already dark. He had lit no candles. There was a sour, fermented smell.

With a yawning sigh he fell into a chair. Anna removed her hat and gloves and set them on top of her cloak.

"I was dancing until dawn," Barnard said. "And beyond the dawn." He lifted a foot. "See my blisters? Heaven's judgment on me. I had to toss my shoes and dance in my stockings. They say a rabble of Englishmen smashed all the lampposts in the Graben-

398

strasse, but I'd nothing to do with it, I'm not even English. I was dancing the whole time." He laid his head back and shut his eyes.

Anna stood in the middle of the room without speaking, in the encroaching dark.

Finally she turned, as if to leave. He opened his eyes and gave a long sigh, and in the next moment was on his feet, gathering her into his arms. A tall man. She could lean her cheek against his chest and hear his heart beating there.

"My little dove," he said languidly. John Fisher had called her that. His fingers touched the back of her neck. "To what do I owe this honor?"

She rested against him. He held her effortlessly. The smell had gone. "Loneliness," she said at last. She tried to laugh. But she felt so sad.

"Sweet Miss Storace," he said. "You of all ladies should never be lonely."

"I only have an hour."

"All happiness is mine."

THE GREAT LEVELER

Lord Barnard, Henry, the future Earl of Darlington, with his big smile and his easy hands, was Anna's near constant companion during her last week in Vienna. He seemed to look on her as a kind of prize, beneficial to his pride and reputation. She, having felt out of her mind for some weeks now, regarded the affair as a final step into dissolution that might yet get her through the days and nights. Embracing Barnard — his drinking, his lust — she embraced the truth. She dropped the weight of longing and loneliness and let herself drift heedlessly down the stream. This was plain daylight, this was her life as she had always been accused of living it. A loose life, a life befitting her wealth and her profession. If she could not be happy yet she could seek comfort, in whatever form or person it might appear. Vienna had enjoyed her and in this last week she would enjoy Vienna.

She saw Mozart only once, at the dress rehearsal for her concert. They were surrounded by people. Stephen talked to him for a long time about the wonders of London. She had warned Stephen on pain of death not to say anything about Lord Barnard.

She wanted to stay awake every minute, to feel everything. But of course that was impossible. Most of the time with Barnard she spent sleeping, as heavily as she had ever slept, and as dreamlessly, and what a comfort it was. This word she repeated to herself — *comfort.* She abandoned everything else.

A few nights before her departure, Anna went with Barnard, Stephen, and Lidia to a masked ball at the Redoute. She danced early into the morning and had scarcely time to catch her breath or drink from the clear, sparkling cider laid out in silver punch bowls along the edges of the dance floor. The hall glowed warmly with candles and the motion of turning skirts and gliding feet and gently smiling faces. The heat of their bodies on this February evening lent to the party feelings of youth and joy. There was nothing the Viennese loved better than dancing. It was good to move in patterns spontaneous and orderly, to be passed from hand to hand by gracious partners, to think nothing of the future or past. Anna's Carnival mask could not disguise her accent or her smile, but her partners were kind enough to make nothing of her fame — except, perhaps, by expressing a whispered word of regret at her parting. She felt she had done little to deserve that regret, but she let herself be touched tonight by their graceful goodwill.

Her limbs were loose and free from dancing. The band of string players in the small balcony played unflaggingly, and since the music did not tire, neither did her feet. Her brother was in a corner drinking with some of the Englishmen who had been here all week. He had no head for drink. Lidia did not engage in the dancing; she felt herself too tall and clumsy, and stayed in the other room playing whist with old gentlemen and dowagers. Anna's feet skipped and turned as if of their own accord and she was not thirsty, though she had barely sipped any cider, and as she turned from hand to hand she could not think of Mozart, nor even of Barnard, though now she was dancing with him again. In his red mask with the big beak, Barnard did not look himself, and thus was more tolerable. But now, suddenly, a drunk officer was pushing into their group, and saying that Anna had promised this dance to *him,* though she had no memory of such a promise. He tried to take her in his arms. In her shock her feet fell out of rhythm and she went hurtling to the ground.

Every spell was broken. She was thirsty and tired. Her mask had fallen askew. And she knew, in her bones, that if she left Vienna she would lose her dearest friend.

To Stephen, drunk in the corner, it looked as if his sister had been struck by the officer. He let out a yell and forced himself through the ballroom and began striking the officer wildly. He made the officer's nose bleed. There was an uproar. The officer was a notable gentleman and everyone attested he had not struck the lady. In a matter of moments Stephen was subdued, arrested, and ordered taken to jail.

"He can't go," Anna protested. "We're leaving in two days."

But it was no use. Stephen blew his sister a kiss and shuffled off in the arms of his captors singing "Rule Britannia." The offended officer retired to the next room with the whist tables, a handkerchief pressed to his nose, while Lidia glowered at him from the doorway. After a moment of hushed hesitation, the dancers resumed their pleasure.

Barnard was loath to go but Anna made him take her and Lidia to the jail in his carriage. Lidia was planning to come with them to London; she had been practicing her English with Stephen and was distressed at his arrest. She kept saying that if she had been there with Anna she could have stopped him.

Day was breaking. Fog hung on the ground and dimmed the streetlamps; the night had turned from black to purplish blue. To their left, the river made its lapping murmur, and somewhere a bird began to sing. The air was damp and almost warm. Spring was coming, spring in Vienna. Last year she had sung in Mozart's *Figaro;* this year she would be in Paris. The air was hushed. Even the citizens beginning their day's work seemed turned inward, their footsteps gentler than they would have been in noon daylight.

Lidia got out first and hurried directly into the prison. When Anna's foot touched the damp cobbles, she slipped, and Barnard had to catch her elbow. The slickness of the stone and the lurch in her belly cast a kind of sobriety over her. She stood without moving.

"Aren't you coming?" Barnard asked, a note of irritation in his voice. "Are you quite fine?"

She held his elbow, blinking quickly, not moving her head but casting her eyes toward the river. The sun was rising by remarkable degrees. A moment ago it had been night. Now it was almost day. There could be no denying it was almost day. Here she stood with her companion outside a jail. The horses snorted and jingled their traces. The air was still damp. Spring was coming to Vienna. Already the day was lighter. Already it was bringing her closer to that thing she had been denying, all these days and nights with Barnard and the rest. She had thought she was embracing truth but she'd only been cloaking herself more firmly against it. There was a reason she was not usually out of doors at this hour of the morning. Unrelenting light — it came so quickly — it changed the world as it had always done. She stood gazing to one side, feeling her quick, shallow breaths, the hand at her elbow.

"Two days, Henry," she said. "I have two days."

"Oh, I should daresay you have a good many more days than that. Look, my dear, if you don't want to go in —"

405

She shook her head. "I do."

They found Stephen curled on a pallet in the corner of a cell. Lidia was already there, talking to him in a low voice. He held her hand through the bars. It seemed they liked each other. They had conspired together during Anna's illness; they sometimes went for walks. One afternoon Anna had happened upon them playing music in the drawing room and had withdrawn before they could notice her.

In his rumpled formal garments Stephen looked the picture of a dissolute young nobleman, although he was nothing of the kind. He seemed to have been dozing. Barnard hung back with a handkerchief to his nose. Anna knelt beside Lidia.

"You should be in bed," he said in Italian. "My dear lady Lidia, how could you let your mistress come to such a place as this?"

"I would have come alone but she wouldn't hear of it."

"Not alone!" He cradled his forehead in his hand. "Neither of you should be here. This is no place for ladies."

"We have Lord Barnard to protect us," said Anna.

He peered at Barnard and switched to English. "If I had any paper I could sketch my companions here. See how that man hunches on his rolled-up cloak against the dove-colored wall? It should make for a pretty picture. Do you remember how I used to draw circles in the ground as a trick?" He withdrew his hand from Lidia's. "See, I will draw one now. Come take a look at this, Barnard. Is it not a pretty circle?"

"Indeed, my good man, the best circle I ever have seen drawn in the muck of a prison floor."

"The muck of life, Barnard. I always said I wanted to see the inside of a Viennese cell before I died. Or if I didn't say it, I should have. I reckon they wanted to give me a proper dispatch. Or perhaps this is their way of trying to keep me here. Well may they try — I shan't waver."

His eyes landing on Anna, his expression altered and he leaned forward. "Are you quite all right, sister? You look as though you've broken your voice again. You haven't, have you? You're not ill? The concert on Friday must go on — it will raise thousands of florins if we're lucky. They'll let me out in a day or two. I shan't miss it."

Anna smiled. "You poor fool, striking an officer."

"Lord," he groaned, "what a bastard. With his spurred boots." He rested his head on the wall. "I thought he'd hurt you. I can't stand the thought of you being hurt, Anna."

"It was dashing," she said. "It was brave. Wasn't it, Lidia?"

"No," said Lidia, in Italian, looking at Stephen sternly. "It was foolish."

He shrugged. "Now here I am," he said, also in Italian, "to meditate upon the muck."

"What have you discovered?" Lidia asked.

He laughed and rubbed his eyes. "It's not so bad. It's not so different being in chains than out where you are. I'm the same man, am I not? With the same heart, the same lungs? And yet how awful to see these bars between us, denying me from you, from all the world. For the bars are always there, are they not? It's only a question of awareness." He ran his fingers along them. "It's music takes them down, music the great leveler, like death." He squinted at his sister and said in English, "See that I get out of here soon, won't you? Funny how quickly one feels oneself becoming maddened."

"It's the wine," she said soothingly. "And you haven't slept."

"And you," he said to Lidia in Italian, "calling me a fool. You'd have struck the bastard, too."

Lidia lifted her chin. "Yes."

"Made his nose bleed."

"Of course."

He laughed. "Good. Let me try to sleep. Good-bye, sister. Good-bye, Barnard."

"Your brother needs a wife and a profession," said Barnard as they were leaving. "You're all he has, is what I mean, and that's a damned shame."

Anna looked away. "And he's all I have." She didn't want to be here, with this strange man. Here was not where she belonged.

"No," Barnard said, and gave her a probing kiss. "Not you. You have everything you desire."

"Do you like my brother, Lidia?" Anna asked later, when they were alone.

Lidia was silent a moment. "Of course. He's everything a man should be."

Anna laughed. "I always thought you loved me."

Lidia smiled placidly and hugged Anna around the shoulders. Her face was smooth and warm as polished wood. "I do. You are both everything you should be."

AMATO BENE

The day of Anna's benefit concert, and farewell to Vienna, had all the feeling of a grand public ceremony — a state wedding, coronation, or funeral — and all for her. One could not find a ticket for love or money. She was more beloved, now that she was leaving, than she had ever been. The attention and gratitude of an entire population fell upon her.

Stephen had been released in time for their departure and after an urgent bath was napping off his hardship on the third floor. Anna had told Barnard she did not wish to see him before this evening. After that she must see him, because they were traveling together. He had finished his European tour and was called back to England. There was no sense in traveling without Barnard, much as it was distasteful to her now. Everything was planned. Michael would go with them, too, to visit his family in Ireland. But Anna

410

could not think of Barnard or Michael or anything but the concert. She would be singing her most popular songs, a few duets, and the aria with Mozart. It would be a retrospective of all she had been to Vienna.

When it was time for the performance her legs weakened and her hands developed a faint tremor. She smoothed them on her skirt and did not resist. The only way to confront such fear was to release resistance entirely; accept her frailty, all the terrors and disasters her imagination could conjure; accept them by releasing her bonds of defense; by allowing herself to collapse into them and not run away. Then her knees became strong and firm. Then her lungs opened and let in the good air, the air that sustained life and sound, and her quarreling thoughts were quieted.

The concert went well. More than well. Then, at last, it was time for the final aria, Mozart's aria, their farewell.

She came off stage and found him waiting in the dark of the wings. He wore his red coat. The collar brushed his jaw. Light from the stage slightly struck his nose and cheek. She embraced him.

"Hello," he said quietly. "Are you ready?"

The orchestra was tuning. His piano waited in their midst, at the front of the stage, the lid removed. He would lead them from his seat.

"Not in the least," she said. She smiled bravely. "Once we begin it will be over."

He caressed her shoulder. "If we don't begin we'll have nothing to remember."

"What if I don't want to remember?"

He tightened his arms around her and put his lips to her ear. "Then you're a stranger to me."

She whispered, "It will go too quickly."

"No, Anna. As slowly as we wish."

"My wish is too great — we'll be dead by the end of it."

"We can't die. There is no end."

The orchestra was ready. It rustled and waited. The audience waited and murmured.

In the wings of the Burgtheater Mozart and Anna held each other. "Now," he whispered. "Now we begin."

Non temer, amato bene; per te sempre il cor sará. "Don't fear, greatly beloved; for you, always, my heart will remain." She wanted to laugh, singing it, for it was no more an aria than the last he'd written her — it was a duet, a concerto, an intimate meeting place for themselves alone. He had created for himself an obbligato part so entwined

412

with her voice that it almost seemed it *was* her voice, that she was spilling into the air from his fingers, all silver and light, and dissolving again in the sweet curl of his ear. They teased and celebrated each other. They spun their hopes into a golden ball and tossed it hand to hand. The notes of the piano tickled her neck and lapped at her toes. Her voice, as he had written it, became a bed for him to lie on, as tender as new moss, and the stream was theirs, as well, and the bright cheerful buttercups, and the air filled with bees and warm fragrance. This was play. This, forever, was the play of their life. When it was over, in the piercing space between the music and the applause, she heard him whisper, "Brava."

There was not time to recover. They must go to the reception in the great, mirrored hall, with the patrons and colleagues and dignitaries; must smile and converse with everyone as though nothing had changed. In an hour or two Anna would leave Vienna. Everything was packed and waiting. They would drive through the night to reach Salzburg by morning.

Benucci kissed her and promised to visit her in London. He had always wanted to go to London. Da Ponte said he wanted to visit her as well. Aloysia Lange embraced Anna and said it had been quite a pretty concert and they would be so sorry to see her go. Constanze said nothing. Dorotea and Luisa burst into tears. Mandini, stern-faced, kissed her on the cheeks five times and told her with a firm shake of her shoulders that she should not forget them.

The Count and Countess Thun had gifts, gold and jewels. The emperor, with an air of long-suffering resentment, offered a box of chocolate and some hundreds of florins. He had circles under his eyes and his breath was bad. Earlier in the week he had given Anna a letter to take to his sister, Marie Antoinette, whose country was tottering on the brink of bankruptcy.

Anna was so surrounded by well-wishers that she could say nothing of meaning nor let slip from her tired cheeks the smile of graciousness and gratitude that held there as if under a siege of trivial beneficence. Mozart was entertaining his own crowd, as if she were not there. She could not go to him, nor could he come to her; there was too much between them. She caught his eyes, across the room, and he smiled and brought his fingers to his lips. But at that moment Lord Barnard was upon her. "The carriages are ready," he said. "If we don't go now we'll never make it."

Mozart and his wife were with Michael and her brother. "Time to go?" asked Stephen.

She could not breathe. It was happening too quickly. "Lord Barnard says so."

"Well," said Stephen. "Isn't this awful."

Mozart gave a short laugh. The mirrors shone about them.

"It was so moving," Constanze said. "Truly I think all of us shed a tear. That rondo theme, Wolfgang, that was so tuneful and kept coming back —"

Alme belle," he said. He looked at Anna and translated the text for his wife into German: " 'You beautiful souls, who see my pain in this moment, tell me if any heart has suffered such torment as this.' "

"Is that what it means?" asked Constanze. "But the melody was so pretty, so light, so hopeful!"

"Then I did well," he said. He glanced at her with a smile and then looked back at Anna. "For you see that's the torment of love — so light, so hopeful, when still she must go away."

"But you'll come back, won't you?" said Constanze with a warm look at Anna and Stephen. "Or we shall come to you."

"Yes," said Stephen cheerfully. "We hope

to have you come to London."

They could not say good-bye like this. Not like this. Mozart's eyes were wet and urgent, and she knew it was because he was trying at the last to fix in his memory the image of her face. Her voice, her touch, her smile. As she was trying to do with his.

At half past two in the morning of February 23, 1787, Anna Storace climbed into a four-horse carriage lined with furs and velvet and bade farewell to Vienna.

LETTERS

LETTER FROM JOSEPH II TO ANNA STORACE, AUGUST 1788

My dear Madam,

As you may have heard, we are at war with Turkey. Therefore have I dissolved my opera company. In any case, madam, as I told you once before, there is no employment for you here.

His Excellency, etc,
Joseph Hapsburg

LETTER FROM FRANCESCO BENUCCI TO ANNA STORACE (EXTRACT), OCTOBER 1789

Yes, the buffa troupe has been taken back into the fold and our Figaro revived. They've got Da Ponte's mistress singing your Susanna. Blowsy voice, no art. Mozart's had to rewrite your arias.

Now they're showpieces. For myself it's like making love to a fondue. Pity me. And Stephen is marrying your maid? Well, I always liked her, though she had no good opinion of me. Congratulations all.

FB

Letter from Robert May O'Reilly, London impresario, to Anna Storace, November 1790

Madam,
Having heard through your brother of Wolfgang Mozart's desire to undertake a journey to England, I have offered to commission him to compose two operas for the coming season in London, at a generous fee of three hundred pounds. I regret to inform you that he has refused me. His wife, he says, is ill. Perhaps we may try him again in the next year.

Robert O'Reilly

Letter from the Countess von Thun und Hohenstein to Anna Storace, December 1791

My sweet girl.
By now you will have heard the black

418

news. We all of us are in shock. When they told me I refused to believe. "That cannot be," I said. "It cannot be that I am living, I who have no use in the world, and Wolfgang Mozart is dead." It is dark here — we have not seen the sun — it rains and snows and all of us rage at the sky and it does no good. He was sick in November but I did not think it would come to this. What have we lost, dear Anna?

You're weeping now, and it's all my fault. I should be grieving in my diary, not to you, who loved him best of all. I know you did. I said nothing but I always knew. I cannot console you. I can see no good in this world. Wrap yourself in your memories. Sing for him, when you can. They say he knew he was dying.

Now the sun is coming out, stealing across my dreadful words at day's end. I want to tear the page. I feel myself crazed. Is this my hand? He was surrounded by friends and his little family. The baby boy! I can't think of it. Why am I writing when it will only cause you pain? Hateful sun — you come too late — you are cold, you mock us, you are gone again. The snow piles.

A day will come when I will have concerts in our house as we used to. Then I will listen to his music and there find solace. Even now I think of the two of you, how you delighted in each other. There my drowning spirits are revived. Let yours be so as well.

With sisterly love, in great hardship,
Countess Maria Wilhelmine von Thun und Hohenstein

EPILOGUE

In June 1801, the promising young English tenor John Braham arrived in Vienna with his lover and collaborator, the soprano Anna Storace, at the end of their four-year musical tour of the Continent. He had met her when her brother, now deceased, had hired him as principal tenor at the Drury Lane theater, where Anna sang. He and Anna had studied with the same teacher. She had an estranged husband who was also named John. They laughed about that sometimes. Although Braham was just beginning his career and Anna was ten years older, it didn't seem to matter.

They had embarked on the tour shortly after the sudden death of her brother, in 1796. She had wanted to visit all of the places where she had sung in her brilliant youth, when she was younger even than Braham. It would feed her memories, she said, and advance his career. They went to

Paris and sang for Hamilton and Napoleon. They spent months in Naples and Venice, and every great city under the sun. Then they came to Vienna.

It was just the same, she said. That was what she'd said of nearly every place they'd visited. Her hand on his arm was rigid. Braham patted it and looked affectionately into her face. Now when she talked of the past he would know where it had happened, be able to journey there with her. He could almost see the past crossing her features now, in this park in Vienna, the past revealing itself to him with more candor and detail than it ever had in her stories. The pretty movement of her dear brown eyes, the furrow in her brow, told all. And there, finally, came a crystal tear.

"You're crying," he said. He loved the vividness of her emotions, her passions, rages, and ecstasies. He often thought someone should paint her in one of her passions.

Anna wiped her cheeks and looked away. She was going to sit on the bench by the lilacs, she said. She wouldn't be half an hour. He might walk in the garden until she was ready. Then they would go see the Thun und Hohensteins and he would sing for them.

"And you, as well, my love?"

Her face was pale. No, she said. She had something in her throat. She could not sing today. The countess would understand.

He left her, as she wished, and paced the orderly gravel paths of the park. The Prater, it was called. They were in a secluded square ringed with trees. She sat by the lilacs. The flowers waved about her. The ribbons on her hat rippled in the air. A blustery day, with gray light. Braham watched her carefully as he strolled the garden paths, but for all the warmth of his attention she did not move or call to him. Drawing out his watch, he saw that it had not been ten minutes. Half an hour, she'd said. Twenty-two minutes to go. He resolved not to disturb her before she was ready. After all, he loved her. He could spare her half an hour.

He turned on his heel to examine a rosebush. Then he looked back again at Anna. She had taken off her slippers. He had not noticed that before. Her feet, perhaps, were tired. Sixteen minutes remained. Under his breath he hummed an aria he would sing later for these famous Thun von Hohensteins. The aria was by Wolfgang Mozart. Anna's friend. Braham had a golden voice. He looked forward to seeing their pleasure when they heard it.

ACKNOWLEDGMENTS

To all those who traveled with me and my Mozart story over the past decade, I offer my deepest thanks.

For inspiring the writing of this book, I am grateful to my exceptional mentors, Keith Kibler, Jim Shepard, Margot Livesey, and Ethan Canin. For their patience, enthusiasm, and wisdom in bringing it to fruition, I am grateful to my extraordinary editors, Susanna Porter and Dana Isaacson, and my superlative agent, Ayesha Pande. I warmly thank Libby McGuire, Dana Leigh Blanchette, Priyanka Krishnan, Zoë Maslow, Nita Pronovost, and all those at Ballantine Books and Doubleday Canada who have supported and worked on this project.

For their cheers, advice, aid, and correspondence, my heartfelt gratitude to: Els Andersen, Peter Aronow, Isaiah Bell, Connie Brothers, Anthony Bucci, Deb Bucci,

Robert Buckland, Austin Bunn, Soman Chainani, Chris Dixon, Rossen Djagalov, David Durham, Anthony Eleftherion, Jeremy Friedman, Ann Foster, Richard Giarusso, Kevin A. González, Julia Green, Chad Harbach, Andy Howard, Deborah Copaken Kogan, Kecia Lynn, Paul La Rosa, Mark Leidner, Samuel Levine, Tod Lippy, William T. J. de la Mare, Marvin Moore, Tyler Putnam, Shannon Rabong, Dan Rosenberg, John Sell, Roman Skaskiw, Isaac Sullivan, Anna Weinstein, Julia Whicker, and Matt Williamson.

Thank you to the many teachers who influenced this novel: Maria Acda, Robert Bell, Deborah Birnbaum, Michael Chance, Lan Samantha Chang, Doris and Richard Cross, Yvonne DeRoller, Tony Eprile, Jill Feldman, Stephen Fix, Jane Hester, Carolyn Kanjuro, Maurice Lammerts van Bueren, Linda Lewis, James Alan MacPherson, Carol MacVey, Randolph Mickelson, Wendy Nielsen, Rachel Joselson, Shari Rhoads, Marilynne Robinson, Alec Tilley, Robin Graeme Thomas, and Jennette White.

My love and gratitude to Amy Blyth, Carol Halpern, Cathy Hubiak, Robin Kibler, Beth Sutton, and Laura Wiebe; to my dear grandparents, Robert and Peggy Moe; and to the Fletchers, Humphreys, Islams, Moes, Ostlings, Riches, and Thorntons.

I am sincerely grateful to the Iowa Arts Fellowship, the Hubbard Hutchinson Memorial Fellowship, the Sun Valley Writers' Conference, and the Writers' Federation of Nova Scotia.

Thank you to all those who care for the arts.

Thank you to the cradle of loving kindness of the Shambhala community.

Thank you to the precious natural world: to the gardens, parks, woodlands, large trees, lakes, oceans, mountains, and songbirds in the company of which much of *Vienna Nocturne* was composed.

Finally, my deepest love and gratitude, beyond expression, to my sister, Alexis Shotwell, my brother, Gordon Shotwell, my mother, Janet Moe Shotwell, and my father, Hudson Burr Shotwell.

HISTORICAL NOTE

When Anna Storace bade farewell to Vienna, in 1787, she was twenty-one, the same age I was when I first began writing this story. In the space of years, I have grown so close to these characters that I sometimes believe that everything I've written about them is true. The bare facts *are* true, at least as far as we know. I stayed as close as I could to an accurate timeline. With the exception of Lidia, Herr Gosta, and the rest of the servants, all of the named characters are based on actual people. Many of the scenes, such as the concert in the orangery and the execution of Franz Zahlheim, are based on real events. The titles of the operas are paraphrased translations of Italian titles. Martín y Soler's *A Rare Thing,* for instance, is called *Una cosa rara* in Italian, and was at the time of its premiere indeed more popular than *The Marriage of Figaro.*

Anna did study singing with a castrato

named Rauzzini, and she did marry a man named John Fisher who was said to have abused her. She sang Mozart's music and was his friend. There is no record of whether Anna and Mozart loved each other, but in the music he wrote for her, especially the farewell aria *Non temer, amato bene,* for which he played the piano solo, I believe there lies an undeniable and unspoken affection.

The thoughts, speech, motivations, and written correspondence of the characters are all my own.

The cantata *For the Recovery of Ophelia* was called in Italian *Per la ricuperata salute di Ofelia,* and was jointly composed by Mozart, Salieri, and someone named Cornetti, who may have been Stephen Storace writing under a pseudonym. This cantata has been lost, and so my description of its music and structure is invention.

When I consider my presumption in writing fiction about Mozart, I am embarrassed. I do not know whether it would have amused or affronted him. I hope, at least, that by writing in such a way I might encourage others to seek out live performances of classical music and opera, to play instruments and sing, and to support musical education and the arts.

It was not within the scope of the novel to encompass all of Mozart's greatest works, and they are the best way to get to know the real man. Another, more direct way to get to know him is to read the Mozart family letters. For this novel I was particularly indebted to *Mozart's Letters, Mozart's Life,* edited and translated by Robert Spaethling.

Less is known about Anna Storace than about Mozart. In historical accounts she is usually called by her nickname, Nancy. She, perhaps most of all, is my own creation. I had to make her mine, someone I loved.

In my research for this novel I drew gratefully upon the following resources: *The World of the Castrati,* by Patrick Barbier; *The Librettist of Venice: The Remarkable Life of Lorenzo Da Ponte, Mozart's Poet, Casanova's Friend, and Italian Opera's Impresario in America,* by Rodney Bolt; *Anna . . . Susanna: A Biography of Mozart's First Susanna,* by Geoffrey Brace; *Mozart in Vienna, 1781–1791,* by Volkmar Braunbehrens; *Daily Life in the Vienna of Mozart and Schubert,* by Marcel Brion; *Mozart and His Operas,* by David Cairns; *Mozart in Person: His Character and Health,* by Peter J. Davies; *English Opera in Late Eighteenth-Century London,* by Jane Girdham; *Mozart's Women: His Family,*

His Friends, His Music, by Jane Glover; *Mozart: A Cultural Biography,* by Robert W. Gutman; *Mozart's Operas,* by Daniel Heartz; *Reminiscences of Michael Kelly of the King's Theatre, and Theatre Royal Drury Lane,* edited by T. E. Hook; *The Culture of Opera Buffa in Mozart's Vienna,* by Mary Hunter; *The Cambridge Companion to Mozart,* edited by Simon P. Keefe; *Mozart and Vienna, Including Selections from Johann Pezzl's 'Sketch of Vienna' 1786–90* by H. C. Robbins Landon; *The Mozart Compendium: A Guide to Mozart's Life and Music,* edited by H. C. Robbins Landon; *Arias for Francesco Benucci: Mozart's First Figaro* and *Arias for Nancy Storace: Mozart's First Susanna,* both by Dorothea Link; *Italian Opera in Late Eighteenth-Century London,* by Curtis Price, Judith Milhous, and Robert D. Hume; *The Eighteenth-Century Pleasure Gardens of Marylebone,* by Mollie Sands; *Angels and Monsters: Male and Female Sopranos in the Story of Opera,* by Richard Somerset-Ward; and, last but not least, "Pots, Privies and WCs; Crapping at the Opera in London before 1830," by Michael Burden.

ABOUT THE AUTHOR

Vivien Shotwell was born in Colorado and raised in Nova Scotia. A daughter of independent booksellers, and a classically trained singer, she has received degrees in music and writing from Williams College, the Iowa Writers' Workshop, and the Yale School of Music.

The employees of Thorndike Press hope you have enjoyed this Large Print book. All our Thorndike, Wheeler, and Kennebec Large Print titles are designed for easy reading, and all our books are made to last. Other Thorndike Press Large Print books are available at your library, through selected bookstores, or directly from us.

For information about titles, please call:
(800) 223-1244

or visit our Web site at:
http://gale.cengage.com/thorndike

To share your comments, please write:
Publisher
Thorndike Press
10 Water St., Suite 310
Waterville, ME 04901